I0671594

Declan Varley is a stunning new voice in the great tradition of Irish literary fiction. Born in 1965, he grew up in the small town of Ballinrobe in County Mayo, Ireland. In his teens, Declan began his career in writing when he established a weekly magazine with a group of friends. That publication gave Declan the motivation he needed to use words as his trade, writing the college subculture novel Kittyland in 1992, followed by Sure It Could Happen (1993) The Elephant's Graveyard, (1994) and Nightmusic (2001). A successful career in journalism followed, writing award winning stories for regional, national, and international newspapers. He is currently Group Editor of Galway Advertiser Newspapers. Declan lives in Galway with his wife, Galway Bay fm Head of News Bernadette Prendergast and their daughter, Giselle.

Acknowledgments

In enabling Peadar Gibbons to come to life, I would like to acknowledge the expertise of my wife Bernadette Prendergast, who edited the manuscript; the generosity of Marek Bluma and the team at Cafe Renzo, Galway who fuelled my inner angst with regular infusions of caffeine while Peadar's life unfolded on my pages; my good friend Eileen Keleghan, who encouraged me to keep going; and the support of my agent Paul Feldstein, for believing in the story.

Dedicated to all those who grew up on our side of town, but who never got the breaks.

First published in 2018 by Dalzell Press.

Dalzell Press
54 Abbey Street
Bangor, N. Ireland
BT20 4JB

Cover design by Paddy Breslin at www.paddybreslin.com

ISBN: 978-0-9563864-1-0

The Confession of Peadar Gibbons

Declan Varley

Dalzell Press

Biography

Lorna T Cuddy was born in Ireland in 1981. She was educated at St Juliens in London where she won the Harcroft Student Journalism Award; and at Oxford University where she studied English Language and Literature. She went on to become features journalist for The Guardian before moving to the United States in 2004 where she has penned articles for Vanity Fair, The New Yorker, Harper's Magazine, Ploughshare, Shenandoah and Vogue. She won the Don Loewright Award for Excellence in Long Form Journalism in 2008. In 2010 she won a Pulitzer Prize for her article The Fallen Families, based on the treatment of the relatives of soldiers killed in Iraq and Afghanistan.

She now lives in Queens with her husband Donald Spitzer and their daughter Ellie. Lorna is Associate Lecturer of Journalism at Richmond University, NJ and Associate Professor of New Media Writing at the Journalism department of Columbia University.

Peadar the Poet

Last year, on his fiftieth birthday, my father's childhood friend Peadar Gibbons, a quietly-spoken amateur poet, walked into the garda (police) station in the small Irish town where he had lived all his life. He went up to the counter, left down the plastic shopping bag he was carrying, and speaking in that fine but deliberate way of his, told them that he had carried out a number of serious crimes and that he wanted to explain why he had committed them.

Having known that Peadar aka Peadar The Poet had only ever come to their attention for throwing a glass at a heckler during a poetry recital session, the garda on duty told him to go home and 'write down' details of the crimes he had supposedly carried out. Reluctantly Peadar quietly picked up the carrier bag and went out through the double doors and into the night. He walked back the five hundred yards to his home, and using the old dusty Remington typewriter that his mother had bought back in the 1950s for writing letters to her pen pal in Yonkers, he typed out a detailed account of his life.

Fifty days after he had first visited the garda station, Peadar returned, with another carrier bag, but this time it contained 300 pages of typed notes. He had a long conversation with the senior officer on duty and was later removed to a psychiatric institution in the west of Ireland. The gardai later described his notes as the "most elaborate written admission" they had ever seen.

This is Peadar's story, based on those notes he typed, and on conversations I had with him after he was hospitalised.

The First Year

It's turned out now,

the shakings of the bag,

the runt of the litter.

Never knew ya had it in ya,

but ya didn't, did ya.

And guffaws

And porter splashes matching

the pats on the back

and the lads saying

Better go see it

get back in the saddle, Jackie

and then a shuffle down the hill

and not knowing whether to laugh or cry.

(Peadar Gibbons)

Here goes. This is probably how it w ent...

'I'm a coont for the biscuits, a pure coont. Sister,' he said, as he shovelled the last of the custard creams out of the packet, jammed it into his mouth, dipped his hands into the basin and then wiped them clean on the arse of his trousers.

"I always have been. Ya see, we never had them when I was young so the fuckin' things are so plentiful now that whenever I see one, I have to have three. A coont for the biccies, I am, excuse my language now Sister, but I'm sure you hear worse above in the Infirmary."

He looked around the room at the gaggle of women there, the midwife, Sr Kellegher, my grandmother, my mother's sister Sheila and at the bed, my mother, panting and pushing, trying to maintain decorum and a front door voice even while trying to push out her fifth child.

Me.

An evil little bollocks.

Eventually, but probably showing signs there and then.

Even though Doctor McNamee had just washed his hands, he picked up the cup again and took one final slurp from it, tea escaping down his cracked lips like a rivulet of the Ganges. He wiped his mouth with the back of his sleeve, and said. "Right so, let's get crackin'. Jaysis, Kathleen, every time we do this I do be tellin' ya not be lettin' Jackie back into the room. You'll have to get a better lock for that door, so you will."

And he laughed and coughed clouds of custard cream crumbs all over her and they landing in the sticky sweat on her legs and on her sopping forehead.

And the roaring was something terrible 'cos it had been a few years since she'd had the last one.

And even he winced at her pain.

And I arrived into this world kickin' and screamin' and covered in someone else's blood... not knowing that somewhere down the line after a life hardly worth living, I might be leaving it the very same way.

My mother collapsed back on the pillow, exhausted but with a lovely radiance in her complexion that prompted Dr Mac to say 'look at the state of her, looking lovely again straightaway. Sure it's no wonder Jackie does be kicking the door in, no wonder at all, the randy aul' bastard."

And they all laughed nervously as he washed his hands in the basin again, and put the cufflinks back in his shirt sleeves.

And when they lifted me I cried ... at the blinding light, the unclear figures. I must have heard the awws and the oohs.

His must have been the first face I saw — The big fuckin' bulbous head on him, the stink of drink off him, the smell of stale piss and tobacco all mixed up in a tweed Magee jacket and a shirt with a design like you'd see on the sums copies at school.

Doctor McNamee was notorious around the town for being a better doctor when he was drunk than sober. Sober, he was cantankerous and careless: drunk, he was operating on fuel.

And although he came from a posh family, he always had great time for my mother, knowing her when she used to be a clerk for one of the other doctors up town; before she got married to my father, the drunken county council foreman, and had to give it all up.

My mother back then caught the eye of all the young professionals in town, but although they'd look, they were never going to be really interested in any girl from this side of the river. And so she ended up marrying my father, in from the country, after a whirlwind romance that saw her knocked up within four months.

My granny had little time for Dr McNamee. I heard her say once that he was present at more conceptions than births but I'd no idea what she meant and when she saw that I'd heard it, she'd given me a clip around the ear and sent me packing for having the cheek to be listening to something she said far too loud, which wasn't fuckin' fair but was par for the course for the way people treated me throughout life.

The room I was born in was the room my mother was born in, and the room my four brothers were born in...and the same room that my mother's father had died in ten years before and the room that mother and father shared in the nights when he'd make it home and wouldn't collapse drunk on the chair and sleep it off in the kitchen. 'Twas known in the house as the coming and going room but I didn't understand that for many years.

It was small as it lost a corner to the rise of the stairs beneath it. My father had disguised the slope in the room by building a set of drawers over it, but no matter how you looked, it was odd and standard for the types of patchwork jobs that were done around our house.

Granny opened the window in the room after I was born, ostensibly to let in some fresh air, but she did it in the manner that people did when someone had died, to let the spirit soar free. And in a way, she did it 'cos a bit of her spirit took flight in exasperation every time her beautiful intelligent daughter bore a child for this drunk.

My brothers Seamus, Ray, Marty, and Kieran were downstairs when I was born and after about half an hour when Dr Mac had been given more tea and biscuits and had regaled them all about his time killing Germans in the trenches of Passchendaele (which he had in his hole), they crept up the wide creaky stairs and went around the corner into the little room, where my mother was holding me, keeping me warm, giving me the kind of feeling I never wanted to be without.

They poked fingers at me and stared and made silly little comments about my nose and my hair and my ears, but really they just wanted to hurry the fuck up and get away out and back up the ball alley for playing games and not shitehawking around with pudgy babies.

I was well asleep by the time Father came back, fumbling in the dark, pushing chairs this way and that; not exactly drunk but doing his utmost to stand up straight lest anyone would think he was, because after all he had just spent the night in Luke Higgins' pub at the top of the hill where he was bought pint after pint of creamy stout and several small Jamesons for continuing the fine form of breeding that his family had become noticed for.

"Sure Jackie what with five lads, there's bound to be nothing here for them in this country. They'll be all fuckin' off to Boston, so 'tis a waste of time feeding the bastards. Should put them on the boat now and let some wan else worry about them 'cos by the time you need them to worry about ya, there won't be a fuckin' smell o' them."

And when he came home, his head was full of all that sort of shite. Depressing thoughts put into his mind by the fuckers in Luke Higgins', who saw nothing wrong in teasing him and making sure that any bit of light in his life would be doused by the sad reality.

And he was so distracted by it all that he didn't even bother trying

11

to ride one of the Kelly sisters that night, publican's daughters mad for his broad shoulders honed from digging holes and filling holes and scratching holes on the Council truck.

And in his mind he knew that if the lads were rising him when he was there, God knows what they were saying about him when he wasn't there.

So when he came in that night, he realised that at 43 years of age, he already knew that he was never going to have much in life, that his kids were never going to have much in life and that the lads in the pub were probably right.

Where had his life gone, just as one more life was starting upstairs?

And he was jealous of the new life, a life that would have chances, chances that he himself had not been afforded.

And as he sat there in the dark, nobody could tell really that he was thinking. The rest of the family upstairs in bed, if they were awake at all, probably thought he was just drunk and sleeping it off, but he wasn't.

He just sat there tormented. Like when ya see a dying cat on the road, you'd have preferred like if someone drove over him proper like and put him out of his misery rather than lying there, suffering until some fucker's wheel took ya out.

Father didn't know then that he had less than twenty-two years to live, but he knew that no matter how many years were left, they were all going to be filled with regret and disappointment and shattered pride and lost opportunity because that was the way his life had worked out so far.

And he longed to be loved again.

That someone, anyone, would love him, a woman, a child, anyone.

He knew he'd passed the age when he might well be ever loved again by someone new.

And so as he heard the soft cries of his youngest son come through the floor above and filter down into the semi-lit kitchen where he sat with a lit cigarette burning itself to death in his right hand, and with his heart trembling and a low howl within, his head shuddered to and fro as he wept for his life and for all that it had amounted to.

The Second Year

Into chaos I squalled

oceans of notions

with their

hear no evil

see no evil

and Delia's screaming wheel

reversing blindly

over a mother's

hopes for a mother.

(Peadar Gibbons)

My arrival had consequences for the family. As I crawled around the floor of the kitchen, listening to John McCormack and Bridie Gallagher on old 78 records on the Pye radio gramophone in the corner of
the kitchen, you could hear the incessant nagging Granny gave Mother. They'd ignore me and even though I was just a kid, they'd turn up the gramophone so that I wouldn't hear what they were saying, as if I'd have a fuckin' clue anyway. So when Delia Murphy was singing out *There Were Three Lovely Lassies In Bannion*, I knew that there was some sort of shouting going on. And then mother would cry and leave the room and Granny would pick me up and bounce me on her lap with her mind not on me but on whatever she'd said to Mother to make her run out of the room and go upstairs where she'd throw herself on the bed, sobbing like a big child. One day when Mother was upstairs sobbing having been reminded of what a shite her life had become, Granny sat me on the big chair near the fire and I toppled off it and into the hearth.
"The child's gone into the fire" she screamed before she bent down and dragged me out, the only mark on me being the ashes that were collected at the front, and not the remnants of the red hot embers which were just inches away from it.
So when that happened there was another row - Granny blaming Mother for leaving the kitchen and not minding the child, always passing the blame onto someone else, because she was used to getting her way. And then Mother would cry again and then I'd cry from the fright of falling into the fire and Delia fuckin' Murphy would be put on again, so much that every time I hear her singing *The Spinning Wheel* I want to get up and fuckin' cry and scream at the bleakness of those days before I was able to speak, but not before I was able to understand.

Years later when I got the chance, I got the Delia Murphy collections and brought them out into the garden and smashed them with a hammer and then put all the smashed bits into the bottom of the fire pit in the garden where we burned all the rubbish.

And as I did it, I could hear the song in me head "Merrily, cheerily, noiselessly whirring, Swings the wheel, spins the wheel, while the foot's stirring." And it was like one of those eels that the more you cut them up, the more they moved.

Granny had always had notions. After all her husband had the second ever motorcar in the town and he drove for the Dunbar family who lived in the big house up the road. For the Dunbar's, Granddad acted as the butler and the driver and general handyman as well. Whatever heiress Audrey Dunbar wanted, Granddad provided. I've no idea if he was ever slipping her a length, but I wouldn't put it past him and his sense of duty. He also drove the officers who were stationed in the British army barracks in the town. And then at other times, against his will, but too terrified to refuse, under darkness, he drove men from the different factions in the Civil War.

He always joked that how the Brits always paid him, but that the patriots dying for Ireland never gave him a bob. He was always careful where he said that 'cos if either side knew what he was doing, they'd have taken him out the Bog Road and fucked him into a turf hole full of water.

It was in 1925 that they bought the big house at High Street where we all were born. It was a series of terraced houses and gateways that they had knocked into one. The house had been owned by an old moneylender woman and up until my 20s, we were hoping that we'd find a stack of money in the walls of the house or the shed. But we never did.

They were a respectable couple around the town and looked grand as they drove on a Sunday when Granddad had time off after bringing Mr and Mrs Dunbar and their son Percy to Sunday service. After that, the Dunbars would just go home and stay in for the full day. So that meant he could bring Granny courting in his shiny car.

So I'm sure you can tell by now they were less than fuckin' delighted that their youngest daughter went off and married a council worker. After all, she'd been very bright in school, had won a story writing competition so maybe that's where I got me poetry from. But what they didn't know was that she was a frisky divil who'd sneak out of the house at night to ate the mouths of poor unsuspecting feckers in from the country who'd never been used to some young wan grabbing them by the mickey and rendering them useless inside a few minutes, wherever the hell she learned that in the 1950s.

She knew that if her father had seen that she had left her room, he would have beaten her to smithereens, but she never did, mainly because her sister Maisie and her brother Liam covered for her in return for her covering for them at some other stage. And she'd be gone for hours, hanging around the dancehall but never going in, keeping out of the street lights in case her father would be walking or driving through the town and see her.

When you think of it, it should have been no surprise when she got knocked up, and Granny never told Granddad about it for it would have broken his heart. She advised her that she had to marry the father straightaway and so the father became Father even though I don't think he had any intention of being a father,

17

as he had plans to fuck off to England and this situation put an end to all that. Especially when Granny called out to his house in the country, threw a hundred pounds on the table and told his mother and father that he was to marry her daughter and there'd be no two ways about it.

And Father's parents were simple country folk mesmerised by this brash woman from the town, so they told Father what he had to do and to put any London notions out of his head. And anyway he'd be getting a grand house in the town. And a beautiful young wife.

So that made Seamus a bastard, but he was treated in the family as 'a honeymoon baby' who just arrived a few weeks premature.

Granny never took to Father at the start – and why would she? Wasn't he the beast who emptied himself into her daughter up against the ball alley wall to get them into this mess and she fuckin' hated the thought of this every time she pictured it in her head, but in time she was taken by his personality, and his lovely smile and his ability to turn his hand to anything, eventually won her over.

Until the drinking and the whoring and the fighting kicked in and he fucking blew all his credit with her.

Her late husband was a strict authoritarian brought up on the principles of good behaviour instilled in him through years of training at the Dunbar house. It knocked the heart out of Granny as well. She knew that her daughter was well set up with a big house but knew that would be fuck all good to her if all she was going to do was breed half a dozen kids for a town drunk.

And so two generations that should have been smiling and happy with their lot were shattered and heartbroken before they even got a chance to start off life properly. But Granny was made from stern stuff. Her family had fought in the Civil War in Galway and took no shit from anybody and she set her stall for a battle in our house.

However as each child arrived – boy after boy after boy, Granny was keen to ensure we would take our morals from our mother and not from our father. And so she implored Mother to make sure I'd be the last one she'd ever bear. Because five kids was bad enough. Six would be making her "as bad as the tinkers," said Granny. And Mother didn't like being compared to the tinkers. And she didn't like being lumbered with a big family when she had seen herself having a great life getting winks out of the young solicitors visiting the office where she worked.

And so with pressure from Granny and exasperation and anger at Father, 'tis no wonder my mother started going slowly mad at that stage.

And so that was how we were perceived in the town. Half respected and half pitied. Half snobs and half waifs. Halfway between being respected and not. Neither here nor there.

The Third Year

Out-turned pockets of the smoky trousers

the heart of crushed Aftons long dead

hang there warning the world is a strange place.

You can run your finger along the fags

broken and bent into the stitching

and you can look at this and feel this,

feast your eyes upon this mixture

of rough Irish tweed and soft foreign tobacco

and black out the rustles and snorts

and moans that break the silence of the night.

(Peadar Gibbons)

Although Granny had told Mother to make sure that I was the last of the tribe, the word mustn't have been passed on to Father. Granny would never have mentioned anything like that to him 'cos she was too prim and proper but she told Mother alright 'cos there'd be lots of hushed conversations in the kitchen but Mother obviously ignored it 'cos she liked the riding too much, even though she'd never have been able to say that to her own mother, so she kept it to herself and had to make do with the constant advice from Granny. The last thing she wanted to do was to make things for difficult for Father in the sex department and have him going off up town to Deirdre Kelly and the likes who'd pull ya off for the price of a bag of chips from Tom Monroe's chipper van. So Jackie Gibbons the randy bastard was thrilled that there was no let-up in the bedroom, even ignoring a little set of eyes in the corner peering out through a jungle of bars and clothes.

Because I was so little, there was no way they were going to leave me in one of the other rooms with the lads in case they threw something hard that hit me or if they fell out of bed on top of me, or any sort of laddish behaviour that would end up with me neck broken, so Uncle Liam built a cot which Jackie placed in the corner of their own bedroom. It was rough enough but was sanded down smooth for me to run my fingers along it. The mattress was a piece of foam rubber that he'd picked up somewhere and cut onto shape to fit the exact dimensions of the cot. This was covered by a piece of curtain and topped off with a flat pillow and a blanket to cover me. And this was to be my bed for the next two or three years, keeping me near enough if anything was to ever happen to me or if I got sick during the night.

And so I'd sleep there, my view of their bed obscured by two chairs that had clothes hanging off them, the thickness of tweed skirts and slacks and the smoky smell off Father's trousers placed carefully over the two chairs so that I wouldn't see anything, though they'd have hoped that I was fast asleep by the time they came up anyway. And so I pretended to be. Wondering what the commotion was.

Night after night, apart from the nights Father would come home drunk, I'd have to listen to them riding the holes off each other. And though they'd try to stifle the moans and cries from me for fear I'd hear, I couldn't avoid the shuffling and creaking of the springs in the large bed two yards away from my cot. The slap slap slap of sweaty thigh upon thigh, the climactic 'fuckeeeeen jaysus' and then when the noise and the heavy breathing would stop, I'd get the smell of cigarettes as the two of them shared a fag and laughed for a while. And I remember it well 'cos 'twas not often that I heard them laughing with each other, or sharing anything with each other or at most times, even tolerating each other.

And I'd stay awake 'cos the noise would have frightened me and I wouldn't have had a fuckin' clue what was going on and I wouldn't be able to sleep with the fright but was far too afraid to call out and ask them to comfort me and save me from the terror. And then a while later I'd hear the tinkle as Father would get out and have a long piss in the bucket we had in the corner of the room. And then he'd let a long low fart out of him before clambering back into bed and my head would hit the flat pillow and try to make sense of all these strange noises and actions in the darkness. And my hands would reach out through the bars and push back the clothes on the chair and try and watch them sleeping and snoring away through the night, with no clue that the child had been listening and shivering all the night with the sound of it.

22

It is strange that all these years on I can remember the feeling of being behind those bars, peering out, listening to the sex noises that would fascinate me all my life, that would drive me to distraction and give me thoughts that would fuck up my thinking and lead me astray. I never told Mother that it was probably all her fault with her riding there beside the child in the cot, and her riding before she was married that resulted in the dysfunction that was passed down to us all. I often thought sure how could we have any luck with that sort of behaviour.

But we had to come out of somewhere so' twas no surprise to think that they would be up to something. And that they weren't this age always. But to think they were doing this with Granny across the landing in her room praying and sleeping with a rosary beads in her hands, while they were tearing into one another.

And to put that beside Granny's strict thinking and Catholic ways that saw her use a hackney driver to bring her to second Mass every Sunday for fear she'd be late and filling her handbag with small Catholic magazines like The Messenger or the big boring broadsheets Catholic Standard or the Irish Catholic and bring them home where she'd leave them on the table. But nobody read them, not Father especially who preferred to get the Sunday Press and the News of the World which he would hide in the cupboard and only take out when he'd be going to the downstairs jacks. The Press would be fecked onto the table and he'd read that for a while, and we'd look at it and try to win the Spot The Ball competition that we never did.

But when he got the chance, the News of the World would be taken out and read in the jacks.

He was afraid the lads would find it and be staring at the pictures of tits and arses and stories about English vicars riding blonde parishioners. In later years I wondered how English vicars and politicians always had love trysts and love nests whereas in Ireland we just had ridin' the holes off one another in the backs of old Hillman Hunters. And when he'd come out of the jacks leaving behind a smell of farts and Old Spice, we'd know that he was going to head to the pub. Sneaking out the back door through the yard and out the side gate so that he wouldn't have to explain where he'd be going but the lads were wide to him. They'd know all his ways and all the stop holes in the walls of the old shed where he used to hide his Baby Powers, small whiskey bottles that he'd use for the cure in the weeks after he'd have one of his bad benders.

They used to hide them on him and giggle as they'd watch him mount the step ladder after weeks of drinking, searching hole after hole in the old wall, sticking his hands in, risking the wrath of the rats to search in vain for his whiskey. But 'twas a waste of time, 'cos if he couldn't find his own, he'd just buy more up town and the money he'd owe to the pub would mount up and the money he'd hand over to Mother would fall and fall and so she'd have to ask Granny for a loan to buy the groceries and pay Mickey the Milk to leave six bottles on our doorstep every morning.

And when Father'd come in drunk, he'd slowly mount the fifteen carpeted steps of the stairs, falling in through the bedroom door, stumble onto the beds to tousle the hair of each of the lads and call them 'astoir' before crashing on into the room where I lay, falling down on the bed with his clothes and shoes on. And Mother would drag them off him with the clump clump of the shoes before he fell asleep in his string vest and underpants snoring the night away.

24

And I'd lie there in my wooden cage and push my head deep into my flat pillow and pick at the exposed foam rubber and wonder if the morning was ever going to come when the light would seep in through the closed shutters, sending a line along the room like the fuckin' chamber at Newgrange on solstice morning - and wipe away the noises and sounds and smells of the night just passed.

The Fourth Year

Poor leftie, rejected.

Left alone.

Left at home

Left unfulfilled

I bring you everywhere

but leftie's left to watch

at what's right with the world

But it's not right that leftie's

Left out

You could have been a writer

an artist, a playwright,

Were it not for the

habit wearer

habit tearer

proclaiming you were not right

And when you're not right,

you're left

out.

(Peadar Gibbons)

Sometimes I felt for the nuns who had to teach us. I mean, when they had their first inspirational thoughts to become nuns, they must have seen Our Lady calling to them to go forth and serve the Lord. They must have thought about lives of prayer and service to their order, spreading the good word and bringing peace and harmony to wherever they served. They must have been filled with a great hope and protection to mind them wherever they went – and they went lots of places, judging by the fact that every time you see a bus, there's a nun on it. — The last thing they would have expected to be doing is trying to put smacht on noisy little pricks like ourselves in an old rambling convent in a small west of Ireland town. But that was their lot and by fuck, did they not waste any time in taking their frustration out on us, determined as they were to get their fair share of bating the shite outta us.

The nuns were to have a massive impact on my life. I didn't have any sisters and apart from my mother and Granny, and the odd visit from auntie Maisie, the only other women we saw were the auld wans in the street, Nonie, Bridgie, Baby Murphy and Gorrie Callanan. They were all old and shrouded in shawls that reeked of turf and piss. In a way they weren't really women at all, 'cos they had gotten so old and bent over and craggy and there was nothing womanly about their shape. It was as if their bodies had blended into their rundown houses, smoke-stained and grey. They were like witches from the kids stories you'd read. If they'd lived in the woods, you could be sure they had a house made out of sweets. But they didn't live in the woods, they lived in our street in small houses built on a hill, with big wooden doors, and big open hot fireplaces that seemed to take up the entire side gable of their houses. And the turf sort of consumed them.

Anyway, where was I? Yes, the nuns. So they were the first real women we came across. Especially the young nuns with their fresh faces and their hair in a bun tucked up in their nun hats and they all having notions and energy that would be soon worn out of them once they got a few nun years behind them.

One thing I knew about them is that they never missed a fuckin' chance to grab a shilling. Whatever event they held, they found no shame in having a nun (normally a sort of simple one who'd been dropped as a child and was fecked into some order or other) with a biscuit tin at the door so that you'd be shamed into dropping a coin into it as you left.

This was even extended to the Black Babies. I'd never met a black baby or a black adult until I started to work in Galway in my twenties, but here was I expected to bring a penny to school every day so that one of them could plant a tree or something that was lost on us. All I knew was that I wondered if you could fuckin' trust the nuns to pass all those pennies on, or would they keep a few sneaky coins to help them buy talc with which they seemed to cover themselves at night when they were alone in their rooms.

But the worst thing they did to me was to stay with me for life and fucked me up in a variety of ways.

She stood over me as I wrote away or scribbled away in junior infants and then without any warning, she brought the stick down on my knuckles, not enough to leave any bruising, but sore enough to make you stop what you were doing. There was Sr Kathleen stood in front of the desk sending the pencil flying, and sending me back into the chair with the shock.

"We don't write with our left hands, Gibbons. We write with our right hands. That's why it's called the right hand. The left hand is the devil's hand for the work of the devil," she said. "It will be left below in the fires of Hell with you. That's why it's called the left hand."

I often wished I could have shown her years later that she was talking through her hole 'cos I could never wank with me left hand, even in those teenage years when you'd lie on it to numb it so that it would feel like 'twas someone else who was doing it. Though even now I don't know if I could ever bring myself to tell her that. She'd have a fuckin' heart attack if I did. But 'twould have been interesting to see the reaction.

Mother never told me we were going to the school. She said we were going to Mass, but I knew that when we reached the top of the hill at Bridge Street and continued up Glebe Street that we weren't taking the usual route to the church. And when the realisation dawned on me that for the first time in her life that she was deliberately lying to me, I started to cry and pull her arm and beg with her to take me home, 'cos she never used to lie to me before about any place we were going, so she must have had a good fuckin' reason to be doing it now. So I pulled at her and went to my knees to stop her from dragging me along, but she hit me a slap across the gob and told me to cop meself on and so I walked with her, sobbing and shaking and swallowing gasps of air as I tried not to panic. And I thought I'd piss myself with the shock, 'cos that had happened to me once when we sat in beside the fella with the bushy whiskers and eyebrows at Mass 'cos Mother knew we'd say fuck all if he was there glowering down at us. I said fuck all that day, even when my socks were soaking with the fright and then she had to bring me out and into the back sacristy to clean me up.

On this morning, when we got to the class, my eyes were dried but many others in the class were there in tears, bawling their little holes off. So then I didn't feel so bad. I could see that they had been lied to as well. Within a few minutes, she was gone off. And although I couldn't be sure, I saw her wipe her eyes as she went down the corridor from the class at the end of the old convent building. She had gone there before when she was a child and she probably knew that this would be the last time she'd be bringing a child to his first day at school.

When I saw this, I stopped crying and just gulped down my tears. And when the nun saw this (a different nun to the one who made me change hands), she gave me a liquorice allsort. And after that, there was a sweet for every child who stopped crying.

We didn't do much that first day, just sat around and played with chalk on big slate tiles that had to be washed down once a week with a wet cloth. So we drew and scribbled and wiped our noses with chalk-covered sleeves and blushed when someone looked at us. And stood confused when we were allowed out the back to the big institution-like yard that you'd see nowadays in those black and white news reports about nuns and priests batin' and ridin' young fellas. Big drab place, high walls with a greyness of the era which made us feel trapped in a cloud of time.

I didn't know it then but those little bastards sitting around me were to feature strongly in my life in the years to come. The kids from up the town, up the Neale Road and the Kilmaine Road and Cornmarket and Abbey Street and Main Street — the way they'd make me feel, the way they'd lord over me and the lads from the High Street and the Creagh Road and the Castlebar Road — with their notions and their big houses and their daddies and mammies with proper jobs like you'd see in the books, doctors and vets and bankers and the like. Jobs that you didn't get ya covered in shit, the likes of what Jackie Gibbons had. Jobs that you'd see in books, like the Famous Five. Enid Blyton had no council workers in her books.

But back then they were just pitiful abandoned kids like meself. And we turned around and looked at each other that day as equals, perhaps for the only time we'd look at each other that way for the next sixteen years. And beyond.

The Fifth Year

Do they think we don't ate proper?

Or talk proper or wash ourselves

all over?

Do they think we drink tay from

chipped mugs with stained gapes

carrying diseases of long dead relatives?

Do they think our musty smell is our smell

and not the scent

of just-once-worn suits and camphorised blouses?

Why were we so long working hard

not being us?

Why did we try to be anything but us,

but something they

thought we were.

(Peadar Gibbons)

"Can ya go to the moon in a helicopter?" I asked the man in the boiler suit and the helmet as he rose the chopper off the Green behind our house and brought us up over the town. All the lads with us gasped as we went up over the river and higher than the church steeple which looked down from the hill over the whole town. "I think I'm gonna get puked, " said Paul Sheridan the guard's son but he didn't 'cos he covered his eyes so that he wouldn't see how high up we were. He was always a weak little fucker anyway, so we weren't surprised that he wanted to bail out. The same prick fainted about fifteen years later when we put on a porn video and he threw up at the sight of all the penetration. You may ask what a bunch of youngsters from Ballinrobe were doing in a US air force helicopter in 1970 but we were — and to make it better 'twas all the young lads from our street who were picked up have the free ride. To hell with the lads from the Neale Road.

Pat Nixon had landed in our patch and we weren't going to be cheated out of any of the benefits.

To be honest, we'd never heard of Pat Nixon or who he was, but He turned out to be a She and that She was married to a He who had a face like a bulldog licking piss off a thistle but who was very important in the world. So you'd wonder how the fuck this Pat Nixon, the First Lady of America ended up in the field behind our house.

Turns out her grandfather had come from a townland outside the town but had fucked off to the States during the Famine and she was visiting to see the homestead and meet whatever cousins she had in the place.

We were never told why her husband didn't bother his hole to come along and visit us too. Father said that he was a thick bollocks anyway and that there was no good in him.

33

She had arrived in the biggest of the three USAF helicopters that landed in The Green behind our house and so the whole townfolk got a collective horn on them with the excitement. There'd been nawthing like this since Grace Kelly drove through in 1961 on her way to visit her homestead in Newport. Father and the other council workers were called in to clean up the park and fence off the stage area for the event.

Pat Farragher the carpenter built a stage but when they realised that was made of chipboard, they put a layer of timber over it to keep all the dignitaries up. Last thing they wanted was the First Lady of America falling on her hole through the floor. After all 'twas just six or seven years after Kennedy had been shot so we didn't want all the Paddys in the White House to be leavin' in a box.

'Cos Father and his council crew had done the work, we were given passes which allowed us up the front with a good gawk at Pat Nixon. She could have been a towering Amazonian with black hair down to her waist for all we knew, but she turned out to be a petite wan with a blonde hairstyle, a tweedy kinda dress with bits of green in it and a handbag which we all assumed carried a gun. We were all given little Star Spangled Banners on sticks to wave at her. She passed by in an instant and mounted the stage and gave a small speech about some shite or other and then left to be driven to the tidy little cottage out the Carnalecka Road where she got the smell of fresh paint and tea poured in fine china and delicate little buns and fruit cake made especially for the day. No big lumps of ham sandwiches for Pat Nixon and her dainty little hands in her dainty little gloves with her dainty little ways.

And it was when they were gone out to visit the cottage and the relatives that the pilots of the two smaller helicopters gathered

34

up a few of the kids in that front paddock and herded us into the cabin. Six or eight at a time, all pressed into the seats, too nervous to sit near the door in case we'd fucking fall out – and that was while we were still on the ground.

'Tis hard to remember exactly how fucking excited we all were, but remember this was a group of kids whose sole experience of any type of flying was limited to the swinging boats in the fun fair at the annual horse show in the town.

We loved it. Up we went and we leant this way and that, as the helicopter went over the trees and past the steeple and followed the track of the river from the town bridge at the Bowers around by the barracks and down to the weir at the Soldier's Hole, the deep dangerous swirling pond at the end of the main river near the Weir.

And we looked at each other and gave little laughs of excitement that only kids do because they're in that age before embarrassment kicks in. And the pilot with his helmet and his uniform and he smiling at us and the big fuckin' American jaw on him and the light reflecting off his sunglasses and ya knowing he could kill ya if he wanted, and his co-pilot beside him the same way saying things to us about what the name the river had and where we went to school. Such was the pure innocence of us all, taking part in a story the likes of which we'd spend our lives insisting was true, even though it just came out of nowhere.

And just as quickly as Pat Nixon had arrived, she'd fucked off again. She'd come back from the cottage where she met her cousins and she was all smiley and like, and she walked along the line of us and patted us on the heads and asked us how we were, but we were too young to say anything of meaning so we just nodded and got the smell of her, the sort of sweet old-woman perfume and lipstick that seemed so perfectly applied to a face between middle age and old age. And we noticed she'd great American fuckin' teeth the likes of which she'd never have had if she stayed around Ballinrobe atin' Macaroon bars and gobstoppers.

And then with a little wave of her gloved hands and a bunch of fuckin' roses or something in her hand, she climbed up the steps of the big helicopter and we clapped and clapped and we stood back as it roared into life and then lifted itself up, up, and up, 'til 'twas higher than the trees and then the church, and it headed to the east and the other two alongside it and we watched 'til it became a little fuckin' dot in the sky and when that dot died and disappeared from view altogether, everyone there just looked around at each other, rubbed their hands together in a 'now, that went well, didn't it,' sort of way, scratched their balls 'cos they'd been dying to for hours but didn't want to take the chance, and set about taking down all the chipboardy stuff and loudspeakers that had been put up for her.

We kinda knew it then but didn't want to acknowledge that this day would be a rare exciting day in the life of this town. You didn't accept this because with every day ever after, you'd have the longing in ya that there'd be a chance of something exciting happening that day, and that it would be something good, not just exciting in a bad way like a death or a fire or a car crash up on the hill where the cars came flying around without looking.

I've looked back in the library on the internet to see if there was any coverage of that event in the papers and stuff, 'cos I did spend me life telling people that we had done this, but most people thought I was talking through me hole, but there's fuck all about it. It was as if the day had never happened at all.

But it did and for one day we thought the eyes of the world were upon us; we rushed home that evening and looked at the TV and Charles Mitchell reading the news on RTE to see if we were on it but there was nothing. Mr Nixon, the woman's husband had done something else that day in Dublin and so they didn't give a shit about what happened in our town.

That night I looked out the back window of the house, across the garden and the fields towards the Green. It was all silent now, there were no flags fluttering or no bands playing. It was as if nothing had just happened. I wondered if life would be like that — great hopes, the occasional excitement but ultimately a disappointment for those of us in life who were passengers and not pilots.

Before I shut my eyes that night, I wondered where Pat Nixon was sleeping, and was she thinking about her visit and her relatives and if she ever really gave a fuck about Ballinrobe.

The Sixth Year

Why do those with more
always want to take more
from those with less?
Why can we never
have more than less.
Do those with more
want less and if
they get our less
does that give them
even more?
More or less

(Peadar Gibbons)

I don't know why I always felt so comfortable in the woods, 'cos if truth be told, they were fuckin' scary spaces. Dark, overgrown branches that looked like they were reaching to grab you. At daytime when we'd be there, I'd be scared shitless and at night when I wasn't there but was at home in my bed scrunched up under the woollen blankets, I'd be scared shitless at the thought of being there in the dark of night.

Father used to bring us there when he'd be cutting timber for the winter. We'd go down in late summer and we'd use two bushman saws to cut down half grown trees and cut them into logs. And then when the logs were cut, we'd chop the round stumps into smaller logs and bag them in hard 10-10-20 fertiliser plastic bags that we'd have got from the mart. The woods were just a mile from our house, so we'd cycle down and cut and chop for a few weekends before he'd borrow uncle Liam's car and we'd fill the bags of logs and squeeze them into the boot and back seat and bring them home to the shed. We'd make twenty or so journeys to get them all home. Maybe the reason I remember it was because back in the days before innocence ended, Mother would bring down a bag of sandwiches and flasks of tea so that we'd get it all done by dusk.

Tea poured into mugs out of flasks that had tartan surrounds; chunky white bread sandwiches with ham and cheap corned beef in them and some salad cream to give them a sting. And then some biscuits. It was the thought of the food that kept us going most mornings and we were always amazed that although we'd had to fight our way through brambles and bushes to get to the clearing where we cut the sticks, Mother used to just appear there, out of nowhere with the bag of food, and not a hair out of place or a sleeve snagged on some fuckin' bramble. She was like the apparition of Our Lady at Knock. She'd just appear.

And then she'd go home with the empties and we'd work on till the evening came and the sunlight above the trees disappeared and the woods took on that menacing feel. When dusk then fell across the woods, the wood became a whole different backdrop from a horror movie. Harmless trees became towering monsters, the slightest noise would be the sound of a wolf awakening, or so Dad'd tell us just to that he could keep us close by and stop us wandering off through the trees.

When he wouldn't be looking, I'd head off through the dense growth to the spot where there was an old stone lime kiln, covered in ivy and moss. It was used back in the early 1900s and had lain dormant ever since. I used to climb up on its arched roof and imagine what it would be like for the lime man, working away here in the heart of the woods, not knowing what creatures had their eyes on him.

That fucker must have been really brave. I wished I had that bravery. Being the youngest, Dad reckoned I was the least brave, but I wanted to show him that I could be as brave as my big brothers who were allowed to wander further in the woods than I was. It wasn't fair that they could do that. I wondered if I'd ever be that brave or would I be scared shitless all my life. Dad had told us that before the lime man worked in the arch that it was a home for a witch who lived in the woods and who used to eat little kids. We were used to hearing shit like that from time to time, but we didn't mind as it was a rare time when we'd get close, all us men in the family. Away from mother and granny always telling us to do things like wash our hands and faces or not to be picking our noses or scratching our holes.

Father loved it too, sitting there around the fire he'd have lit in the fire-pit, sharing cheese and corned beef sandwiches and flasks of tea with his four sons, the boys who would grow into men and care for him when he was old and infirm. At break time, he'd sit for ages, smoke four or five Carroll's, tell scary stories about the woods and ruffle our hair?

He was in his element, sitting there puffing away with his nicotine-stained fingers, the smell of the woods off him, the shavings from the timber all over his jacket and in his hair, and we gathered round him like you'd see in the movies, laughing with him and joking with him and the lads minding me, putting their arms around me 'cos I couldn't understand what they were laughing about, but I joined in anyway. I just knew that Dad was happy, that there wasn't a smell of drink off him, that he was being the kind of dad that you'd expect to have – strong, brave, responsible, caring, and there when you wanted him. And so we sat around proudly as he went on and on.

But as he'd do it, you could tell there was a sadness about him. And although we were happy, there was a sort of sadness about us too that these days happened so rarely and that there was nobody there to see us acting like a real family, doing things together. One good day, he even helped us a bit with our camp-building which thrilled us because it meant he acknowledged that we had to have some playtime even when working in the woods. He used some rope to tie it together and make it even more sturdy. Then he cut down some more branches to put inside to make it even warmer, so that the wind would not whistle through it. He helped us to camouflage it, so that you'd barely see it until you were right upon it. Father was fierce proud of it. It was if he too felt the uniqueness of those days together in the woods. It was as if he didn't feel that he was a proper father, sure he knew he wasn't with his drinking and riding and whoring around.

So we were surprised and he was probably surprised at what we all felt when he came along and built our camp. And for the next week, we had our lunch in there and even Mother squeezed into the darkness when she arrived with the food. Camp Gibbons we called it.

Then one day we got there and the place was knocked down. Some cunts from the town had obviously found it and ripped it apart. They had taken a lot of our timber as well - a week's work down the drain. 'Twas either the knackers or the pricks from the Neale Road, but they wouldn't have stolen the timber, so we'd no clue. We were devastated and I cried. And the lads cried.

Dad took this very badly and went on the whiskey for a few weeks. When he did this we went to the wood ourselves and rebuilt the camp, this time using bigger branches. But it was never as good as the day that he made it. We brought the bushman saw and cut enough timber to replace the stuff stolen the previous week.

We didn't have Liam's car and didn't want to take the risk of the timber being stolen again, so we hung two bags on the bars of the bike and made dozens and dozens of journeys home. Mother was very pleased and let us go to the pictures that night.

We ate Emerald sweets and Perri crisps and drank Cadet orange and watched Clint Eastwood in T*he Good, The Bad and the Ugly* and wished we had the guns and the coolness to shoot dead those pricks who had knocked our camp and stole our timber.

And as we ate and drank we were thrilled by Clint and when we came out onto the street we ran mock gun battles with the other lads who'd been at the pictures.

But just as we were enjoying the games all the way down Bridge Street, we found Father slumped drunk in a puddle of his own piss up near the bridge and I ran home crying.

And I cursed the lads from up town for always fucking our family up and for ruining the few good moments we all had together.

And I still do.

The Seventh Year

Lies are like little rabbits

once you've two,

you've four,

then eight,

Lies ride like bunnies

needing the fur of their subversion

to cover the other

Needing the fluff of one

to create another.

(Peadar Gibbons)

A big shaggin' pencil, the likes of which you'd need two hands to use. As useful as tits on a bull. About foot and a half long, an inch wide and a map of Ireland all the way around it, with the usual boring locations marked on it. The bloody Rock of Cashel, the Blarney Stone, Clonmacnoise. This was obviously a pencil designed for some yank to buy in Bunratty and bring back to his home in Missouri and hang over the fireplace as a mark of respect to some long lost grandfather called Michael Martin O'Mahoney or something like that.

I have no idea who gave me the fuckin' thing. Probably Granny 'cos she usually shopped in Miss Dee's, the shop opposite the church which sold a whole host of religious shit, statues, Children of Prague (is that the plural for Child of Prague), Blessed Martins, St Bernadettes, the lot. If there was ever a martyr who gave his life for God, Miss Dee had an alabaster version of him or her. She had them from five inches tall to five feet tall which you could put in your front hall and it would scare the shit out of ya if staggered in late and half tore any night.

Miss Dee was about ninety but was still running her shop. I used to be bored out of me mind when Granny brought us in there after Second Mass. 'Cos there was nothing in there to interest a kid at all, apart from the little snow globes of Knock and Lourdes. And a Sacred Heart picture where the eyes of Jesus would follow you around the room and which had a special illusion where you thought the eyes were open and then shut. Fuckin' thing used to freak me out, especially after she bought it and put it on the wall in the sitting room. And do ya know, that to this day remains the only room in the house where I didn't ever have a wank, gas isn't it? I was afraid that just before's ya'd come, you'd say 'Oh Jayssiiiiss' and the picture would say, "yeah, what?"

45

Well, whoever gave me the pencil gave me a five pound note as well. Big brown thing that I didn't know how I'd spend. But I wanted to treat everyone. I never had money that big before. Real money like grownups had, not the two pennies that I'd get to buy Taytos and Perri and the likes. No, this was the kind of money you'd use to buy people something they'd like. First thing I did with it that evening was buy a big apple tart and a bottle of Lucozade. I was hooked on Lucozade at the time, though I've no idea why now. Strange fuckin' taste off it. But it kinda counteracted the badness of ating' an apple tart. Like, this will make me a fat fucker, but the Lucozade will make me fit. Or least that was the shaggin' theory.

The flutes from the Neale Road all arrived for the Holy Communion dressed in little suits and mini ties. It was like they were all going to a court sitting for dwarves. They looked like mini men with their suits that matched their ties, and their little hankies that matched their suits.
I was wearing reddish trousers, a grey cardigan and a shirt with a little dickie bow that had been handed down from brother to brother. I felt then that I looked like a spare prick. As I hold the photo here in my hand now, I know that I looked like a spare prick. In fact when I look back at all the photos from my younger years, I looked like a spare prick all the fuckin' time.
I rarely wore new clothes, having to settle instead for hand-me-downs by the four brothers. By the time they got to me, not only were they wrecked, but they were also about half a decade out of style. I was like the singer in that song *Rock and Roll I Gave You All the Best Years of My life*, when he finally caught up with the trends, they had moved on. "You were changing your direction, and I never really knew, that I was always just two

46

steps behind you."

And he was fucked 'cos in the end he sold his guitar.

That was me, but I'd no guitar to sell. 'Cos nobody would want my clothes. I felt that my clothes were just for other fellas to laugh at.

Mother didn't give a shit whether we were in fashion or not, as long as were warm in winter and cool in summer.

If there were some times in life that I excelled at anything, then First Confession was one of them. We were brought down to the church by the mouldy auld nun who used to slap me around the place and made me write with me wankin' hand. Then she acted out as the priest in the confessional box while we went in the other side and recited what imaginary sin came into our minds.

I know that I made up some longwinded sin that involved theft, avarice, pride, selfishness, a bit of sloth and a slight bit of lust thrown in for good measure – all I know is that when I was finished, she sat there, with her big mouth open, her dentures hopping up and down on her gums and she opened the door of the confessional and dragged me out, looking around at the empty church before lashing me across the face.

"Now that was one of the best sins I've heard all day, but if I hear you talking about that sort of dirt again, I'll be telling your mother."

I wanted to cry but was too stunned. My sin had been creative, much more so than the "I told a lie, Father' type that the rest of the class had used. They had just gone in for the boring option, but they had gone for the type of sin that the teachers wanted to hear, not stuff from outside the box.

For the first time of many in my schooling years, my ability to throw words together had landed me in the shite.

47

"You've a great way with the words, Gibbons. You might amount to more than your father yet," she said.

I knew she was being a mean auld cunt the way she said that, but it was some sort of praise so I took it for that. 'Twas better to be noticed than not be seen at all. Oscar Wilde said that. Or something like it.

First Communion wasn't any more pleasant.

When I went up the aisle with the classmates and lined up to take the host from the priest, I came down to Mother and said 'yuk, it tastes like paper, Mammy." I wondered if this was what all the fuss was about. And Mother was sitting there beside me with the cream handbag she kept for days like this. Father always went to a different mass, if he went to Mass at all. Either way he wasn't there that day.

All the other kids seemed to be going to the Valkenburg Hotel or the Lakeland Hotel for dinner, but the guys in our street were just eating at home with their families. I was looking forward to this, being the centre of attention for a day. Eating our tea in the sitting room, where we normally just went for Christmas. I hoped that we'd all sit around and share the apple tart; the apple tart that I had bought with my money. I was going to slice it up and share it out but when I got home, Father had just stumbled in the door from the pub. He had been off celebrating my Communion without the rest of us.

Granny told him he was a disgrace but he told her to keep her fuckin' nose out of his family and his marriage and that he wished she was dead.

And that he hoped she died from a cancer that rotted her hole.

And had her screaming 'til the life left her.

And then she screamed and cried in the way that only an old woman can cry.

Horrid, witchy sort of way.

You don't often hear really old women cry.

Or should ya either.

And then he picked up the apple tart from its little foil plate, and fucked it against the wall, the crumbs flying everywhere.

Mother screamed at him but he told her to fuck off as well.

And I just stood there, oblivious to the shouting and the screaming, with me Holy Communion badge on me, and I just looking at the bits of apple stuck on the floor and on the wall and running down the face of the Sacred Heart picture with the funny eyes.

And I swear to fuck, I think it winked.

Good on ya, Jaysus.

The Eighth Year

Don't Prods get old
and young again
Their aged skins softened
by lyrical
pulpit ramblings
and psalms that sooth the soul
while our blood vessels burst
in our cheeks at rage and fear
of overriding guilt
at over-riding
spat down at us
by padres who despise us.
And the soft skins soft spoken and gentle
cover their ears as they pass our doors
for fear of shaming us more

(Peadar Gibbons)

Now that I've been saying what I've been saying, you might be thinking I was a cheeky little fecker in and out of trouble, but if truth be told I wasn't like that all at all.

I can well remember the first thieving I did, proper stealing like. We distracted Katie Jennings in her sweet shop and stole a Gateaux Chocolate Log and a Tipsy Cake which was a kind of a Battenburg thing but just made up of all the odds and ends from the Gateaux factory with a dollop of brandy fecked into it, hence its name. The bloody thing was gorgeous, but you could never eat more than slice of it, so it was pointless stealing a full one 'cos you'd be throwing the rest of it away.

But I was just eight when I performed my first act of proper illegality – we stole apples from the big rambling orchard belonging to the Dunbars, the only remaining gentry in our town. I have no idea why kids steal apples. I mean you can only ate two or three of the bloody things at any time, so nicking them in bagfuls seemed a bit daft. I'd bring them to Mother and ask her to bake me an apple cake, but she soon copped on that we hadn't bought the apples and slapped it out of us where we got them.

She was horrified when she found out we had stolen the apples 'cos her father used to work for the Dunbar family who owned the 100 acres of orchard and woods just two minutes from our house. "Your grandfather would be twisting in his grave if he knew what a brat you were to steal Mrs Dunbar's apples and he the poor divil who probably planted those trees for her," she said to me as she slapped me across the face, giving me a right stinger and nearly catching me into the eye with the side of her ring.

So Mother made me march up to Mrs Dunbar and apologise for stealing them. She was a little old white-haired lady who had those Protestant good looks, you know the way they age beautifully so much better than us Catholics do. That kind of perfect skin and lively eyes even though the rest of them is deteriorating; the Prods are fuckin' masters at that kind of progression. The Catholics just get drunk and wrinkled and fall over and can't work or walk. But the Prods just get older yet are still able to fuckin' work as hard as ever. That was the likes of Mrs Dunbar, Audrey Eleanor Dunbar, but nobody ever called her that.

The era in which her family had dominated the town was long gone and now she just rambled alone in the big house, getting the occasional visit from her sons and daughters who now lived in England having been Oxbridge educated. Even though she probably had enough money for the rest of her life, and certainly enough to hire a few helpers around the house, she just paid a gardener to act as bailiff and did all the pottering around the house herself. She spoke with a wonderfully plummy accent and always said hello to us 'cos she knew us out of our grandfather who had chauffeured her around when she was a young wan.

I was an age waiting for the door to open, knowing that it would take her a few minutes to get from the scullery right up to the hall, and as I stood there on the top of the steps, I was aware that any other fuckers passing by would see me and be wondering what I was doing at the steps at the front of the house. They'd be thinking I was going in to inform on them all, to name and shame all the lads who had stolen her apples. But I wasn't. I was just going to name and shame meself and to take whatever was the consequence of it all. In a way, guards, ye can see certain parallels with what I'm doing now. A sort of take it on the chin attitude that I get from time to time. Though it gets me nowhere.

She didn't make me feel at all bad. She knew all the stuff that Granddad had done for them at a time when it was not beneficial for any Irishman to be seen to help any of the landed gentry and so she wasn't about to torture his grandson over a bag of few mouldy apples, when she had thousands more in the orchards and probably more falling in the wind than were ever stolen from her.

She said she'd forgive me if I'd help her sort out some stuff in the house. And she'd pay me. She felt that her possessions needed to be organised and that she could do with a young lad to gather things for her. Mother trusted Mrs Dunbar implicitly so she had no problem in letting me go along and do some odd jobs and carry dirty old boxes smelling of fuckin' long dead life. She gave me gifts of books like The Wind in the Willows and Lorna Doone. I loved that one. Scottish families fighting and rowing. And I loved that name too. Lorna.

None of the other lads in the street were made to go and apologise. If truth be told, most of the other parents on the street had no time for Mrs Dunbar or were intimidated by her. They'd found themselves unable to talk to her when she'd say hello and stop for a conversation.

"People around here think I only want to talk about the weather. They stop and look at their feet and probably wish I hadn't said hello to them at all," she told me one day when I was lugging boxes of documents down to the cellar for her to go through.

I was scared shitless in that house though. And especially of the room at the end of the house which had the windows all barred and the door locked. Since I was knee high to a grasshopper, we'd all been told the story about the card game that had been

53

played there 50 years before, when a row ensued and a stranger who was playing the cards stood up, startling the men there who looked down and saw that he had cloven feet. Then just as they shrieked, the stranger disappeared into the night. For ever after that, the room was barred up, never to be used again.

And although I knew that the story was probably a load of auld bollocks told about every landed gentry house in the country, I stood there and stared at the door to this locked room. And because of that, something drew me to turn the handle and try to get inside, but I knew I'd never be right after it if something horrible was in there, so I quickly turned around and ran back up the stairs.

I spent three weeks in that house helping Mrs Dunbar organise old records and sheets of music, and old maps and musty old newspapers and letters which seemed to have been sent from across the world and which she was storing in a series of old biscuit tins around the house. I had no idea what any of these things were about, but she gave me four big albums of rare stamps when I was finished. They had belonged to one of her sons, but he didn't want them any more as he was now in his fifties and living in England. I brought them home and kept them in my room and for weeks afterwards, I'd go through them all to see if there was any Penny Black stamp in there that I could sell for a fortune. And although I had a few scares that I might have found one, in the end I didn't. But they were lovely and I still have them.

There were yellowing old letters in a silken bag that she showed me, and they all started with the line 'My darling Aw." She said they were from the only man she ever truly loved and when I looked down at the name at the end, it wasn't her husband

54

George who had signed them but someone called Trevor who lived in India. And when she looked at them she looked like she was far away, and she often cried that if she had the chance to change things, how much she would have. And something about now being too old to be loved by anyone anymore. And then she'd go off into long chats about life being a series of crossroads and that the direction you take alters the destination you find. All of which seemed pretty obvious to me at the time.

A few months after I helped Mrs Dunbar with her documents, she fell down the little stairs leading down from the kitchen into the scullery and she broke her hip. She was lying there for a day before she was discovered and she was rushed to hospital in Castlebar. Her family came home from England to visit her and to arrange for her to move into a care home, far from the house where she'd lived and grown up and where she'd amassed all those wonderful things that she'd spent the last few years of her life sorting out.

She never went back to the house again, and she died in the care home. The once fine grandeur house went to rack and ruin. It was later sold to some club and was left in shite, turned into a clubhouse pub with people pissing in the hallways during drinking sessions and card drives.
And fuckers the likes of whom would never have been let into that fine house by the front door stubbing out their fags into the wood turned by the finest of dead craftsman.

I wonder if the devil ever turned up there again....
Maybe he did,
And they just never saw me.

The Ninth Year

Sun squinting through the prism made

by Harry throwing shades

Over pews and altar

Leaving my face a canvas for colours

the green on top of the blue on top of the red

put there by fear of dropping the patten

on some auld wan's toes.

The smell of priest and crimson wine

dyed into the sleeve of my dead brother's soutane.

(Peadar Gibbons)

I hated missing the end of Opportunity Knocks. There was no fuckin' point to seeing any of Opportunity Knocks if you didn't see the end of it. That would be like watching the Eurovision and then switching off the telly after all the songs had ended. No, we had to leave Opportunity Knocks so that we could go to the Legion of Mary meeting. They clashed at the same time every Monday evening, so just when the Cotton Mill Boys or the Duane Family were getting into their swing, doing their bit for Ireland, we'd have to get out the door and head for the meeting in the Sacristy at the back corner of the church.

At different stages, Mother had enrolled us in the Legion 'cos she felt it would make us better kids. She felt we should be doing good things for other people and the Legion had a stipulation that every week you had to do a good deed for some poor auld bastard in your area. And then you had to relay this to the meeting and get approving nods from the worthies who ran the meetings.

I normally chopped sticks for Delia Fahy across the street. She lived on her own in a small terraced house and hobbled around with the aid of a stick. My brother Kieran thought he'd killed her once when he kicked a football through her window, just months before she died. He thought that some of the glass that shattered from the window might have gone into her sugar bowl on the table inside and that she might have swallowed this. But, 'twas a heart attack that killed her, and not a spoon of glass fragments tearing open her throat.

Another good deed I had to do was to get messages for Tommy Walsh in our street. Messages were not like real messages, but the word used to describe errands for groceries. Peter Murtagh's cousin home from America for a holiday once asked us what the fuck we were talking about when we said we had to do the messages for our mothers. But he was a yank so we didn't expect any better. He wouldn't play soccer with us or anything. Just sat and ate like fuck - the fat bastard who tried to run but couldn't. Murtagh said 'Jaysus, I'd say he walks away from a fair shite."

And if you were in the Legion of Mary, you had to be in the altar boys or the servers as we were called. Mother said that I'd have to do that as well, just to make use of the immaculately clean soutane and surplice which was handed down from the boys. Kieran only got to wear it for a few years and it hadn't been used since then, 'cos later on Mother lost the heart for a while and didn't talk much to us. So I had to wear my brother's soutane and she cried when I put it on and left the room and Granny patted me on the head and said 'you look like a little priesteen, Peadar, a little priesteen."

I was in group C led by Gerry Kellegher. He was the one in it the longest so as each leader left, the next longest serving server took over the role of captain. There were three masses on Sunday in the church — early, middle, and last Mass. You started doing last Mass, then the next week, you did middle Mass; the next week First Mass. If you did First Mass, then you were on for all the daily Masses during the week at 8am and 7.30pm.
If you did all that, then there was a week off.

I thought I'd fuckin' hate it, but I didn't - I loved it. Ok, I was nervous the first day when I had to walk out there in front of the whole town, all dressed in their finery and me thinking that all they were looking at was me. And I was afraid I'd shit in me trousers or something. I knew I was red the whole way through and the blushing in me put me heart racing and thumping and I was afraid it was going to burst in a heart attack because I thought that was how people got heart attacks and their arteries exploded. But after a while I'd see they weren't all looking at me and then I thought they mightn't give a shit about some young fella from the High Street anyway when they had their prayers to be saying and their Holy Joe impressions to be giving.

I think I liked it 'cos there weren't any pricks from the Neale Road doing it. No, the mass-serving was strictly the preserve of the lads our side of town. Maybe it was because the priests felt that we needed a bit of guidance and moral teaching that four years in the Mass-serving might do to us.

Each member of the group was allotted a different task – you had to go out and light the candles first, which wasn't too bad although I was afraid I'd bring down the High Altar candles with the extinguisher which was a long pole with a brass cup on top that would snuff out the flame.

The Consecration was the most dodgy job – as you had to hold up the water and the wine for the priest and not drop anything. This was seriously front of house as well as you were right beside the altar.

Bells was a handy one, you just had to stay awake and catch the key words and moments when you would twirl the four bells around in your hand for about five seconds. It meant you had to be on the fuckin' ball, 'cos if you missed the cue, the priest would look at ya and then the whole fuckin' town would be looking at ya.

I loved bells because it was something the whole church noticed, although we spent most the time trying not to be made laugh by the smart Neale Road fuckers in the top rows alongside their mammies and daddies, glad that they didn't have to do the menial jobs like Mass serving.

They'd be teasing me during the week saying that I was only in it because the priests were ridin' me, but that wasn't the truth at all. The priests were grand. No ridin' or dropping the hands or smiling funny at ya the way the others did. There was a parish priest who was a boring auld lad with long winded sermons that he'd be better off giving to ecclesiastical students in Maynooth, rather than a small parish in the west of Ireland. But the two curates were great gas, always in mighty form, singing and joking their way into the sacristy where they'd don their robes. Then we'd line up and the sacristan would ring the bell and out we'd march, turning to genuflect at the High Altar before turning and making our way down to the low altar where'd we take a side each facing the congregation.

Maybe this was the happiest time of my life 'cos here I was in front of the whole town, 'cos it was something I could do well and something that no rich fuckers could take away from me. I used to bask there with the light streaming in through the priceless Harry Clarke stained glass windows, the morning sun throwing a rainbow of shades across our pallid visage.

On the weeks when I was doing the early morning masses, I'd run from my house up the Bowers by the river and up the hill to the church. The sacristan Jack used to live near us and he'd set off cycling at the same time. Each morning, my aim was to get to the church gate before he did, by using a series of shortcuts. And then with the birds singing in the trees on the Mound near our house, I'd set off with the early morning's sun in my eyes, racing up the town, the cares of the world behind me, and thoughts of school afterwards banished from my mind.

Then when I got home afterwards, Mother would have tea and bread toasted on a fork in the fire and we'd sit there and share breakfast together, just the two of us, proud of each other and she'd be hugging me and holding me and the warmth of her body against mine and the heat of the fire and with the crinkly just-right texture of the toast, I'd feel the most loved person in the world, even though I'd no idea why. And when I want to think of those days, I get a fork and stick a slice of bread on it into the embers and watch it curl up, the way Mother curled her arms into me on those sunny morning when I was as content as I would ever be in my life, but of course I didn't know it at that time.

Everything was just about to change.

The Tenth Year

Rap rap rap

a knock, just a tap

and another

and then a shush

a look

a sigh

a shuffle

a grab of a duffle

and the beginning of an end

a pat of a shoulder

then a scream

a roar

a childhood no more

(Peadar Gibbons)

I knew there was something wrong when me uncle arrived at the class door, and spoke to the nun. She looked down at me and went outside for a minute. She never looked at me much so I figured I'd fucked up something. I'd just learned the word fuck from Peter Cuddy. That and bra. Bra were the bumps on a woman's chest. I'd said fuck and bra a lot in the last few weeks just to be cool. He had been saying them a lot before that. I said Christ too, even though the nun slapped Kevin Sheridan for saying that. Was Christ worse than fuck and were they both worse than bra? I felt bad about saying Christ. That was the worst one, I thought. I wonder was that what the nun was worried about. Was that why Uncle Liam was here? He went to Mass a lot so he would be mad if he heard me say fuck and definitely if he heard me say Christ. He might not skelp me but he'd tell me father and he would skelp me, so either way I was fucked.

I said fuck under my breath. And then Christ when I saw her walking towards me.

"Ciunas," she said to the class, and came down to my desk. "Put away your stuff, Peadar. You've to go home." And she never called me Peadar before, so I knew something was wrong.

Uncle Liam had the car with him, a black Morris Minor with a rusty number plate. We used to borrow it on Sundays and go for a spin across country to the cousins in Galway who lived on the farm.

This day he made me sit in the front and said "your mother said to collect you. Something's happened.'

He wouldn't tell me what, so after a few attempts asking him, I gave up. I reckoned that Granny might have got sick or something, 'cos he didn't say Father said to collect me. And since Granny was Liam's mother as well, maybe they just did things

63

like that.

But Mother was screaming when we got to the house. Which was strange for her 'cos she never said much loud really. Most of the time she'd be just talking in that low voice of hers or sighing the way she did when she'd be doing the dishes at the sink or chopping the spuds. Mother sighed a lot, but today she was screaming and breathing a strange sort of noise that was neither talking nor screaming. Like a scream from the neck. I thought she'd swallowed something and was choking, But she wasn't. Mrs Fahy had her arm around her and helped her into the chair beside the fire. When Liam brought me in, I stopped to look, but he brought me through the house and out the back garden. None of the lads were there, which was strange.

And then he put his hand on my shoulder, and went down on his hunkers in front of me, and rubbing his other hand through his hair, he said.

"It's Kieran…he fell into the Soldier's Hole…. and they haven't got him out. They're looking now," he said.

"Is he drownded? Did he drownded in the Hole?" I asked.

He didn't say anything, but nodded.

We'd been told never to go near the Soldier's Hole. It was a big swirling pond right at the end of the River Robe, just past the salmon weir. The story went that back in the 1900s when a British infantry soldier was stationed in the barracks just up river, he jumped into that pond and drownded himself. We never figured out why someone would drownded themselves. Wouldn't that be a fuckin' stupid thing to do. It's one thing getting drownded but doing it yourself would be terrible. That river was full of eels and they'd be swimming around your body and taking little bites out of you. I wondered if the water would be dark black if you fell into it. and if you went to the side walls to climb up, wouldn't you be scared shitless that you'd put your hand in one of the holes in which the eels lived, the dirty bastards. Charlie Ward the knacker who lived in the caravan in the big field once caught one and showed us that even when he cut it up into a dozen pieces, it hopped around alive on the frying pan on his fire. We reckoned if you couldn't kill one when 'twas chopped up, what chance had you when 'twas wrapped around your leg or your neck in the dark of that river, or in the deepness of The Soldier's Hole.

I wondered if Kieran was fighting off those eels now. I wondered if he was alive and collapsed on some part of the riverbank, exhausted from falling into the Soldier's Hole and finding himself downstream away from where the people were looking for him. I wondered all these wonders and then I took off from Liam down the bottom of the garden, up on the branches of the big pear tree and out over the back wall.

I ran across the fields towards the river 'til I got to the tarmac path that ran beside it. Up ahead I could see a lot of people at the weir, one of them had a long stick with a hook. He was dragging something across the water. I know they said I shouldn't have seen that. I heard them say that later on. "The fuckin' child shouldn't have seen that… Liam was supposed to be fuckin' minding him. He came along just as they were dragging the young lad outta the river."

Kieran's face looked fat and white and a bit blue and he wasn't moving.

I suppose I should have shouted something or started crying when I saw that 'twas Kieran they were taking from the water. Is this because I'm not right? Would a right child have cried or

65

something? Was I not right even back then, not able to cry when I should have? The oddness in me head stopping the tears from getting to my eyes. Or had I just seen Mother crying and sighing too much to realise that this was the reaction you had when you were sad. Me other brothers were crying and my father was shouting to the sky and calling God a cunt. And me mother was at home making that strange noise.

So I just ran away back across the fields and back over the wall into the garden and hid there in the trees. I looked at our back yard with the various bits of bicycles and the football that we used to play with and there was nobody playing there today, not a sinner.

Kieran slept in the bed beside me by then. He was older so when he'd come in later at night, he'd tell me to turn into the wall 'cos he didn't want me breathing in his face. So I'd stare at the wall and the little luminous stickers that I'd look at to tell meself I wasn't blind when the light went off.

But that night he wasn't there. I'd the whole bed to myself so I could lie whatever way I wanted. So I did. I slept on my left shoulder and faced out, the whole bed to myself. His pyjamas were there under the pillow, so I took them out and put them in the press so that they wouldn't be reminding me of him.

I felt a big sore pain in me chest that night, I remember like a sickness but I didn't want to puke out. I thought this pain was a strange one. It came and went. When I tried to read my Beano comic, the pain stopped for a while and then came back when I put it down. So I picked it up a lot and read it a lot in the hope that I'd have no pain at all in me belly.

None of the others went to bed early, and there were people coming to the house all night. The knocker was going rat a tat

tat for hours and there were the murmured voices and I'd hear
Mother wailing, but she stopped being as bad after Dr Mac came
to see her and gave her something.

And the priest came to see her.

And that night, Father didn't come up to rub my head and say
'sleep well astoir".

The Eleventh Year

I hate when something

knocks the good out of life

Turns it upside down,

shoulders it and watches the good

roll out of it, and down the street

There are fuck all things

with good in them to start with

without losing any goodness

to stupidity

or selfishness

or greed

or sadness

(Peadar Gibbons)

Mother spoke to herself a lot more after Kieran got drownded. She'd be at the sink and I'd hear her whispering but there'd be no-one there and when I'd ask her was she talking to me, she'd say nothing but wipe her eyes with the back of her hands and carry on. Then Granny would tell me to 'go out the back and play" 'cos Granny seemed to know what Mother would be saying to herself and she'd shoo me with the back of her hand 'cos she didn't want me to be hearing Mother whispering to herself. Granny was the one who was always minding me from hearing things being said all my life. She always be the one who said 'mind the childer" when some fisherman would be sitting at the fire and talking about "fucking cunting pike" in the lake atin' all the trouts.

Although he was only one of us, the house was a lot quieter after Kieran died. You could hear the clock ticking in the kitchen all day in a way that you couldn't hear it before. And when you heard it tick, it seemed to make the day go slower than when you didn't hear it tick. Maybe the clock had some arrangement in the homes of dead people that it drags out the days, so that they would feel fuckin' miserable for longer than the 24 hours in every day.

And they felt that way because whereas before there'd always have been a smile or a laugh from time to time. Now I'd be waiting for that and waiting and eventually you'd give up wondering if you'd get a hug again which as the youngest I had been getting regularly all my young life. And because I had no hugs, I had to sort of grow up and spend more time with meself in the garden, climbing trees and the like. Even the lads I played with were funny about me, as if I had some sort of fuckin' disease or something. I wanted them to act as if everything was normal, but they knew it wasn't and I knew it wasn't, so we just played

69

on with our own little awkwardnesses.

I felt the days long that year because Father used to go on his benders a lot more than he did before. We'd never know when he'd be home. When I came through the door of an evening, me heart used to lift when I'd see him there in the chair or even better if he was out the yard making things. When he'd gone on the benders that year I hated walking home from school in case we'd meet him lurching from pub to pub. And when he'd see us, he wouldn't say hello or anything as if he thought he was doing it unknown to us.

And when my friends in the class saw him pissing one day against the cinema wall, they laughed and then stopped when they realised I was there with them. I hated them for laughing. I wanted to bate the heads off them but sure there was no point, there he was pissing and growling at them to fuck off.

They walked on but I stopped and looked at him and wondered if he even knew what he was doing to us with his drinking. I shouted at him "Dada, stop and go home..." but he just turned and went in the back door of the pub. I felt a pain in my heart and then ran after the others, with my head low and my face a bright red. And they said nothing to me about it out of shame and embarrassment and pity.

Granny was great help to Mother in those days before it all went bad. I'd see Mother crying in her arms in the way she used to hold us when we cried. It frightened me to see Granny and Mother hugging each other 'cos 'twasn't natural to me then. But I knew then that Granny and Mother were the same relationship as Mother and me, and so that's where my hugs were gone to. Mother was getting them and Granny was giving them, but either way, they weren't coming to me.

Then Granny fell and broke her hip and had to go to hospital a few weeks before Christmas. And we had to take Liam's car to go and see her. I'd never been in a hospital before and it smelled of Dettol and piss, and she was lying there with her leg in a cast in a big ward and she looking so grey and pale in these big white-walled rooms, with some woman in the next bed coughing and farting all the time and shouting out 'mind me Josie'. And me feeling sorry for Granny 'cos it was a far cry from her comfy bedroom with the floral wallpaper that her husband had put up 30 years before. I felt sad that she'd be stuck in here for a while, having to put up with the people in the ward. And I felt sad that we didn't have any power to change things for her. When you go into a hospital, you realise you've no fuckin' power at all. That you're nobody.

And we didn't get a turkey for Christmas that year. We got two ducks but Father said there'd be fuck all on them, so we got some chickens as well that they boiled so that they could bring some to Granny in the hospital where the food was "utter scutter," he said.
Because we had to visit Granny, Christmas wasn't much fun that year. The sack of presents was smaller and more simple. I heard Mother say to Granny in the hospital "sure I haven't the heart to go buying stuff when one of them can be snatched just like that." I didn't know what she meant – Was someone snatching our Christmas bags, but later I reckoned it was probably about Kieran. And I was wondering what she had to do with Christmas presents anyway as they always just appeared like in the sitting room on Christmas Eve when there'd be a big bang and Mother

and Father would shoo us in to see what the noise was about -
We'd all rush in, the lot of us, the eldest ones letting us going in
first cos they kinda had copped on to what was happening. But
this year, we walked in slowly and the bags were smaller, much
smaller.

On other years there had been socks and toys and annuals and
comics and Ludo sets and Snakes and Ladders and chocolate
Santas, but this year there were just a few things in the bag. But
nobody wanted to say anything cos we knew no matter how
small was our present, it was far fuckin' more than Kieran had
below in the graveyard around the corner and he frozen solid
with the cold.

I wondered had the worms got through his box yet or was the
wood still holding them out. And I wondered if even for a second
he woke up and realised he was stuck in a box under the ground
and no matter how hard he'd try, nobody would hear him and he
wouldn't be able to push the lid up.

And then he'd just give up and wait to die again.

But then maybe Hell was being alive in this box, always
wondering if you'd get out. But those thoughts frightened me so
I didn't bother thinking that kinda stuff anymore. And I'd shake
my head to try and shake the thoughts away.

Granny was in the hospital for about four months 'cos she'd
never manage the stairs in the house if she came home and her
hip wasn't healing the way it should be, the doctors said to
Mammy, who was talking to herself even more now that Granny
was not in the house and there was no-one to understand what
she was saying and say 'shush a gra shush' to her.

Then in March, Granny got out of the bed one day and leaned on
the eating trolley that was on the bed and didn't it go from under

her, and she fell and hit her head on the side of the steel bed.

Daddy and Mammy took Liam's car down to the hospital to see her, but she was never able to talk to them again, and she died the day before St Patrick's Day. People came to the house that night, locals and people she had worked with when she was young. Auld wans with the smell of camphor-y fur coming in and drinking tea because mother wouldn't let any drink in the house with the way Father was.

So the next day we sat in the house, as the town parade went by the front door. Dozens of bread vans from the local bakery and the music of Sr Frances with the school band and lorries with loudspeakers and Irish dancers all having the time of their fuckin' lives while we were in the house inside in the dark with the light off crying our hearts out that there'd be two empty chairs at the kitchen table for the dinner from now on.

The undertaker came to see Mother to arrange the funeral but when she went to ask Father, he was gone up town, gone to the bars, borrowing money from one publican to drink in the pub of another one.

I grew up that year ' I had to, 'cos I was on my own. No more baby shite out of me.

And from that year on, I could never bear the thought of people drowning the fuckin' shamrock.

The Twelfth Year

A gentle sway
just an inch this way,
then the other.
A desperate glance
at the sliver
of the letterbox
that brought light
but never warmth
And then a silence.

(Peadar Gibbons)

My father wasn't the biggest drunk on the street. In comparison to the others, he was quite tame, actually. He'd just have his benders a few times a year and the other times, he'd just have a mild pint and be home at suppertime. He wasn't like Gerry Byrne and Tommy Walsh who lived across the road in the terraced houses who were pissed all the time.

They were the classic drunks, the type you'd see in the films. They'd wobble down the street. Byrne would be using the walls to hold himself up and then he'd fumble at the front door that his wife Maisie had usually locked. So he'd stand there for an hour calling her a hatchet-faced cunt and a hoor and then she'd let him in out of shame. And then he'd flake her, and the guards would walk down from the barracks and take him away and let him sober up in the cell in the station. And she'd be there to meet him and bring him home and make his tay.

The cell in the station had a small opening through an outside wall that dated back to the British days – 'twas used then for putting food into the cell without having to open the door. We used to use it to shout abuse in at the prisoners, usually knackers or drunks. Once, Gerry threw out some money for us to go get him a Baby Power, a small bottleen of whiskey. We had fierce trouble being served for it, so we made a distraction in the bar and stole it, keeping the money for ourselves. Rich fucking publican, no loss to him. And Gerry got his booze.

Tommy Walsh on the other hand was the kinda drunk who knew he was drunk and was fighting a constant battle to walk a straight line. He'd have the cautious gait of a fella trying desperately hard to convince everyone he was sober, even though the red face of him and they way he'd rasp at ya to 'fuck off' was a dead giveaway. He lived in the fourth house down across from us. His mother was one of the oldest women in the street when I was younger. She had two daughters who were married over in England and 'twas just Tommy and herself at home. He didn't drink as much when she was around and he cared for her awful well. He'd carried her around the house when the stairs got too much for her. He made sure she had grand dinners, cooking mutton stews which she loved. Filling her hot water bottles and making her cocoa. He always sent me to get the RTE Guide and the Mayo News for her. And a Club Milk for myself.

When she died, he was lost without her. The sisters were in England and had no interest in the house so it fell to him - and he lived there on his own, drunk most of the time.

He had some work as a part-time postman but he got fired from this when one Christmas after getting too many festive drinks from householders, he was seen going along Bridge Street with his flute out and he pissing away. When the postmaster heard about it, he called him in and fired him.

After that Tommy just went to rot altogether. He was killed with the loneliness, the fear of the dark nights when he'd shut that heavy door on the little house and seeing nobody but himself until the next day when he'd make his way up town again, using the drink to paint a false picture of the reality he was facing.

The Legion of Mary had told me that visiting him and doing the odd messages for him would count as one of the good deeds we had to do each week to stay part of the Legion.

So I'd call and ask him he needed any messages brought down. I'd bring in coal for him from the backyard, carry the odd bale of briquettes even though it nearly killed me and cut my fingers and legs when I was in the short pants. He'd give me the odd 10p for the work, enough for two bags of Tayto, which was great. And I didn't declare this to the Legion who'd probably have taken it to send off to buy vestments for the missionary priests to wear out in Africa.

Some days he'd be full of chat, others he'd be just sitting there by the fire, his head in his hands. He normally said fuck all, but a few times, I caught him crying.

"Stay off the fuckin' gargle, young fella" he said to me one night when my mother sent me over with an apple cake that she had made in between talking to herself. Of course, he took one slice of the fuckin' thing and left the rest there. So I ate it. Food was never that important to him. I never saw him bringing in any shopping anymore so God knows what he used to ate. Apart from fags.

Every so often he'd send me to the shops to get fags for him. Twenty Carrolls and Twenty Majors and to the butchers for peppered steak. Twas something new the butcher was selling, but Tommy loved it though it used to burn his tongue.

"I'm so fuckin' miserable you'd never know, gosseen. This house is so fuckin' quiet. I can hear me head clicking away. Do ya ever hear a noise in your head, a sort of ringing or a clicking like your skull is cracked and creakin'?"

I shook me head, 'cos I hadn't a fuckin' clue what he was talking about. All I knew that he was very sad. Like Mother was since Kieran died. A sadness had come over them. Like someone had reached into their bellies and ripped out their hearts and their souls or whatever it is that gives you that little bit of urgency. No, they were both slowed down by their lives and none of them old.

The day he did it, we were playing football on the street 'cos back then there were damn all cars. I could see him coming for a good while before he got to our street, walking along in that fake straight way he had when he was pissed. He growled at us when he passed and then struggled with the key on that green door before pushing it in and disappearing into the darkness of the empty house.

A few hours later when the smoke was rising from the chimneys on the row of terraced houses on our side of town, and when I could smell the coal fires and the smoke was going straight up in the still of the teatime sky, I headed over.

I needed a few bob to go to the pictures that night and had thrown together 20p of the 40p admission fee, so I decided to see if he wanted any messages.

I went around the back and in through the kitchen door. I knew he never answered the front door to anyone. "Nosey cunts," he called them, those who came to the front door. The priest, Legion of Mary types, St Vincent de Paul types wanting to know if he wanted the Meals On Wheels or just someone to chat to, to pray with. But I knew he never prayed or went to Mass or believed in Heaven or Hell and he felt they could " wheel the meals on wheels up their holes," he told me, so that's why I knew he had no time for do-gooders.

His neighbours and those few he could trust always used the back door anyway.

'Tommy, I called out. Want any messages?'

No reply, so I pushed open the narrow double doors into the kitchen. There was the usual smell of cigarettes and stale drink.

I heard a noise in the front hall, near the bottom of the stairs, just inside the door.

There he was, standing on the back of a chair, with an orange rope around his neck, tied to a beam that ran across the hall. His face was red and his eyes bulging as his legs tried to kick away the chair. But 'twas stuck on the bottom step jammed against the banister and wouldn't budge.

"Tommy, Tommy I'll go and get some wan," I said, but I knew that if I did, it might be too late 'cos his legs were flailing at the chair and so my mind had me running between standing still and sprinting away but I didn't move. I couldn't move. I grabbed his feet above the ankle and he kicked me on the shoulder, but he didn't mean to, so I tried to lift him upwards so he could free himself. But he was heavy and I could only hold him for so long. His feet went back onto the back of the chair. I was shitting meself in case the chair would fall and then I wouldn't be able to go and get help.

"Kick it," he grunted. "Kick the fuckin' thing."

I didn't know what to do.

"For fuck's sake do me this favour and take the fuggin' chair..., please."

It was the please that shocked me. He'd never said please to me at any time before when he'd ask me to do the messages.

He said it again.

"Please."

He looked at me as his hands grappled with the rope around his neck.

I looked at him again, his face bulbous with stress, the eyes bulging, the leg lashing out still trying to kick the chair while standing on it with the other.

"Fuckin' do it," he said again... please."

I was twelve. Fuckin' twelve. I shouldn't have to make these decisions. Go for help and he might die. Or be left a bloody vegetable. Do what he says and he would die. And I thought of all that torment talk he had thrown at me in the nights when he'd ate fags and I'd ate Club Milks.

And of how miserable he had become, the last one of his family left there, battling with the darkness, night after night, hoping fruitlessly that the sliver of light that filtered through the letterbox from the street light outside would expand with the arrival of someone who cared.

And so with all those thoughts in my head, I looked into his eyes, looking grey with tributaries of blood moving outwards....

I grabbed the chair leg which had been jammed into the banister of the stair and pulled it free and onto the floor at the bottom of the stair.

Then I ran without looking back but I could not avoid hearing the gasping and the grasping and the kicking and the swinging from the hall.

And the roar like a cow.

A noise not speech nor shout.

And as I ran through the yard and over the wall, I wondered at that moment if he was regretting it and was willing me to come back in...but I wasn't going back in 'cos maybe 'twould be too late to do anything now and if he didn't regret it, I'd be left with the haunting sight all me life, instead of the haunting sight I have of him on top of the chair and him begging me to do it.

Once I was over the wall, I stood there for a minute, then wiped the tears from my eyes and made my way around the house and onto the street and home for the tea.

Later I went up the stairs and leapt on to the bed, stifling the howl within me, the howl just asking me to open me gob so it'd be heard, and reaching under the mattress for the piece of Kieran's pyjamas that I'd put there a few years ago. And I thought

80

of him in the river and of Granny in the hospital and of dying and how easily and quickly it came to our street.

Once death gets its claws into you, it just doesn't let go.

The Thirteenth Year

They didn't even have the guts
to say it'll be our little secret.
Or that they loved me in a special way.
Could they not even make it day-cent
with tenderness, and not the rough grab
of the lobe to disguise the pinch of skin on hand
the sharp bristles against my soft chin,
and the hardness beneath to
replace the softness.

(Peadar Gibbons)

'Twas nawthing strange for them to feel your balls if ya didn't know your Peig. I know it might seem strange now, but we were fuckin' used to it and never really gave a shit about it happening to us. You might say it affected us a bit but sure it's hard to know if we'd be the same mad eejits we are if we didn't have our balls squeezed by the teacher. In a playful manner of course. I never thought of it that they might be getting any pleasure out of it.

I never looked to see if they were excited, though I do remember feeling the Brother's prick through his trousers in sixth class when he'd bounce me up and down in his lap and rub his bristly chin against my smooth face for not knowing sums. We took it all as a punishment, not that we were being fucked in any way by these perverse bastards, which is what I now know they were. And if they were alive today I'd say it to them, or I might.

But then I think they'd scare me as much today as they did back then and I was never the type for causing a scene or anything or for being confrontational. So maybe I wouldn't say anything to them. And I can't say for sure that if they tried it on with me now, that I'd reject it in anyway. That maybe now I wouldn't mind anyone sticking their hand down my trousers and getting pleasure out of it. Maybe they wouldn't now 'cos I was cute back then and they were attracted to that. They mightn't feel the same doing it to a grey haired middle-aged man. And so I'd feel shit about myself and in a way you'd yearn for the days when you were attractive enough to have someone to feel your balls.

Maybe that's how they've fucked with our minds.

And so I think of it all when I think of Peig. I'd take the dog-eared book out each day not knowing the fuck what it said 'cos it was written in Kerry Irish. It wasn't as if we even had Connacht Irish 'cos all the fuckin' Christian Brothers were from all over and each spoke a different sort of Irish. So you could be right and at the same time you could be wrong. You'd just stare at the page and try to understand one word in ten and muddle your way through it.

Anyway, in case you don't know, Peig Sayers was this miserable auld wan who lived on an island in Kerry. She had the most depressing life to befall anyone. She seemed to have her own personal cloud to follow her around. Every damn thing she tried to do failed her. Ya know, we had been hoping that if she had her time again that she'd have caught the mail boat to America instead of missing it 'cos one of her ducks drowned or some stupid reason like that. If she'd fucked off to America, she'd never have written the book, or if she did, it would be a more joyous one, and not one that brought misery to us in the dark pissy wet days of the 1980s...and then we'd never have had our balls felt or our heads slapped 'cos we didn't know what she was on about.

And because one or two of them felt 'twas alright to squeeze your mickey and did it out in the open as a sort of punishment, none of us thought 'twas wrong or anything we'd tell Mother about. They wouldn't believe ya anyway, and if you said it too often you'd get the fuckin' head beat off you at home to make things worse.

'Twas only the lads from my side of the river who had their balls felt. If you were from the Neale Road where all the rich houses were, the new style bungalows, then you just got the odd slap, or had a roar thrown at ya. And they were always spoken to in a different way, sometimes in Irish, 'cos the Brothers knew that if they gave out to them too much, then they'd have to deal with a different sort of parent. They always called those kids by their first name. Theirs were parents who actually gave a fuck about what their kids were doing in school, because they wanted their kids to go to college after school. Whereas ours just wanted us to be normal and happy and educated enough to have cop on.

But because we were the only ones getting our balls felt and they weren't, we didn't know whether we were fuckin' privileged or victimised and that they didn't deserve to get the same treatment. We didn't know whether to laugh or cry.

And so we'd left messed in the heads about sex and things...and the lads would go around punching each other in the balls as well because they knew that if the Brother could do it, then it must be alright.

We ended up more curious than anything else. There was a science book with a drawing of a vagina in it, but it didn't look in the slightest bit sexy, but we all memorised the page number and would be staring at it during Science class trying to wonder what the fuck you'd do with it if you ever came into contact with one. And then we'd be comparing mickeys.

John Herlihy asked if me if I'd show him my mickey...so I did on condition he would show me his.

And 30p.

So we sat down at the back of the empty class one Friday evening and took out our mickeys. He said he'd never seen another one before and I couldn't tell him that I was surrounded by the things in our house and was sick of seen them flopping around the place. I just looked at it and looked at it and he did the same to mine.

And we didn't say anything to each other.

We weren't tempted to touch each other's or anything, we just sat there with our flutes in our hand. And then we said 'grand' and fucked off home. And I spent the 30p on crisps. And then we wondered if we were gay and we threw each other strange looks in the classes after that. But with the ugly head on him, I knew I'd never fancy him so I knew I wasn't gay at all.

Still the desire to find out more about sex drove me on daily.

Course it had to be Cuddy who involved me in his next escapade. He ran to my house one day to tell me that he'd found a sex book in his house, in his parents' bedroom. *The Joy of Sex*, 'twas called and 'twas in the locker beside his auld pair's bed. They were gone out the country getting sticks, so we went in and got it and read through the pages. 'Twas fuckin' amazin'. The likes of which we'd never seen. No photos but drawings of some beardy fucker lashing into some young wan. He was on every page and I couldn't be sure that she was the same young wan, but he was doing her from all angles – back, front, under, top, sideways – and she seem to be lovin' it too. He was a serious hammerman, this beardy fucker. The lucky bastard.

There was some strange shit in there. There was one page about a fella who was putting jam on his cock. Jam, why the fuck would ya do that? Is it good for the length, like? Is there something in it that gives ya girth.

Yet the next page he was hammering some other young wan so it must have been good we thought, so we went downstairs and looked for jam in the press in the kitchen... the two of us up on chairs with the horns on us, raking through the sugar and the tea and the biscuits to find the jam.

But they only had marmalade.

So we reckoned that might do the trick, so up we went to the jacks, and lathered our knobs with Little Chip Orange marmalade and waited and watched to see if anything would happen, but it didn't. Nothing grew any bigger. It didn't even feel strange, just sticky. He said that maybe it would work after a few

86

minutes 'cos the fella in the book had a massive knob on him by the next page, even if it was only a drawing.

But we were just a minute or so waiting when we heard the car outside, so we had to rush the book back into the locker and pull up our jocks and shorts with the marmalade all over our balls.

And when Cuddy's father came in, he said 'right, the very men, I've a job for ye." He'd a load of timber in a trailer that he wanted to be put into the shed. And so for two hours we had to lash in blocks of timber with the marmalade all over our balls. It felt shit. I wondered how the fuck could anyone do this to themselves just to get the ride. I resolved there and then that if I was ever to have sex ever, that I was never going to put jam or marmalade or porridge or fuckin anything from the kitchen on me knob. I wanted to leave it the way it was and take my fuckin' chances.

The Fourteenth Year

Dead windows winked at me
from the gentry cottages.
The red door of the big house
puckered its lips and blew me a kiss.
The ivy-ed walls waved at me
and the mangy mongrels
from the Bog Road snarled
a sort of knowing growl,
saying we know you
and what you are
and what you've done.
And I know they know.
I looked through them all
and foisted them up
there on my shoulders.

(Peadar Gibbons)

That day I was just fishing for pinkeens - the little bastards would gather near the edge of the river, near the weir bridge where there were stone steps leading down to the water's edge. The lads from the Neale Road had proper pinkeen nets to catch them, but we just had buckets. Little buckets that we'd tie a rope to and feck into the water and then pull them in. Then we'd take the pinkeens out of the bucket using a bit of a pair of tights that Gerard Kelly found in his house. His sister's he said, but I'd say the fucker was wearing them at some stage, or smelling them. Either way they were better than any net.

I don't know why we spent so much time catching pinkeens 'cos there wasn't much you could do with the fuckers. You couldn't ate them or sell them. 'Twasn't like the grasshopper trade. We made a fortune selling those little bastards. I was expert at catching them. You'd hear them rubbing their legs together and making their grasshopper clicking noise and then you'd follow the noise until you saw them, perched on a blade of grass. Then you'd grab with your hand until you had him, taking care not to crush him, then lift the lid off the jam jar which you had filled with some grass and fecked him in, with all the others.

I used a knife to punch holes in the lid so that they'd have some air and wouldn't suffocate in their glass prison. And the grass made them feel at home, or so I thought. That made me feel better. That they'd a place to live in for the last day of their lives. For 40 grasshoppers we'd get a pound from the fishermen above in Luke Higgins' pub where all the anglers gathered after their day's fishing on the lake. When I think about it now, 'twas a cruel thing to be doing. The 'hoppers would end their lives on the lake with a hook plunged through them to act as bait for the brown trout. And we were complicit in their deaths.

They must never have known that one minute they'd be happily clicking away on a blade of grass, and the next they were almost cut in two by a hook and then used as feed for a fish. I often wondered if they died when the hook went through them or did they know they were dying when they bobbed away on the water. They'd surely have died by the time the fish got them, but then 'twas their little legs flailing that caught the fish's attention. So maybe they brought their deaths on themselves by doing what they did, maybe they deserved it 'cos if they didn't move their legs, they might have saved themselves and eventually they might have healed up from the hook through their belly. And if they didn't make their fuckin' stupid clicking noise, we'd never have tracked them and caught them.

Some people do that.

Do things that bring on their own deaths.

Stupid things like pushing people too far.

Not thinking about what could happen.

I believe that and when you think about it that way you don't feel as bad about it.

Not bad like you feel when they don't deserve it at all.

That thought makes me sad.

But this doesn't.

That day I was pinkeen hunting on me own. Down the steps near the weir, when the plastic bucket came crashing down on me head. And then I saw him, standing above me, up the steps from where I was bent over, leaning into the water, dragging the tights. "Gibbons, ya little retarded cunt, fishing for pinkeens. Will ya ate them will ya? I'd say ya would ya little prick."

Twas Terry Ward — who gave me a flaking every so often.

For no reason, just 'cos he felt like it.

And because he could.

90

A bad knacker. I hated the knackers 'cos they always picked on me 'cos Sheridan was the sergeant's son. They'd never bate a guard's son, but they'd no problem bating a friend of a guard's son when they caught me on my own. So I took a lot of beatings 'cos I was a friend of a cop's young lad, a Peeler's brat.

"The best of you Gibbons was left runnin' down your mother's leg, ya prick. "
And then he spat at me and got me in the face. I hated that. Dirty fucker could have had any disease 'cos he smelt shite and he lobbed another one at me into the face as well.
He'd bate me about four or five times a year, normally a few slaps into the face or a kick in the hole or a knee into the leg to deaden it.
But today he seemed like he really wanted to bate me.
And he always finished off by spitting in me face, dirty fuckin' knacker's spit.

He came towards me and took a swing at me and caught me on the side of the face. It was more a slap than a punch. My ear hurt and felt red and he came again with more. He pranced around like a boxer 'cos all the knackers thought they were great boxers but most of them were shite, just that everyone was afraid to hit them, 'cos if ya hit one, twas the same as hitting them all, as they'd gang up on ya when they got ya on your own.
But Ward had found me alone and he knew I'd be no match for him and he just felt like dishing out a flakin' and I was gonna be on the end of it.
He hit me again and kicked the side of my leg. I tried to get away from him and was too afraid to hit him. I just wanted him to stop, but he didn't. He had his mind set on giving me a good thrashing.

91

He stood outside me, on the edge of the stone parapet beside the river, swinging and spitting, his face getting redder.

I knew I had to make him stop 'cos he looked like he was out of control, so I lunged at him.

Last resort. I had to fight back.

He slapped me into the face again.

And then took up the gait of a boxer, holding up his fists and daring me to come at him.

But if his fists were up around his face, his balls were unprotected.

So I kicked him up into them and he bent over crouched and then I punched him up into the face. It caught him on the nose 'cos I felt that on my fist. And it kind of went soft with the punch.

I knew then that if he recovered he would surely kill me. He staggered, and getting up on one knee, he started to come at me, but I looked around and saw that no-one else was there so I ran at him and shoved him just as he was halfway up – and he tumbled back, his legs trying to support him but he disappeared over the side of the river and down the seven feet into the water. He fell awkwardly on his side and seemed to swallow a lot of water 'cos he gasped as he looked up at me from the water.

He tried to shout but the current took him, first five yards away, then ten yards, the water getting faster the nearer it got to the weir bridge and the old timber and steel sluice gates which were open.

I looked at him, heard him give a muffled scream as the rushing water took him into the first sluice gates, he hit it hard. I heard that noise of bone on stone.

He tried to get a hand to it but the wet timber didn't allow him a grip. Then he disappeared through the opening to the far side of the gates, and the concrete fish run. I watched as he went through this, his body battered by the force of the water as it slipped down the run into the lower river. I still thought he'd kill me if he got out.

There was a lifebuoy a hundred yards from me. A series of them were put up after Kieran died.

But fuck it, I wasn't throwing one to him.

Not one put up for Kieran.

If he got out, he'd tell everyone and he'd come after me. They'd burn the house down and tear me to pieces. His body was surely broken by now.

I looked into the lower river and there he floated lifeless, his head bloodied and to one side. The sluice gates must have broken his neck. Either way he was fucked.

And I didn't give a shit even though my heart was racing and my head seemed to be filling with blood.

The river flowed around the bend, under the barracks bridge and on down to the Soldier's Hole where Kieran drowned. I wondered would he end up there, the same eels that wrapped themselves around Kieran dragging him down now and taking little bites outta him. Bastard. He deserved it all and worse. He fuckin' died roaring, but I knew 'twas something I could never tell anyone about for years and years. Til now.

But it's something I've never forgotten, the sound of it, or the half sound of it or the full sounds of everything happening at the same time.

I didn't feel too bad about it. I learned then that you can fuckin' do anything if you can live with it.

For as long as you can live with it.

But like the grasshopper, he didn't do anything to stop himself from dying the way he did.

Like them, he'd waved his legs and invited it and made it impossible for anyone to care enough to stop him from dying.

The Fifteenth Year

Dawn hits the brain
with the realisation
that nobody would give a shit
if I just stayed here,
lay here, scratched me arse
and turned over. Let the orange glow
of the rising sun be for someone else
who needs it to light their way of purpose.
Leave me be. if I don't care, why should they.

(Peadar Gibbons)

I don't want ye to think I'm phobic towards tinkers. First they were called tinkers, then they were itinerants and then they were knackers, but I didn't really like that last one and itinerants sounded too fuckin' academic, so I called them tinkers even though most of them had never seen a piece of tin. I got on well with most of them 'cos they didn't see us from High Street as being much different. They saw the guys from the Neale Road as being very different, like from a different planet. But not us. We were just a notch above them – we just lived in houses. They had great time for Father 'cos he used to go down and fix their battery sets for powering their lights. And they'd see him drunk coming home so they knew there was no snobbishness about us. When I was much younger they used to camp on the side of the road about half a mile down from our house – you'd see the smoke rising from their fires between the caravans each evening. So in the main they treated us as equals because we had fuck all and were fair to them most of the time.

But then there were the bad tinker fuckers, who just seemed to relish in being cunts. They'd bate ya and spit at ya and stop ya when you were on your way up town, and they'd keep slappin' ya til ya handed over your money to them, feck all that it would be.

The town was known as tinker town so they were nothing strange to us, and we regarded them a bit like you'd regard the pissin' rain – 'twas always there and you could do nothin' about it.

So when I went to school they were there in the classes, sitting by themselves in one corner of the room, not giving a shit about whether they annoyed the teacher or anything. One of them lit a fire in the desk one day to keep warm, just burning auld sweet papers in the shelf under the desk so that the smoke came up through the inkwell like a chimney. Mickey Connor got beaten around the head for that. Hard slaps that had him lying on the ground pretending he was dead. And so he stayed there for an hour, the blood pouring out of his nose. Until the next day his father came in and battered the Brother who did it to him.

Mickey's dead now too.

He was rotten with the fags and died of cancer.

In jail for robbin' and batin' three auld men.

Dead.

They did life in a strange way and they did death in a really strange way. They had their graves all in the same place against the wall at the back of the graveyard. Big fuckin' headstones higher than any of the others, all gilded with colourful stone and photographs and candles that never went out, and dozens and dozens of bouquets as each member of their family wanted to ensure that nobody thought they were a mean bastard when their father died.

Even though the graveyard was just around the corner from the house, I'd never go there at dusk or after dark. But some days I'd be sent there by Mother to clean up the family plot, if you could call it a plot. She had felt that it was in a shockin' state when Granny died a few years ago. But we hadn't a chance to clean it. Death does that to ya. It just creeps up and before you know it, you're caught up in it and that there's people shaking your hand and wanting your tay and biscuits and you just wanting to get yourself a black suit or a black dress with black tights, and you know you can't 'cos there's things to be done, and ya can't leave the house and you're too ashamed to ask someone to get them for ya. And one of the things you can't do is clean up the family headstone and it's probably the worst thing to leave uncleaned 'cos there ya have a few hundred of people who know ya, standing around a hole in the ground and not wanting to stare at anything apart from the mildew and the bird shit on the headstone where your father or mother is buried. Fuckin' cruel prick, is death.

'Twas just a double grave where Grandfather and Granny were buried and where Mother and Father would probably go. The headstone was donkey's years old and so every year 'twas covered in green mossy streaks so I'd have to take a wire brush and a bucket of water, and scrub it til twas clean and grey again, just like it was when 'twas first erected back in the 1950s. I'd have to refill the bucket from a tap just inside the gate. And the path back brought me past the tinkers' graves.
And it was there I saw it. His face. The fucker. Staring out at me from a little gold frame in the centre of the headstone.

Terence Ward - Died Tragically. Taken from us to lie with the angels.

Lie with the angels! Lie with the fuckin' angels, me hole. I'm sure the angels were well wide to what sort of a fucker he was. Thieving and robbing and stealing and arsoning. If the angels really wanted him to lie with them at some stage, they'd have surely saved him from going through those sluice gates and breaking his neck as he was swept through the concrete pillars. Maybe the angels were looking out for me, 'cos if they had saved him, he'd have killed me, and his family would have killed me again and they'd not have bothered calling the guards. They'd have just kicked the shit outta me and fucked me in the river too. Shit, I worried they might see me here and put two and two together but then there's no way they could connect me with what happened so I told myself to stop worrying and to calm down.

But I moved soon enough anyway 'cos twasn't the done thing to be seen mourning near the tinkers' graves. Most people who went there were settled people wanting to have a gawk at the ostentatious nature of the headstones, probably feeling guilty themselves for not mourning their own relatives in the same manner.

Still, where did they come up with these lines? 'Spose they thought he'd just fallen in while fishing; that he was trying to catch perch or eels or something. There was no mention of anything ever suspicious about the way he died. Just that he might have been drunk.

I had deliberately avoided going to visit these graves before – or Tommy Walsh's. His was over further in the centre of the graveyard in one of the old graves. The ones that were just plain slabs, no crosses or anything, just the basic message painted in a fading white on the front.

I knew from the funeral that he was buried somewhere in this area. I'd had to help with the mass-serving when the sisters in England paid us five pounds sterling to help the priest. The priest was looking at us in a 'what the fuck are ye doing here kind of way," 'cos he never used to have altar boys at the graveside service, but Tommy's sisters Angela and Helen obviously thought that was the norm and had come up to us after the Mass and asked us to do it. We had some job trying to cash that English fiver, but Mickey Hession in the shop gave us six Irish pounds for it so we spent it on cake and shit in his shop. Although we stole another fiver's worth when he was gone in to get the change.

I went over to see what they had said about Tommy on his headstone, but there was nothing. Just the names of his mother Delia Walsh, his father John Walsh and then below them just the line "and their son Thomas" and the date of death.

Fuck! How cruel was that. Tommy wasn't the worst, he just died of a broken heart really. 'Twas that that led him to do what he did, and what made him implore me to do what I did.

I wondered why did Tommy not get a decent line like 'lying with the angels" as he deserved it much more than that other fucker.

Tommy was lucky to have his name on it at all. Angela and Helen in England had paid for the inscription when they came home to sell the house. And a family had moved into it without having any idea what happened there in the front hall.

I'd looked in through the door a few months back and it was all repainted, much brighter - they'd torn out the old kitchen and replaced it with new stuff. Now it was going to be a bright happy house and not a dank musty auld place that drove a man to hang himself at the foot of the stairs.

I felt sad that Tommy who was a solitary scholar, and who had lived all his life in this house, was gone and there was no trace of him at all in it.

And now the same in the graveyard.

His sisters too ashamed to give him a euphemism.

She didn't want to say 'took his own life', which is just as well 'cos strictly speaking 'twasn't true and I wouldn't want him to have a lie on his headstone. But nevertheless the embarrassment of the sisters meant his life was summed up with a few words – his name and the date he died.

And the fecker who'd never gone to school or learned proper words and who acted the bollocks had the best lines of them all.

It just wasn't right.

The Sixteenth Year

I seek love but despise its chores
the way it drags me in by the collar
luring eyes and vows of heart healing
of honeylike slides down
the beanstalk to my core.
But fear the darkness of the shadows
cast by the fear of when
it slips away from me
abhorred by me
its hollow cackle
a sword of ice in the night
making me huddle
I never fear love more
than when it is just before me
waiting for my fat fingers to pet it
as it evaporates.

(Peadar Gibbons)

102

Can ya die of an erection? I mean, is it possible to pass out there and then 'cos it has nowhere left to go in me trousers. My heart was racing - I'd had them before but never when I was in close proximity to what had to be the most perfect pair of breasts that the Lord had ever made. If he made breasts, I mean. Della Horkan had to be first in the queue. Jesus, there was no way this thing was going down for hours. I tried to think of boring things like Monsignor Mitchell's sermons on church stuff that bored the arse off us on Sundays, but nothing could help me.

When she leaned across the desk I could feel the softness of her breasts on the back of my arm, so I left it there, enjoying the feeling, but I could feel the excitement rising in my trousers and the more it continued, the more the erection grew.

I feared I was going to faint. I squirmed in the seat trying to adjust its direction without alerting Della, or the others who were jealously watching me having the craic with Della Bainne as they called her. Della Bainne with the creamery trucks, they called her, but every one of them would give his right testicle to be sitting where I was now, even if my right testicle was having a battle of its own to make room for the erection which was threatening to strangle me.

Every Thursday we went to the convent for geography and a crowd of girls came to our school for chemistry. 17 of us going in either direction. I hated geography but I hated chemistry even more so I fuckin' had to go. The convent was so much better run than the Brothers. The heaters worked for a start. They all wore slippers, and the first week we were there, some of our lads got in trouble for fuckin' dozens of the slippers out the second floor window, so our weekly trip was almost cancelled.

The nuns brought us in and allocated seats to us, surprisingly offering us to share desks with the girls. I was mortified. What

103

would I say to one of them if they started talking? I didn't have any sisters so I didn't know what to say to them. They knew fuck all about football and shit, so I'd just have to sit there and blush and try not to get excited. Which was failing already.

Della smelt nice, fuck she was nice with a gorgeous smile and smelt lovely. I had ended up sitting beside the girl who every lad wanted to sit beside. Fellas in the class spent their nights tugging the pricks off themselves at the thought of her and her enormous perfectly rounded jugs. And here she was sitting beside me, the nice girl that she was, chatting to me and my red face and me trying not to stutter any words out or look at her tits. But I could feel them with the back of my arms and fuck was that a good feeling. Then I told her a joke and she laughed and that drove the lads even more daft. The good looking lads, the guys who actually had a chance with her; the lads who would have no bother asking her to dance at the disco in the Town Hall on a Friday night. I'd die if I had to ask her to dance or any good looking girl or any girl 'cos they'd take one look at me and tell me to fuck off. So I didn't bother me hole and just stood there gawking, wanting to dance but not wanting to dance when every girl I faced turned away from me lest others would think I was with them. And so I blushed and blushed and wondered if things would always be like this. Would I be always trying to get things I'd never have a chance of getting. Maybe I was gay after all 'cos John Herlihy had showed me his mickey and there was no chance of any of these girls doing the same for me. Not their mickeys now, but ya know what I mean. And so the discos made me feel like a right outsider, and you could say that's how I've stayed, living on the fringes, barely visible. Not having an opinion that was worth a flying fuck.

One night I ran home in tears 'cos I thought I'd spilt paint over

104

me jeans not realising that 'twas the ultra violet light that had picked up the bleach off them which happened when I put them in the bath and threw Parazone over them to make them have that stonewashed look that was cool.

I hated the discos because they made me feel even worse about meself. I felt such a loner 'cos the lads I hung around with had no bother asking girls to dance. Even girls who smoked. I remember falling in love with Marissa Curran from afar. She went to evening Mass with her parents every evening in the church, so we'd tag along just to get a look at her. And she was fuckin' gorgeous. She wore this green woollen coat, and she had brown eyes and curly brown hair down past her shoulders. Her teeth were slightly protruding, but in a sexy way, not in a fuckin' goofy kind of way.

I truly loved her even though I'd never spoken to her. I tried to but then I reckoned she'd freak out if she thought I fancied her. But the fact she went to Mass meant there was a chance she'd take pity on poor fuckers like me. And so I lived in hope.

There was a Valentine's Card that came to me with a proclamation of love but I couldn't be sure that 'twas her who wrote it or the lads pullin' the piss, so I had to steal a copybook from her bag to compare the writing. But even then I couldn't tell. I told myself it was, but twas probably more likely a sister of one of the lads who helped with the prank. Cunts.

Then I saw her at the disco. Now was my chance, but I saw she was smoking. How could she? How could this angel who went to Mass and looked so perfect be smoking fags? I was gutted, and even more so later when Donal Murphy shifted her, atin' the face of her against the wall of the Town Hall, in the dark corner, thrusting his groin against her, and she seeming to like it. And she thrusting back and the two of them grinding each other against the wall and no sign of the wan who went to Mass about her at all. To be fair Murphy was a good looking fucker; he'd been born in the States and came home with his family, so he was well able to talk his way into getting his hole. And he smoked as well, so fuck it, maybe there was something wrong with me that I didn't smoke — and Father atin' fifty a day. Fuck, why couldn't he have taught me to smoke proper like.

I hated it and ran home but the house was dark. Mother was sat in the kitchen, knitting by the light of one dim lamp. She smiled at me, not wondering why was it strange I was home early. Father of course was nowhere to be seen, but ya could be sure he was having far more fun out in town than I was. Mother was humming softly to herself. Still not the same as she used to be before Kieran died. She knitted...plain, purl, plain, purl, staring into space, only stopping to ask me to 'put the fire out'.

Every night she insisted that the fire be quenched with a pot of cold water in case it started up during the night and burned us all in our beds. The smell of the water on the hot ashes was rank, the former fire reduced to just a mess of ash and water, a stinking mess in the middle of the large hearth in the kitchen.

I went to bed and cried for Mother, and cried for Granny. It seemed they both had gone and left me...and I cried for myself 'cos Marissa Curran was a smoker who was with someone else.

Women were determined to break my heart and I wondered if I would ever understand what I had done to deserve this.

The Seventeenth Year

Others shouldn't matter

in that incessant chatter

you fire at yourself

to bring calmness to your soul.

Years spent teasing

aimlessly pleasing

those who surround you

just drain your needs.

Your needs. Not theirs.

And then when they smile

and forget to thank you

you know you really

shouldn't have bothered

your hole

bringing calmness to their soul

when you needed it more.

(Peadar Gibbons)

A lesson I took with me throughout life came from a bit of a stupid prank we did in fifth year. Well it seems stupid now but to us, 'twas hilarious at the time. I wasn't to know that it would provide me a sort of justification for the way my life turned out. And bejaysus I needed one, as I'm sure you're thinking right now. There was a new parish priest in town, a new sort of priest, the kind of fella who didn't look or sound anything like the boring ecclesiastical feckers we'd had for years, spouting out theology at us as if we were cardinals in Rome or the likes. This new priest was into the youth. I don't mean he was ridin' us or anything, nothing like that at all. He was just keen to do things for us, to get down with the kids as they say it nowadays. He restarted the youth club, he got the pool hall reopened in the Town Hall so we had somewhere to hang out on Friday nights, he organised bus trips to Castlebar to the cinema where for the first time in a decade, we could see proper films on a big screen and not just the same auld Top Gun and Gremlins shite that was forever being shown on the video in the youth hall.

Fr Christy Gilhooly was his name, from Galway or somewhere. He'd used to play hurling for Turloughmore or some team like that, but he never played hurling when he came to us. But the fact he played GAA at all meant that the likes of Father and the other men in town had great time for him, not afraid of him like they would have been with the other priests who used to intimidate them or scare the shite out of them from the pulpit.

Anyway, Father Christy was a fierce hoor for giving complicated penances in confession. Fellas would get sentences such as ten Hail Marys and cut the grass at the front of the church; or an Act of Contrition, three Our Fathers and chop timber for Delia Kelly for the rest of the week. They were crazy fuckin' penances altogether. I'm sure the Pope hadn't approved them, but Father

108

Christy didn't give a shit 'cos he was doing his job and getting other bits done for lonely auld divils around the town.

However, after a while, it dawned on us that he wasn't giving the feckers from the Neale Road their share of the shit jobs he used to throw into the penances and I'm sure their sins were just as bad as ours, just that they may have committed theirs in better clothes than we did ours. We knew they got handy things to do, like sweep leaves in their own driveways.

We didn't have driveways.

Or leaves.

Still, there was no doubt that he was going easier on them than on us.

So we decided to test him out to make sure he was equitable in his penance giving. A dozen of us went to him in Confession, and we decided to all give the same sin which was 'I just can't help touching myself, father and it feels really good." We'd made a pact to be honest with each other when we came out so that we could compare penances. Three of the Neale Road lads joined in with us as they thought it was some weird experiment, but we hadn't explained it all to them.

So we started and in we trotted, trotting out the same line about touching ourselves and how it felt good. Awful good. And how we couldn't stop doing it and was it true we'd get warts on our hands from doing it so much?

I was third in line to do this and by the time I came in, I could tell that he smelt something was up. He gave me four Hail Marys and a leaf-sweeping job in the church grounds.

The nine of us from down the hill side of town all got prayers and manual work to do, while the three fuckers from the Neale Road just got prayers to say.

So, we were right, he was afraid to give work penance to the precious pets from the rich families with their daddies with proper jobs and their mammies with wrinkled tanned skin from being off playing golf and their houses with gardens at the front and back, and roses and tulips and hydrangeas growing out in them carefully tended by mammy when she wasn't off fucking golfing. Yes, they were getting off lightly, but what could we do about it? Not for the first time and not for the last time, we were powerless in the face of the fellas from the right side of town. And I suppose we kind of realised then that there was no point in trying to take them on at their own game. Eventually when we'd all get to leave the town, we'd get to leave behind the prejudices and insecurities that your hometown gives ya; we'd have a chance to wipe the slate clean and start afresh where nobody would know your name and what sort of fucked-up state your family was in. No, when you go away, you leave all that behind you, and it'd only haunt ya when you come back again inside the town boundaries.

But there was a development the following week that I've never forgotten and which I've used to clear out this fuckin' head of mine from time to time when it'd get all full up of guilt and noise and shite and shakes and thoughts about hurting people.
Just a few days after, who comes into the class but Fr Christy. He used to breeze in without a yay or a nay to the teachers in the staffroom. He used to do that. He didn't give a fuck about what classes he was disrupting. He'd just burst in the door, nod to the teacher and roar in a bellowing voice "now, boys, what year is this?" Cuddy got a box in the ear for replying "1981" to him one day. Smart fucker. But worth it for the laugh.
Because he came into the class the week after we all told him we

loved wanking, we were kinda shitting ourselves that he was going to report us all, but we knew that he couldn't, cos the Pope would fuckin' fire him if he told things that he'd heard in the confession box.

But there was no escaping the fact that 'twas connected. He stood up in front of the class, when the teacher had stepped out and he says to us. "In confession, there is no need for the sinners to list out their exact sins. It is more important that they feel guilt for them rather than having to recount the exact details. The moral is that the sin happened and not how it happened.

"From now on, I want you all to bear this in mind and remember that some sins can be classified as being selfish, and that is all the description I need in the confessional. So in future, the phrase 'I was selfish' will suffice."

And then he went with a blessing and a bye, but it stuck with me, his message.

When you thought about it, every fuckin' sin you commit could be put down to selfishness. Selfishness is the act of doing something to better yourself over others, to deprive others of something, to do something that you feel is right, and that if it feels right then it must be good and if it feels too right, then it must be fucking selfishness.

And this is how I managed to live with myself through all the things I've done in my life. I didn't and don't really see myself as a bad fucker, though you'll probably think I am when you get to read all this, but I'm just a selfish fucker. I prefer being selfish rather than evil or bad.

And I've a dead priest to thank for all that. I wonder if he knew that day that while he thought he was just saving himself embarrassment, that in reality what he was saying was helping someone like me wipe away guilt for proper sins and have them absolved under the canvas cover of a single word.

He did in his hole.

But he said it, so I followed it.

The Eighteenth Year

See me, please
look and feel my skin
put your hand here flat and feel
the rise of my heart under
the geansai that defines me
as someone you should not see.

Peer into my eyes
and see the walk forced on me

and ask why you do not talk to me.
Just a glance and a nod
something to tell me that
I am someone
who should hear you.
A look just to let
me know that I exist

(Peadar Gibbons)

I hadn't seen Mother beam like that for many a year. She took the letter from me and smiled and then without a warning, she reached out and put arms around my shoulders and started to hug me and pulled me closer to herself. And then she kissed me on the cheek and said "I'm so proud of you."

I'd been expecting some reaction, but not this. I hadn't bothered me hole showing the letter to Father as he never took an interest in writing things or school things. He'd left school after primary himself and so had Mother, but at least she was always correcting my grammar and all that. Very strong with the correct use of 'presently" and "currently' and that a person can be hanged but not hung.

Father didn't care or get involved at all with our schooling. Or grammar, even though he talked a lot and despite this, I'd never heard him saying things wrong. He looked up with a curiosity as I showed her the letter though. But it would kill him to ask what it was about. He reckoned if 'twas important enough he'd have been told anyway.

She read it with that intense way she had when she was reading something, as if 'twas a meal she had to consume slowly. Then she read it again...and again. And with each reading I felt more and more proud and I hoped the words would sound better with each reading, that like seeing that a play over and over, that every time you saw it, you'd see something you'd missed the previous time. I'd showed her my results earlier and they were shit. But nothing more than I'd expected.

I'd gotten an F in English. A fuckin' F and that was the one subject I thought I'd be the best at. I didn't even think they went down as far as F. Normally that would be marked as an NG as in No Grade, but no, the cunts must have reckoned I was worse

114

than that. They must have known that I'd skipped the last hour of the examination to head home and watch West Germany play Austria in the World Cup in Spain. And if I'd known what a shit game it was going to be or that the fuckers had stitched the game up to be a pre-arranged draw, I wouldn't have bothered me arse.

The day we got our Leaving Cert results we were all told to call up the Brothers' house in the afternoon. I'd been in there a few times, sent in to get books or pass on a message to the housekeeper, but this was the first time we'd actually be summoned to it, as real people like, men of the world and finished school.
The house was over a hundred years old, heavily carpeted, with the smell of the Brothers off it. You know the smell of chalk and talc they had off them. I wondered if they even used talc or whether they just brought home the chalk dust from the classrooms and used that to dry themselves after their bath.

The principal Bro Dorgan was sitting in his office as we went in one by one.
The letter he handed me said that I was "an intelligent and honest student with a zest for learning" and that I would be "an honourable employee as I came from a good family."
 Wow, that must have been the first time that I saw anything written about our family, never mind anything positive. Did they really think that? Fuck. We were just one of those families in our side of town who were kind of invisible, living under the radar so to speak, with the only seeming perception of us as being the family who lost the young fella to the drowning a few year back.
And that description would invariably be said with an "arragh"

added to the end in the absence of 'the poor crayturs'. Sometimes I wondered if 'twas better to not be mentioned at all, than being mentioned with an air of pity about us. But the air of pity was as good as it got at that stage, so there was no other option. We weren't suddenly going to be elevated to a family of people spoken of with pride and envy or anything like that.

"Young Gibbons, Peadar, here is your reference for yourself. You're not the worst of them, you've talent but you just need to be less giddy and more focused.
"You're good at the English and the words. A bit too smart sometimes so it makes no sense that you did as badly as you did, but you have the words in your head and maybe at some stage, you'll get to use them for some positive purpose. I'm wishing you the best of luck in the world," and he shook my hand.

I smiled and said thanks, not knowing if what he had just said was a compliment or an insult. He'd never shaken my hand before. Anytime he'd taken it before would be just before he lashed it with the leather strap he carried on his belt. So I shook his hand back and took the letter and said "thank you Brother," and left the room.
And as I walked down the carpeted corridor that ran along the front of the house from the private oratory to the front door, I clasped that letter with its kind words and its encouragement and the fact that all of them were written and meant about me.
And I didn't want that envelope to bend or get creased so I held it straight in my hand.
Holy fuck, I'd never had anything like this before – a written commitment from the Brothers to back me up if I needed a job. To think that they had held this opinion of me after all these years

116

was making my fuckin' heart leap with excitement. I folded the letter neatly back into the envelope and walked quickly then broke into a trot, then a full-fledged sprint across the Curate's Field, through the church grounds and down the Bowers and over the River until I could see the wall of my back garden. I climbed over it, sweating and ran into the house where Father sat slumped in the chair beside the fire.

By the gip of him, I could tell that he'd been jarring up the town. The smell of porter off him only confirmed this. I was afraid to hand him the letter in case he'd take some kind of notion and tear it up. Especially after the time he'd fucked the apple tart against the wall on my Communion Day and when he fucked the turkey into the garden on a Christmas Day some time back. So I wasn't taking any chances.

Mother was far more receptive and shocked me when she gave me the hug. And me 17 and not got a proper hug for years. From any of them. When she'd read it, I took it up to my room and sat on the bed and read it over and over again. I'd not normally lie here for such a long time without having a wank with the Bo Derek picture I'd pulled out from Woman's Way, but today I wasn't bothered as this made me feel good itself.

It was only on the fourth or fifth read that I noticed that the Brother had misspelt the word 'potential'.

He'd typed it as 'potentail.'

Fuck.

Would this come against me if I was going for a job?

Would they dismiss me as being some sort of fuckin' eejit if even my reference had a spelling mistake in it?

I thought about going up to the Brother again and asking him if he could retype it for me so that it'd be right, but the thought of telling the Brother that he'd got something wrong scared the shit out of me, so I sat there bothered and decided to have that wank after all – getting solace from Bo Derek, but to be honest, it did nothing for me.

'Twas the following day when I saw Mother and Mrs Cuddy at the door and they both laughing and chatting. They each had a sweepin' brush in their hands and holding letters in the other. When I got closer I could see that 'twas my letter my Mother was holding, and Mrs Cuddy had another one and they were both thrilled that their sons had done so well.

Mrs Cuddy tousled my hair and Mother put her arm around me. "Our two sons, the pride of the street," she said.

And then I saw Cuddy's reference. It roughly said the same as mine, and looking at it closer, I could see that 'twas saying exactly what was said in mine.

He too was "an intelligent and honest student with a zest for learning" and that he would be an honourable employee as he "came from a good family".

Fuck.

It's mine.

And then I saw it.

The same fuckin' mistake.

'Potentail.'

Fucking potentail.

The same mistake.

And it dawned on me, the fuckers hadn't bothered their holes to make out individual references, they'd just copied them all and handed them out. And hoped we'd never notice, because soon enough we'd all be scattered to the winds to England and Boston and New York.

118

I found out that evening that 'twas only the lads from our side of town who got them. The lads from the rest of the town didn't fuckin' need them cos they were off to college, but there was no college for us. And the career guidance teacher wasn't behind the wall in telling us that either.

When she asked me what I wanted to be, she looked surprised when I said 'a writer.'

Then cocking one eye and sighing, she looked at me and said "well, Peadar, have you ever thought of just being a council foreman, like your father?"

The Nineteenth Year

Am I a loner because of me

Do I enjoy this solitaire

Or is it because this world rejects me

Slaps me in the face

Each time I try to break

through the curtain.

Do I expect

too much of myself

Or is it the world

that disappoints me

Or does the prospect

of both terrify me?

(Peadar Gibbons)

I couldn't believe it when Cuddy told me he was going. And couldn't believe it even more when he told me the reason he was going. Seemingly he'd knocked up the guard's daughter. Swear to fuck. I never even knew he was getting the ride. Never mind getting it off the guard's daughter.

Lovely girl.

Pale face.

Teresa Sheridan.

Lovely skin. Like milk.

Alabaster they call it in the books.

Alabaster which is some kind of delicate china.

Well, he came to the house and he told me.

Was a weird conversation. I didn't know what to say to him. Didn't want to say how did it happen. Had ya a johnny on ya? Or what? I didn't want to talk sex to him. It's ok when it's about sex that none of ye were getting, but sex that he had and had resulted in some consequence.

And especially when it's sex with one of the nice girls.

And the way he was talking she might be his wife at some stage and it just didn't seem right.

So we stood there, awkward.

And the funny thing was that I sort of felt cheated on. It was if we were some auld couple and he'd gone off with someone else. I know it sounds crazy but that's how it felt. And a double whammy. Bad enough he was leaving and he didn't know where, but probably England.

I was meant to meet him to play handball up in the old Ball Alley but he never showed and so I played there myself, lashing a half-solid against the base of that battered wall. Bang, bang, bang, chasing a fucking small hard ball around a vast concrete court.

Just by myself, each thud a reminder of how fuckin' ridiculous my life had become.

A sea of nothingness with the tidal waves just a thud of a rubber ball against a cracked wall.

And then he came around the corner and his jacket on him and a bag with him. He hadn't told his father but he was going to ring his mother when he got to Dublin. He was going to get a job over there and sort out his head and pay for the child. He said he was going to work his hole off and send money home and do the right thing.

"Cos I really like her, I really do," he said to me. S'pose that was the closest he was going to get to saying he loved her. And if he loved her and he was leaving, then it kinda fell to me to mind her a bit for him. To keep an eye on things. To act as a go between. To be his friend. Just a friend over here. Fuck, I wished he wasn't going.

I didn't want a friend over there. I wanted a friend here, where I live, where we live. Why do we have to go away, any of us?

I didn't pity him telling his father though. The father had a wicked temper on him. Fierce. I knew there was a time when we had built a camp down in the father's woodpile and we put a roof on it with bushes and then covered that with the long grass that had been scythed down in the back field. It was lovely, until Cuddy decided that it would be great if we had a fireplace in it. To toast conkers. And bread. Not the fuckin' brightest idea and when his father came back the woodpile was ablaze.

I thought he was going to kill him. He chased him down the garden and flung the claw hammer he was carrying at him, catching Cuddy around the legs with the claw and drawing blood from his calf. And when he caught him, as he did easily when his son fell to the ground, he started kicking him in the hip, telling him to get up, but he couldn't get up 'cos that cunt of a father of his was kicking him in the hip. And deadening his leg. And he was crying. And bleeding.

Then he started slapping him and batin' the shite outta him and there was nothing I could do to stop the big fucker lathering into my friend. So I just roared "I'll get the guards if ya don't stop," and he stopped.

But then I ran.

And thanked the Lord that he'd never known about that day we had his marmalade on our balls.

Cuddy ended up getting a job in Neasden working for some fucker from Ballinasloe. And he used to send me the money and ask me to give it to Teresa. And I did. As she got bigger she used to go for strolls along the river and I'd hand her packages. She asked me about names. She liked Laura if it was a girl but I told her that Lorna was a better version of it. I didn't know any Lornas, apart from the one in Lorna Doone. So I gave her that book to read. And she did 'cos she used to talk about it and how sad it was in parts. And that she could see parts of herself and Cuddy in it, him being away and all that.

And then later, I saw her walking up in The Green with the baby. Lorna Teresa was her name.

She'd given her the name I said. And that made me feel like a sort of a father, just a sort of a one.

She was a fuckin' dote of a child. With big brown eyes like Cuddy and pale skin like Teresa and a mad flapping of her hands when she saw me and the big happy head on me.

Cuddy would write to me once a month and send a copy of Shoot

123

with the money tucked into Page 20 every time. A hundred pound sterling.

He told me he was as bored as fuck on Sundays 'cos there were no GAA games and how he knew damn all. So he'd walk around the parks in London and all who would be there were families with kids and he'd think back to his own kid. And he wished to fuck he was back here and walking around a park but he knew that if he came back he'd be a bit ashamed for running away in the first place.

So he'd get a fierce feeling of guilt and he'd send me money to buy books — kids' books and he'd ask me to pass them on to her because he didn't want her growing up a useless amadan.

"I want her to be smart, Gibbons. Book smart like you are. I want her to be able to have people not say to her that she can't do something 'cos she's thick. I want her to be given the list of college courses that we weren't. So you'd know what books to get her."

And so I bought kids books in Nellie Walsh's paper shop and I'd deliver the books to Teresa when she'd be up the Green with the pram. And she'd look so gorgeous and innocent and happy even though she was on her own and hadn't been with any bloke since Cuddy left.

'S'pose she hadn't the fuckin' time but I got the impression that she just hadn't the inclination. That she liked him as well, even though he'd fucked off.

And she'd be asking me things about what I was doing, as if she genuinely cared. I think she did. And then she'd ask me about what Cuddy had said to me and what he was at. And I'd tell her that Cuddy was a nice fella but was scared and ran and that he had great time for her and little Lorna, and that he'd told me that as soon as he'd be sorted he'd come back and get them and make them a proper family with a house, and that she wouldn't have to live at home anymore and put up with shite from her mother.

And then I'd put my little finger in little Lorna's hand and she'd grasp the fuckin' thing real tight. Tighter than you'd expect a baby to do, to be honest. And then she'd pull at it and laugh an infectious laugh, which felt great 'cos it meant she was alive and well and strong and she was seeing me as a person even though she was just a baby and hadn't a clue what I was like really or the shit that was going through my head.

And I wanted to pick her up and hold her but I was afraid I'd drop her and I didn't want that to happen 'cos I didn't want her life to be fucked up by some eejit dropping her.

I wanted her to grow up to be everything we weren't. I hope she has.

The Twentieth Year

Where d'ya stand

on the windy stair up

to the place where you'll be asked

if ya bothered your hole

to earn the dole

by playing your role

and do ya stand

with the knacks

or the farmers

or the wideboy townies

who'd tell the guards they were

getting threatening letters

if they were offered a job.

Where d'ya stand?

Or do ya sit and if ya do

do ya look lazy, like too lazy

to look for work.

So ya stand but where?

(Peadar Gibbons)

Myself and the Mother looked at the fridge. Just some milk and two eggs. But 'twas Thursday and that was dole day. To be honest I'd never thought I'd end up signing on the dole, but then I'd never really thought I'd get a proper job in this town either.

"Your father paid enough tax over the years, so you'd not be worrying about signing on while you get yourself fixed up," she said one day when I burst into tears and told her that I thought my life was properly fucked up, although I didn't swear in front of her, even though Granny was dead, 'cos she hated me saying fuck or shit or bastard or piss. I looked at her that day, her hair greying, her prettiness fading into lines on a well lived-in face.

It only seemed a few years since she had that 1970s prettiness and when she was less plump and when herself and my father cut a handsome couple. I had looked at a picture taken about fifteen years before and she looked much happier then. I think that when the house was fuller she seemed more content; when Granny and Kieran and the lads were here. And when Father wasn't fulltime at the drinking ever since he got let go from the Council.

Because he was hanging around the house all the time now and annoying their holes, Ray and Marty had fucked off to England now and had written to say that they were working for McCarthy laying cables in Hackney, the brown McCarthy not the green McCarthy. Different sides of the one family, I think.

They sent home money for the first two months but Mother told them not to be daft, that she had enough to go on and that they were better making a life for themselves over there.

But the truth was she hadn't enough to get through and whatever she got from the pension and whatever I bought from my dole and butter vouchers meant that the fridge was bare by the time Thursday morning came around. Father used to collect his own dole now and we'd never see a bit of it, even though he'd regularly swan in and demand to be given a breakfast or whatever else he felt like to line the stomach for the night's drinking. Mother was very glad that Granny didn't get to see him this way, totally fucked up and broken, totally a shame to the family. She knew that she could never love him again the way that she once had, he'd broken her fucking heart just too many times. He had shamed her by going off with other women in the town, right auld mangy fuckin' dogs they were, and then when he'd disappear to Galway, there was no finding out what he was up to.

So because of this and her great fear that we'd all end up like Father, she wanted the lads to make good lives for themselves in London. She didn't expect that they'd ever come home to live so there was no point in making them starve themselves over there where they had hard jobs to go to. She felt she'd make the sacrifice for them, just as she had when she'd put up with all that shite years ago.
But I knew from Cuddy that Ray and Marty were drinking themselves silly over there, that every penny was being spent in The Crown in Cricklewood. I thought of them and of Father who had been ruined by the drink and thought they might have had enough fuckin' cop-on not to go the same way.
I wondered would I go the same way, would I start drinking when the realisation finally came upon me that I had no future in this town, that I needed to escape the reality that we were on this side of town, that Father's drinking would be the one fuckin' thing that he'd leave to the rest of us. I thought about going to London too but then Mother would be all alone in the house with Father and although he'd never hit her over the years, he was

turning into a right bad cranky auld bollocks and there'd be no knowing what he wouldn't do to her.

She kinda modelled us all on Seamus who was off married in Tipperary and only called a few times a year when the kids weren't doing something on a weekend. He'd a good job cos he went to the technical college. He seemed happy, with a nice wife Catherine and four kids. But to be honest Catherine seemed to have no time for us and was kinda shocked to find out just how different Seamus was from the rest of us. He was clean cut, non smoker non-drinker, with a great sense of right and wrong. Maybe he got this after Kieran died, 'cos after that he was forever badgering us about what we were doing in school, had we summer jobs, were we brushing our teeth properly, that kinda shite. Yeah, it seems Seamus had bailed out of home after he saw the mess that we were in.

And on days like today, I pitied the mess that this family had gotten into. Dad didn't hand over anything anymore, maybe the odd fifty quid, so all we had to live on was the £28 I was getting on the dole, plus butter vouchers. And whatever I'd earn on the side from doing things like painting houses and cutting grass. And even though a lot of the town was unemployed, I felt like shit having to queue up every Thursday morning, to sign my name on the form and to answer the question that I was available for work and to swear that I hadn't worked in the last week. What sort of fuckin' question was that? Sure they had to know there was no proper work in this town.

To make the money stretch, I bought a load of shit food. Big big packets of fish fingers and processed cod fillets and big fuck-off packets of custard cream biscuits and butter, loads of butter with the vouchers.

I got a few days work in a clothes shop when a friend of mine was sick, but it paid feck all and I had to hide at lunchtime when the clerk from the dole office would be passing by to his lunch. I'd have to 'sign on' first without the tie on me and the anorak buttoned up to the last and then into the shop to sell slacks and Farah jeans and socks and ties and to measure up fat cunts who were in for suits for a wedding.

And I cut grass, loads of fuckin' grass for auld wans and not so auld wans who'd be at home alone during the day. There was this wan who was about 40 or so and she was a bit stout with glasses, but she'd a great pair on her. I wondered many's a day if she'd come out and seduce me like Lady Chatterley's Lover. Did she fuck? She only came out to pay me half the normal rate 'cos I'd done the grass in half the normal time, 'cos I'd the stalk on me for looking at her inside the house so I made sure I passed the window as many times as possible.

And then she gave out to me for taking the grass away with me 'cos I used to sell it by the bag to Gerry Hanratty for his rabbits. So I went from lusting after her to hating her to lusting after her again. But when she went into the house to get me the money to half pay me, I stole a few pairs of her knickers from the wash basket and shoved them into me jacket.

And although I had only earned enough money to go to the pictures that night, I did so wearing the frilly garments and prayed to fuck that I wouldn't get hit by a bus on the way home. This town was driving me fuckin' cracked.

The Twenty-First Year

I've my life too
for living,
to do things cos I can.
I want to
belong to myself
and not to you anymore
You've owned me
grown me,
pushed me out of you
and away from you
the ball of string you handed me
for all those years
has reached its end.
I was yours to hold
but you cannot expect me
to mind you just
because I was once yours.

(Peadar Gibbons)

And so I left. I just couldn't take his shite anymore and although I felt bad about leaving Mother at home, I felt that she probably would come to her senses and kick him out for good, even though she'd probably be too wary of what the fuckin' nosy auld hags on the street would be saying about her, and they haggard after nursing alcoholic husbands all their lives. 'Tis good to have the bit of auld hardship,' they'd tell her. 'Offer it up, agra, offer it up. 'Til smarten ya up for the life hereafter,'
She didn't believe it and neither did I. Fuck the life hereafter, and fuck offering it up, so I decided to do something about it and left.

The bus was on time getting into Galway, so I'd some time to kill. The place looked so open and noisy and colourful and strange and frightening and so different to what I was used to. I made my way down from the bus station and onto the grass in Eyre Square and looked at all the young people like me having fun, 'cept I wasn't having fun. Foreign types with long hair playing guitars and flinging frisbees. So I sat down on one of the benches, put my bag beside me, feeling kinda happy in my suit. I'd typed out a CV and stapled that to a copy of the famous letter from the Christian Brothers with the 'potential' spelt wrong. I thought about Tippexing out the error but then they say if employers see Tippex on a reference, they fuck it into the bin.

There was a man in his fifties sitting on the end of the bench. He looked the country sort with a tweed jacket on him, shirt and tie, smart out, like a bachelor farmer, like an auld guy with a sister at home who'd make sure he was turned out well. A guy who minded himself. He told me he was from Ballyhaunis and was waiting for the bus home.

132

"Great day. Lovely here watching everyone enjoying themselves, isn't it?" he said.

"Tis, " I said, happy at myself to be engaging in conversation so soon after I arrived in the city.

Things were looking up already. I was feeling more confident, chatting to people and job hunting. Sky's the fuckin' limit, I thought.

"Up looking for a job, are ya?" he asked after I'd told him that I'd arrived on the bus and was just taking a breather before going from shop to shop.

He was very chatty and told me about how often he came to Galway and loved sitting here...and then out of the fuckin' blue, he says to me...

"Tell me, do ya give himself an auld pull, now do ya?"

"Sorry, what'd ya say?"

"Your lad, d'ya give him the odd pull now, like I do meself,"

Then I could see that his hand was in his pocket, but was rooting around in his groin.

"'I'm doing it now, so I am, but ya must yerself now, at home like, do ya?"

"Arragh, fuck off," I said and got up to walk, but then I saw he was coming after me, probably thinking I was going to hop into the jacks there where I subsequently found out, young fellas blew off auld fellas for twenty quid.

I walked faster and he walked faster, but then I broke into a jog, then a sprint and made my way down Shop St. Once I left the confines of the Square, I could see that he had given up and walked back to the bench, in the knowledge that all he needed to make his day was one positive answer from one poor innocent fucker.

133

I could tell that handing out CVs to most of the big shops was a waste of time, although some were fine about it. There were some shops that made me feel like shit and as I walked the streets in the sunshine, I knew that in a city famed for its welcome and inclusivity that it was the worst feeling in the world to be an outsider. The happy smiles of the people and the happy fuckin' heads of the buskers only made it worse, as if you had to be a member of a club to enjoy this place. People walked by in twos and threes, sporting sandwiches to eat in the Square, and I envied them. I knew nobody, and nobody looked at me. It was as if I was fuckin' invisible, not mattering to anyone.

I felt hot in my suit, the suit that'd I'd bought for Seamus' wedding in Tipperary. Everyone seemed to be in shorts and summer gear. I felt I looked like a spare prick.

It got easier when I got the city bus out to the suburbs to try the factories and the wholesalers. It seemed cooler out there as if there was more space for the breeze to blow around in and fewer buildings for the sun to bounce off.

The receptionists in the factories said they'd pass it on to their human resources departments, but I knew that the achievements listed within were unlikely to encourage them to give me a call for interview.

I must admit I was surprised when the foreman in Mortons the wholesale plant started to talk to me.

'What work do ya want? Office?"

"Any type. I'm not fussy."

"Is it office work you want, cos you've a suit on ya?"

"No, that's just because I wanted to look respectable."

"Respectable, is it?

"Aye."

He looked me up and down and then said
"Well respectable or not, I've no office jobs but I've floor jobs."
So I took it... I hadn't even asked how much it paid or what I'd be doing. I was being offered a job, a proper job with other people and with pay at the end of the week.

Floor jobs turned out to be working into this massive warehouse stuffed with all of the items that were sold in every large and small shop in the region. The shops would tick off boxes in a big order book listing all the stock they wanted and each floor team leader would be given a book and have to travel around on long forklifts putting the order together.
I fuckin' loved it cos I got to drive the forklift and fill the steel cages with boxes of biscuits, confectionary, household goods. The more orders you got completed during the day, the more I got paid. I sped around like a mad flute knowing that the more I filled, the more money I'd make.
Another bonus was that for breakfast or lunchtime, we could eat any of the goods that were in damaged boxes, so if the lads fancied Jaffa cakes, they'd put a box just behind the wheel of the forklift and bash it in, therefore making Jaffa cakes available for a post lunch snack. God, we ate such shit for lunch. 'Twas great craic and the lads were good to work with, especially the country lads, The city lads were lazy pricks always trying to get wan over ya. But I steered well clear in case they'd make me lose the job or anything like that.

When I got the job, summer was starting, so there was plenty of accommodation because the students had left. I scoured the small ads in the Galway Advertiser and found a bedsit at Moneenageisha for forty pounds a week. It was very small, and had a one-ring electric plate cooker and a kettle, with a shared bathroom. Each week I left the rent in an envelope under the door of an adjoining block and when I came home each evening it was gone. I never saw a sinner in the place. I came and I went. I managed to learn how to make a mean egg mayonnaise, so for that summer, I lived on the fuckin' stuff, reading books 'til my head fell down. I got this library book called The History of the World which was about 800 pages long and gave me a basic knowledge of every major thing h happened since the beginning of time. A little bit of knowledge about a lot of things. Enough to get by. From Herod to Hitler. I'd read that, eat the egg mayonnaise and toss off to the new Suzanne Vega album cover. I'd a mad fuckin' crush on her, but I knew nothing would ever come of the relationship. So instead of heading to America to stalk her, I'd wank off to the sound of Marlene On The Wall and Luka til' I couldn't do any more and fall asleep.

I loved the job. If you were ten or fifteen minutes early you got extra pay so I'd be there at 7.30 each morning instead of the 8am start, getting a good lead over the others, getting more orders done. I was doing about ten books a day within a month of starting, taking home more than 400 pounds a week. Crazy money. I mailed a hundred home to Mother every week, but like the lads she told me not to be wasting my money on her and that she'd be grand. But I still sent it anyway – it would go a long way in meeting her bills every week, as long as Father wasn't pissing it away. And I was happy as a pig in shit with the two hundred or so that I had for living my life in Galway.
I went to the pictures twice a week, in the Claddagh Palace and the Town Hall, rundown fleapits that I'd be scratching me hole from for a week or more, but I loved it - the freedom, the

136

satisfaction that whatever I eat or drank or bought or watched was from money given to me by someone else for doing a job for them. And when you came from a long life of scratchy jobs, that meant something.

I used to buy myself salad rolls from Lydon House and eat them above in the Square. I hadn't met any more queers trying to ride me so I sat there in the grass, drinking Coke and eating my rolls, feeling for the first time like an insider.

Now that I was settled there in the city there was no feeling bad about where I came from or who my family were in the town. It was like a clean slate and I'd lie back on the grass, squinting at the sun and wondering why the fuck I hadn't done this years before.

The Twenty-Second Year

Big sweaty hands pushed into mine
Grabbing wrist, heart, and head
with bulging eyes, some alive with
the energy of the man in the varnished box
Spitting out sympathies and some pities
staring at us lined up
dark crumpled suits and punchdrunk heads
and red eyes and a yearning for
the gold screws to be fastened tight with a final squeak
so we could get home and eat sandwiches
that feed our souls white pan and fatty ham
and lashings of butter spread with the tears of aunts.

(Peadar Gibbons)

I had no idea who the fuck she was, but there was no doubt she was one of the fattest women I'd ever seen. It was 5am and I don't know if I'd ever been awake this early or up this late. 'Twas the knocking on the door that woke me. Even though all the bedsits were full, I'd still not seen anyone in the block, so when I heard the knocking I thought I was dreaming.

"Are you Peadar? Peadar Gibbons?"

I nodded.

"Yes."

"There's a phone call for you."

I followed her down the hall. Still wondering if this was real or some fucked up dream where I'd be led by a fat woman and conned into riding her by some weird cult. Moonies or something.

I picked up the phone.

It was Mother.

"Hello love, that you love?"

"Yes, mammy, are ya alright?"

"Love, I've some bad news for ya.

"What?"

"Dad is dead."

I took it all in.

"What. How"

"Heart attack."

"When did it happen?"

"A few hours ago. Can you make your way home..."

I hung up the phone and went back to the bedsit. It looked even smaller now. The walls seemed to have moved in a bit since I went down to take the phone call. It was if some of the smart fuckers from the city had pushed in the walls by a foot all around

139

and made it even more suffocating. I sat on the bed and wondered if it had really happened.

Dad dead.

And it didn't feel sad, at all.

Not a bit.

I went in and showered and showered, even though at this hour the water was cold to middling. It was hard to comprehend. A man who had been there all my life was gone, snuffed out. There were many times when the drinking was bad that I'd wished he died, but then there were so many times that he was like a real father, like they had on the Neale Road. I wondered had he died there in the chair where he'd lie slumped with his head forward like he did for so many of the 22 years of my life. But then even as I thought of that, I thought of the woods when he played with us in the camp and of the times he brought us and taught us how to catch grasshoppers and daddy longlegs for the fishermen. I thought of the many nights in Luke Higgins pub when we sat bored but wide-eyed at the foreign anglers and their colourful clothes and the exotic smells of their cigars.

He was like a knacker's dog in that everyone knew him and had time for him. Even though they knew he was an insufferable drunk, he was always first to help anyone in time of crisis. He would paint their houses, dig their gardens, use the Council diggers to fix drains and water pipes. And at times to us, he was the best father in the world. So much of the life in our house revolved around him and the many characters he introduced to our lives, council workers, craftsmen, fellow drunks, errant criminals that he'd have met and offered them a place to stay.

And now he was dead. I sat back on the small bed and thought about it. Shit, I needed music for this. I needed music for everything. There should be a soundtrack to life that bursts into voice at times of emotional need. I took down the three-in-one radio-cassette player and shoved in the black cassette – the soundtrack to my favourite film *Once Upon A Time in America*. It was the last film that I'd watched with him, and a film that reminded me of the days in the years before he died when unknown to me, things were changing around me, more actors were leaving the stage. And me with no lines. Or having ever seen a script or a helpful hand from a fellow actor.

As the Morricone music played, I sat and cried and cried...

Father looked strange in the coffin. His face was very purple and red, not gaunt and yellow like any other corpse I'd seen. The doctor said that was common with people who'd died of heart attacks or brain haemorrhages.

At the funeral, we all sat in the front pew, flanking Mother with Uncle Liam and his wife at the other end. The priest stood up and said wonderful things about Father even though he probably knew fuck all about him. And as he said he was a great character, I knew that he meant drunk. But 'twas only in later years that I wondered what was it that made him drink. Twasn't the fuckin' thirst. No one is thirsty for forty years.

That day seemed to be the final day that I felt we were a family anymore. The lads had come from England for the funeral but had gotten scuttery rotten drunk the night before, the heartless bastards, and so were unable to stand up for the removal and when they did, they stank of beer and whiskey.

Seamus had come from Tipperary with his family, but they didn't want to stay around long. They came to the pub for the sandwiches and soup, but then he gave Mother a hug and said 'we'll be off' and off he went. Back to a house where there was a family, and some happiness, and some hope. He was always a little bit embarrassed about where he came from. He didn't want his friends or indeed Catherine, to know that we came from a house that had no indoor jacks, that we'd piss into a bucket in the room at night and then empty it in the morning.

When he met Catherine first and he brought her home to meet Mother and Father, he had actually physically threatened Father into staying sober for the Sunday. He never brought her to the house for tea. They always went somewhere else, somewhere out, one of the restaurants or hotels up town. He slapped me on the back and told me to mind meself. He didn't bother with the lads.

Uncle Liam told Ray and Marty to fuck off back to England after their behaviour and got a slap in the face for his efforts. But they did fuck off. They got the CIE bus from outside the Ulster Bank in the morning and were back in their bedsit in Olive Road in Cricklewood the next day. Kevin tousled my hair even though I was 22, and he gave me a ten pound note, an Irish tenner. "There, a mac, take that. It's fuck all good to us back in England."

They headed for the back of the bus where'd they be able to stretch out and have some kip before the boat journey back to Holyhead. Before they lay down, they both gave me a sort of wave, one of those hand signals that the cool truck drivers used to make - a sort of flick of the hands with the fingers flailing out. I tried to do it back to them, but failed miserably... and then they laughed and gave me a proper wave before their heads disappeared low into the long seats at the back.

Though they didn't rise again before the bus left, I ran after it all the way to the corner of Glebe Street, where it turned into New Street and disappeared out the Kilmaine Road.

I didn't know then as I saw the lads red faced and awkward in their cheap suits, stagger up the steps and onto the bus, that I'd never ever see them alive again.

The Twenty-Third Year

Any eejit can run

It's the slowing down

after the run away

that shapes you.

It's the

stopping

strolling

shaping

schmaltzing

that defines you.

The lack of sweat on the brow,

the speed of breath.

The pace with which you

return your heart

to the humdrum beat

is the brush that paints

the dark shade of your soul

'Tis not the speed you run at

that matters

but the balance you have
when you stop.

(Peadar Gibbons)

I loved thumbing. And I loved the buzz of a Friday afternoon when I'd work the early shift and get finished early. I'd run back to the bedsit and grab me bag and head over to the Headford Road. If there were students there already you had to walk past them to take the furthest spot. And the furthest spot was normally the place a driver was least likely to pull in. And if there were any birds thumbing, you'd never get a seat 'cos they got all the early seats.

'Cos if a fella had a choice between you with your mad look about ya and a fine bird, you wouldn't stand a chance. So sometimes, I'd thumb before the birds so that you might have some chance of getting a seat.

I never really thought about the concept of thumbing. After all it's just a glorified form of fuckin' begging, 'cept that instead of money you were asking for, you were seeking the use of their car and the use of their conversation, and the invasion of their privacy. I wondered if one day I'd have a car and if I did, would I give seats to dodgy-looking fuckers like meself. I thought I might, but probably would still go for the good looking birds.

In general, I'd get a seat in about half an hour. If you didn't get one then, I'd always start walking out the road, to sort of psychologically shorten the journey but to also increase my chance of getting a seat.

Once a priest gave me a seat and starting saying the Rosary and was impressed that I knew the run of it, especially the Sorrowful Mysteries, 'cos 'twas beaten into me at home by Granny who made us all go down our knees every evening and make us recite, not just one batch of decades of the Rosary, but two and sometimes three. I was always amused by the Sorrowful Mysteries 'cos to me they were all sorrowful fuckin' mysteries.

146

Jesus was dying and crucified in most of them, so it sure wasn't a comedy.

I blamed that for the way I spoke fast, 'cos I'd rifle through the Hail Marys and the Our Fathers so that it'd finish early and we could watch TV. None of my friends said the Rosary in their houses which was just another fuckin' reason why we were different. It made me sad too to think that the Rosary was always the mark for Father to head off up town drinking. As soon as the 'Glory be to God' was finished, he'd be up off his knees, into the jacks for a piss, a splash of Old Spice and a run of the lacquer through his jet black hair.

On the day I want to talk about, I was a bit cranky from early on anyway. At work the lads were getting more and more pissed off that I was coming in earlier and earlier and getting more books filled. By the time they came in at eight, I'd have eight or nine aisles done with my forklift, filling the cages with stock for the shops. That morning after my tea break I saw that they'd taken half of my load off the trolley and put it back on the shelves. So I didn't know what I'd gathered and what I hadn't 'cos I'd the stuff ticked off on the books as I went along. And then I could see them sniggering at me and covering their mouths when they thought I wasn't looking, But I knew they'd done it and that I couldn't do anything about it. It took me two hours to get it right, and so instead of getting the credit and a few more quid for the weekend, I ended up getting a bollocking from the foreman John, who I hated anyway just because he was a proper cunt. He was always onto me. He was more friendly with the lads from Mervue than he was with me, and used to give me grief when there was no need to. But there was nobody to complain to. The previous foreman who'd taken me on had moved upstairs but I

147

knew that once you complain, then you'd might as well head for the door. So I took the humiliation of the morning and I took the bollocking from John and I was sad as I left because I thought when I had left home that the sort of shite done agin me would stop and that a new slate would be there for me to make my mark.

And when I got back to the bedsit the fat lady I met the night Father died was at the door saying she hadn't got the rent due the night before and when I told her I'd put it under the door, she said I was a liar. Jesus, I felt like hitting her. I needed to hit someone. I swore again that I'd put it under the door and I showed her where, and then we spotted it. It had gone under the lino at the door. She mumbled a sorry and fucked off back into her kitchen, probably to eat more shite, but 'twas just that sort of day, I'm saying like. The sort of day that wasn't going at all well, and none of it, none of it was my fuckin' fault.

By the time I got on the road, the place was full of students but one by one they got picked up and after 20 minutes I got a seat.

He'd a big black car, not new but well kept.
"Where ya going?"
"Ballinrobe."
"Hop in, I'm going that way anyway. To Ballina and then Sligo."
First thing I noticed is that he smelt grand. Expensive aftershave and a pink polo shirt with the collars turned up. Real mod like. This fella had money and wasn't backward at coming forward about it. The car was beige inside, nice soft leather with an armrest between the two front seats, on which he left his left arm. We chatted.
This and that.

Football and politics.

Shite talk like. He laughed and smiled.

And told jokes.

Filthy fuckin' jokes.

Which was kinda weird given that I'd just met him.

And then he said...

"Don't panic now, and hear me out. I'll give ya a hundred quid to pull me off."

A hundred quid. A fuckin hundred quid. I was down forty quid for what the lads had done to me at work.

I said nothing for a minute.

A hundred quid for something that was just one step from pulling myself off.

Nobody would ever know. Fuck, what to do.

He looked at me again in case I'd make a grab for the door or start screaming or hit him.

"Ok."

"What?"

"Ok, I'll do it for a hundred quid. I want it upfront though."

He rustled in his pocket and took out a wad of notes held together by an elastic band. There must have been a thousand quid in there. He didn't look like the type who'd need to be whacked off by someone he gave a seat to. He looked like the kind of fella who'd have no problem getting the ride, especially with a car like this and money like that. Or that he'd want a fella to do it. Queer fucker with money heading to Mayo. You couldn't make this up. Could only happen in Galway.

"Sound, we'll go somewhere quiet so," he said, kinda surprised I was going for it, I'd say, 'cos he had a strange smile on him. A cat who got the cream smile. A cat who was about to be creamed smile. And I was smiling too but feeling weird about it too. But sort of excited. How could such a shit day turn out this way? Swings and fucking roundabouts.

At that stage I wondered if I'd made the right decision.
Five minutes later, he turned down a boreen that went on for a few miles before he drove into a forest area. He stopped the car at the edge of a small clearing, handed me two fifty pound notes and opened his trousers, slipping them down as far as his knees. I grabbed his cock and started to toss him off. He'd a fine schlong on him to be fair now. Bigger than John Herlihy's anyway. And mine. He lay back in the seat and started moaning . "Fuckin jaysis, that's great boy, kape at it." I thought I'd have him off in a minute but there was no sign of anything. I hoped to fuck he wouldn't be like one of those porn fellas that can keep going for hours.
Then he leant over and grabbed my head and tried to push it towards his groin. He held onto my hair and tried to force me down again, my face in his crotch.
I jerked up, the back of my head crashing into his chin. Fuckin' sore. But his face changed and he seemed angry and out of control.
He tried to push my head down again. I flailed my arms.
"Go on, ya little fucker. Go on."
Then I punched him hard into the balls and he loosened his grip, before hitting me a hard slap against the side of the head. I went at him, grabbing his head and pushing it back against the window, then sharply bashed it against the dashboard. He was stunned so I did it again, this time his eye connected with the indicator handle, he let a roar out of him ' me fuckin eye" so I pushed him again, me having a good hold of the back of his head.

150

He protected himself from the protruding indicator handle but I pushed him again, his head bashing against the dashboard, and again, and again, and I got into a rhythm so I did it five, ten, twenty times and each time, I pushed him, the easier it got. And then I thought of myself and the possibility I'd be seen but there was nobody around. So I continued to bash him against the dash, til his face was a bloodied mess. And blood ran down his nose and out of his mouth, dripping onto his exposed balls.

I could not tell if he was alive or dead, so I continued for a few more minutes.

To be sure.

And then I stopped. And looked at him and how different he looked when he wasn't conscious.

How he didn't have that confident away about him now, slumped there, blood running from his nose and mouth and eye and his trousers half down.

I know that if I was caught here or seen here, there'd be no way I could ever explain it, even if I told people what he'd done. So I had to get away. Fast. I made sure I hadn't dropped anything or touched anything but there was no way of knowing, so I just rubbed the door handle inside and out. Then reaching down into his pocket I took out the roll of money and shoved it inside my jacket.

I knew I'd have to make my way through the woods without being seen. I found a pathway that ran into gorse so I tore my way through that 'til it came to a clearing and from there the road led away to Glencorrib and over the hill into Mayo.

I walked all the way into Shrule, then bought a coke and a Snickers in Mullins' shop and headed to the other side where I got another two seats to bring me home. And in those cars I talked shite and acted normal and didn't even break a sweat on me...as if the people who picked me up were ever going to be testifying or anything. Daft as it might seem. But I felt I had to be extra normal and be sure there was no blood on me or anything.

And when I got home, Mother wasn't there so I let myself in and went upstairs and went into the toilet and puked up all the Coke and Snickers and whatever other black fuckin' liquid that was in the dark part of my soul.

And then I sat back and waited for the howl within
and waited...
and waited.
'Til the thought of it didn't make me feel bad about myself at all.
'Til I could feel right again and not give it a thought.
'Til my head fell out of my hand and onto the pillow.

The Twenty-Fourth Year

At four am, the world slows down
and all the scrambled fears I try to quell
rise up and in an ordered line
make sense in ways I don't want to hear.
And as I scrape my scalp with anguished hands
and stare through panes at darkened fields beyond
I see them march four strong along the troughs
to rip away the shells of my defence
and leave me weeping tears
that fall through the night onto my hands.

(Peadar Gibbons)

For the year after that, I'd be bothered. Real bothered.

Sort of waking up in the middle of the night and having to ate loads of digestives covered with butter and drink lashings of milk bothered.

Going back to bed with the belly swollen on me bothered.

Tossing and turning and flinging the duvet off myself and then waking up cold later bothered.

Not bad dreams or anything, it was as if I didn't want to leave this pillow. That is I wanted to push my head into it as far as I possibly could because that's where I was only truly comfortable. And when I lifted my head from it, it bothered me. So I left it there for as long as possible every morning.

And they say if you're bothered about shite and you've a way with words, you should put it down on paper, so that year I threw myself into the writing, proper writing. I'd seen someone say somewhere that you have to write about what you know in terms of emotions and stuff, 'cos that's the only way you can be sure they're true or honest. There's no point in me writing about love 'cos I've never been in love and then all I'd end up writing would be made-up shite about feelings I'd never know are true because for all I know, someone who had been in love would read them and know that they were fake. And then they'd know I was talking through me arse.

I'd often wondered what those fuckin' real writers and poets know about shit. Their poems are full of angst and love and hate and desire and you know in your heart and soul that none of those fuckers ever experienced loss and love and hate and horror the way that I had. So if having all of these things qualified you as being angst-ridden, then my angst was certainly having the hole ridden off it.

I'd always been pissing around writing. I did some kind of three-

154

page book using crayons and pencils when I was about eight. It was called Pigeons Come Back. I've no idea why I called it that or what the story was about and whether there were actually any real pigeons in it at all, or was I just being a surreal little prick long before I even knew what surreal was all about.

But then I wondered if actually having lived through all this shit, you'd be no good at writing about it. 'Cos people would expect you to be good writing about stuff like that, just because you were close to it and had lived through it. Bit like former football players being shit managers and all that.

So maybe, because I've done all this stuff, I'll be a shit poet and writer. Maybe I am. Maybe you're better off if you haven't experienced any of this stuff, because then you'll have to use your creative imagination to conjure it up, whereas I'd just be using memory.

And they're two different things 'cos the creative imagination allows you to float across things with just a gossamer touch, whereas the memory of such stuff can be as unsubtle as a sledgehammer hitting someone on the side of the head and hearing that dull thud that you'd only ever really know if you'd done it.

You see, the people who have seen or done terrible things often don't want to see them as terrible things. They might want to forget them or to justify them in some way, so writing poetry or stories about the events might be too painful, and I know you'll be saying "fuck them and their pain if they've done terrible things," but you've got to be able to understand anyone before you can make a value judgement like that about them. Value judgement means an opinion by the way. So I tried to write about things that I knew little about, like love. And to see if I could

155

understand it. So I wrote about the love my mother gave me when I was young, way back before Kieran got drowned. And I wrote this.

The Thread
A thread, softly woven,
Weak but strong enough
Short but long enough
A thread that put me there
And made me look into your eyes
And see the love that begged me
To let you go.

D'ya like that? Sorry, maybe guards aren't into poetry and the likes. I wondered if ever people will be analysing my poems like we used to do in English classes. Yeats and the others. Interpreting what he meant. What a load of bollocks. He wrote what he meant. So why the need to interpret? Fumbling around in the greasy tills meant just that. Yes, there was a broad explanation but sometimes English teachers were looking for fuckin' meaning when there wasn't any there to get. Just trying to throw shapes.
I'd look at some poems and not get anything from them at all, apart from the actual words on the page. And I knew I couldn't answer the teacher when he asked what is the meaning of that, and I'd say "well sir, the bicycles were going by in twos and threes to Billy Brennan's barn, so I'd say the meaning of that is that the fucking bikes were doing that sir, not causing ya any offence sir?

But that was my problem with poetry, so I decided to do it my own way. I couldn't write about what really happened, so I'd try and pick the opposite emotion that I felt at the time and use that to create a sort of poem that was full of fuckin' meaning for me, but might be so complicated that nobody in the outside world would be able to make any sense out of it at all. So if I wrote about love, I meant hate. If I wrote about him, I said her. If I wrote about her, I meant him. If I wrote about calmness, I meant absolute roaring fucking terror. If I wrote about friendship, it was about hitting a head off a dashboard so many times until the head stops chattering and asking me to stop. Poetry was like that, complicated, not really meant to be understood proper like, just fucking arseways so that people would have to work to find a meaning in it because after all that's what proper poets did.

And so it was because of that, to show ya like what I mean, I penned this poem to Terry Ward. Bet he never knew he'd have a poem written about him, apart from the long maudlin shite that his family put on his headstone. And as I wrote it, I thought about him flailing there in the water, his arms out, his mouth unable to say much before it got filled with dirty eel-pissed water.

Floating
A wave from a friend
A wave that swallowed her
A wave that said goodbye and help me
In an order I cannot remember
A wave that said you will never forget
the fear in my eyes as I sweep away from you
A wave that I ignored as I turned away

I did that to have a little laugh myself at the lines on his headstone. Bet the angels he's lying with are enjoying that one.

The Twenty-Fifth Year

How do you know when you're in love?
Is it when she taps ya on
the arse and says 'you're in, love
or is it when she looks at ya and knows and hopes
that you'll not be the last man she'll sleep with.
Or will you drown the nagging sound of loyalty
with the slap of thigh on cheek and close your
eyes and think of far away.

(Peadar Gibbons)

Suppose it is a sign of things that I had to wait this long. For the proper thing. The full ride. Not just the feeling and groping and trying to get a feel through layers of jumpers. And then when I started, I couldn't get enough of it. Like the Pioneer fucker who went on to become an alcoholic. And especially when they thought I was a bit of a dark horse. The quiet flute who writes the poems.

And I dressed for the part.

I'd bought a pair of khaki army pants in the Army and Navy Stores in Galway and wore shirts with braces and jackets with leather on the elbows and scarves. I'd learned how to tie a scarf in a very queer kind of way - Make a loop and then pull the scarf through and you looked the dog's bollocks.

The bank girls loved it. This arty fucker who had a way with words and was alright in the sack. The town was full of bank girls back then when working in the bank was something you could be proud of. Not now when everyone thinks you're a cunt for working in the bank. Every small town had girls who worked "in the bank." They were everywhere, normally blow ins, girls with good maths and boyfriends back home who'd never do to them the things they really wanted them to do to them. 'Cos they were good bank girls and good bank girls didn't drop the hand on your knob or let you put their hands up their skirts. And we'd joke with them about withdrawals and deposits and lodgements and the likes and some of them got it and some of them fuckin' didn't, 'cos there were varying types and levels of bank girls.

And because the lads in the town weren't exactly subtle in the romance stakes, I looked kinda different, more cultured, more polite. I used to stand up when they came into the room or when they left, and open doors for them and let them out first. And hold their coats for them. Course they thought it was 'cos I wanted to look at their arse. They used to titter when I'd tell them what I was doing and they'd say 'Go on, Peadar, tell us some more about good manners and things to do."

So I'd tell them about how to eat at the table and start the cutlery from the outside in, and how you're supposed to tip your soup bowl away from you and not towards you when you're down to the last few drops. And how to speak properly and not say 'them things'. That used to drive me daft about them. They were all so brilliant at maths and knew how much everyone had in their bank accounts, yet they spoke like boggers 'cos when you had to fill in those difficult bank application for the jobs, it couldn't tell that you were a bogger. I'd filled in a few of them but my handwriting was so bad ('cos of that fuckin' nun who changed my hands when I was five) that it looked a right mess and I knew straightaway that the bank wouldn't entertain it for a minute. And I wasn't sure if I wanted to be in the bank at all and be sent to some God-forsaken hole like this town.

The bank girls had great handwriting so that's how they moved up the pecking order. Anyway to cut to the chase, the one I broke my duck with was called Sinead. From Longford. They were probably all called Sinead. Good auld innocent names. She wasn't a great looker but she had a lovely laugh. She was about ten years older than me and was built for comfort rather than speed, and had a great pair on her that'd give a horn to a snowman. On top of this, she used to drink wine. And I'd never drank wine before. And she knew the names of all the wines. Both of them. Chardonnay and red wine. And the more we drank the more stupid she seemed to become. I mean if she was anyways thick before, there was no talking to her when she had the wine onboard.

161

She was never backward at coming forward, but the night she grabbed me and dragged me into her room, I was shitting meself in case I'd let her down. I'd been reading her a poem I'd written to her when she just put her hand over my mouth.

"Shut the fuck up," she told me and pulled down my khaki trousers and whipped off her skirt and knickers and then she climbed onto me,

"Take the bra off," she said and I didn't know what to do with it. 'At the back" she said but I couldn't make out what sort of fuckin' button or clasp was at the back, so I just lifted it from the front and put it up over her head.

Then they were there in front of me, the tits I'd been admiring for a month or so, there slapping against me face so I grabbed them and started kissing them and licking at them and sucking at her nipples and I was getting hard.

Then Sinead who was good at maths sat up on me and "Say nawthing ya poetry fucker ya."

I was saying nawthing.

"Just kape yer mouth shut and grunt for me. Like you're some sort of feckin animal or something."

Grunt for me?

What the fuck?

Animal?

What kinda shite were they into in Longford?

Like a fuckin' animal?

So I started grunting and making out I was enjoying meself which I was, and after a few minutes I didn't need to fake grunt as her fat arse started pounding me into the bed and the tits slapping up and down and me praying to God that I'd stay the course.

And she kept lepping on me and I was on such an angle near the end of the bed that I was afraid she'd break me fucking legs 'cos they were hitting against something. And that kinda stifled the urge for me to erupt, so I'd take the pain and yowl like 'twas the sex but twas really the hard board at the side of the mattress that was hitting into me arse every time I moved. 'Twas like on one of those dodgy seesaws where you hated and loved both the ups and downs.

And then I went and thank fuck a minute later, she let out a moan the likes of which you wouldn't hear out of a cat on a winter's night and then leant forward and started kissing me and she whispered "that was feckin' great." and me there thinking that I'd done fuck all to make it great. I'd just lain there but I felt great that she'd thought 'twas great, and then she snuggled her head into my shoulder and turned herself back into the quiet one from the bank with the great handwriting and the good maths that she was twenty minutes before.

And then I'd realised I hadn't used a johnny and what if she got knocked up, but then d'ya know what, I didn't give a shit whether I did or not. She didn't look like the type of wan you'd catch the AIDS of and I certainly had never caught it meself, so I lay there, happy. Not grunting anymore.

And then she said,

"Write a poem for me. Write a poem about the love we just made."

So I did. One of those long rambling one with no rhyming, with stuff about clouds and skies and rustling winds through summer forests and she smiled more and more and snuggled more and more into my shoulder.

And before I got to the third or fourth stanza, she was gone asleep.

Snoring into my neck.
Like some sort of an animal.

The Twenty-Sixth Year

Our crib, an old radio, valves ripped
replaced with fake straw
A backdrop cut from a magazine
sent home by yanks to prove that they can read
And statues wobbling to and fro as
we knelt and stared through decades
mysterious, sorrowful and the rest.
Behind the wise men stood a window frame
I wondered what lay beyond and
If I were out there looking in,
would I see the world any different.

(Peadar Gibbons)

The house was like something out of a magazine. Hello magazine. Not Woman's Way. No, one of those ones with celebrities and shiny happy faces sitting around in fancy jumpers and dresses and legs that go on forever and kids looking like they'd have their faces washed for hours and hours. And a dog, there was always a big shaggy dog sitting there in those pics. Yes, it was like that in Seamus' house. In Tipperary. With decorations and trees. He had three fuckin' Christmas trees. A big one in the hall; another in the sitting room and a third white one on the landing.

When I went in the door, it dawned on me that I'd never ever spent Christmas away from home, and that maybe we were missing out in a big way. Was this how the rest of the world celebrated Christmas, while we just sat at home, eating turkey and watching shows on a borrowed TV set?

Seamus had done quite well for himself, but despite all that, Mother hadn't that much time for him. Yes, he was her oldest son, the only one to go to college. He'd went off and got a Diploma in some type of architecture or something. Not in a proper university but a technical college, but it didn't matter to him, to him it was the biggest thing in the world, his ticket out of the town and away from the family. He was the one who got on the worst with Father so he was determined to get the fuck out.

He wasn't full of notions, but he knew what he wanted and whatever it was, it was to be the furthest away he could get from us. He'd met Catherine in college where she was doing a minding kids course and she had opened her own Montessori in a big extension attached to the house so she didn't have to pay rent or anything.

He had done the drawings for the house and the Montessori 'cos he was a fuckin' genius with things like that. He'd won prizes for it in school and it was him that myself and my brothers were always being compared to when we'd be shite at school. "Pity ya wouldn't be smart like yer brudder Seamus and not just a smart alec, Gibbons," I'd often hear from some auld mouldy smelly fuckin' teacher before he'd squeeze me nuts.

Back to Catherine. She was very pretty but when she was talking to ya, ya felt like she was doing ya a favour like. She wasn't a snooty cow really though Mother said once that she 'thought her shite was chocolate'. I was a bit younger then and thought she must be a terrible stupid fucking bitch if she thought that. And that I was fucked if I was ever going to accept any cooking from her. But later I copped on that 'twas just an expression, but still 'twas a strange thing for Mother to come out with, given that she never swore much or spoke bad about people. So Catherine must have been a right cunt.
She spoke to us with a kind of a grin that didn't look real and then when she wouldn't think I was looking, she'd look at ya like you were something the cat brought in or dirt that would stick to your shoe and you'd bring around the house.

I was surprised that herself and Seamus invited us down for the Christmas. Think he did it 'cos he knew the lads weren't coming home from England for the holidays and after all, how bad could it get just having Mother and myself there without them making a show of him. I was still earning decent money in Galway so we were able to get the bus down and Seamus picked us up in the middle of the town.
Because we'd a few quid, we managed to get presents for the

kids, not Santa Claus ones but ones they'd open in front of us on Christmas Day. I looked around at all the trappings of a comfortable Christmas and thought of our house back home, empty this Christmas and quiet and even the electric crib made from an old radio set, plugged out and the lights dimmed on the skimpy skinny fake tree.

It was the centre of happiness and joy for so many Christmasses. But then I also thought of the many Christmasses when the day would be ruined by Father, drunk and cranky all day from spending the grocery money on beer and whiskey the night before. And probably wishing that he was somewhere else with someone else. I'd found out fierce young that he'd been riding one of the Kelly sisters from the pub so he probably spent Christmas Days wishing he was with her, even though he knew himself that he looked fuckin' ridiculous with a young wan twenty years younger than himself.

One year he'd fucked the turkey out on the lawn before storming out of the house on Christmas morning, trying to find a pub open up town, and being let in the back door of Kellys for a while. But he was home again an hour later, cursing in his mind that there were no Kelly sisters there to tease him.

And I'd to go out and pick it up and bring it in and wash the dirt off it and put it back in the oven. And then we'd eat it later and there'd be a sort of stifling of laughter 'cos we knew our hearts were aching and shaking from the sadness of it all.

And we could tell he didn't want to be there.

And Mother was crying and Granny was crying and praying to God asking him how the fuck her daughter was married to this animal. She didn't say 'how the fuck' really, but she had other words.

And the harshest words she was capable of were the ones that she never uttered to anyone but herself. And you could see in her face that the thoughts she was thinking were something she didn't want us to be party to.

But it was the same for many Christmasses - Father would get paid a few quid more so he'd go to the supermarket up town, get four or five bags of groceries and then head to the pub next door where he'd drink the rest of the money. And I'd be sitting there with him, sipping a Fanta and feeling that this was fuckin' Christmas Eve and that a young lad like me should be at home watching the Miracle on fuckin' 34th Street on the telly, if we had a telly, instead of being stuck here in the smoke and smells and seeing through the big Harp sign on the window and looking out at normal families doing normal Christmassy things. And so he'd send me home alone after a while when Triona Kelly would come out serving and so I'd walk down the hill home, eating a bag of Perri crisps and crying and hoping to fuck that when I got bigger I wouldn't have Christmasses like this. That I'd have normal Christmasses like those other families.

Later he'd arrive down with the shopping bags, half the stuff probably stole out of it by miserly fuckers on the way down the hill. And he'd arrive in with the goodies, expecting us to greet him like the arrival of the Queen of fuckin' Sheba and when we wouldn't, he'd get all thick and flail his arms and storm off to the jacks every few minutes to take a swig from the baby Powers he kept in his pocket. And lettin' on we didn't know. What did he take us for?

Now he was gone and here I was in a proper Christmas and to be honest it didn't feel as nice as I had thought it was going to be.

I looked over at Mother sitting here at the fire in Seamus and

Catherine's massive sitting room, with Perry Como on the telly and a glass of sherry in her hand and she having the radiance in her face I hadn't seen in a long time. And there was an ease about her, a sort of calmness that for one Christmas after a life of worrying, she did not have be concerned about how Father would fuck it up. But I knew that deep down, she had the anxiety that she'd always had and that it would probably never leave her for the rest of her life.

We stayed for the few days and Seamus and I had some long chats. He was worried that I hadn't got a decent job and he asked me if I considered going back to college to study as a mature student and get some qualification. It was something I hadn't thought about as I thought I'd be too thick to get into college now that my learning days were over and because I'd been shite at school.
I told him about the poems and was going to tell him about riding the bank girl, but decided not to. 'Twasn't something he'd have done himself. He was too straight. Not a bad bone in his body or not a bad bone in anybody else's body. He thought the poems were grand but said 'they won't put butter on your fuckin' bread.''
Despite the fact that he was talking down to me, I loved being able to chat to him like a man, even though he seemed to be getting older faster than I was. I thought that once we all became men that we'd all have the same outlook on life, but not at all. The twelve years stretch between us just seemed to be widening and his oversupply of commonsense was getting to me.
I longed to be back in Galway in the bedsit writing, and going home at the weekends to see if any of the bank girls stayed around. Which they probably hadn't.
And then I resolved that I hated fuckin' Christmasses good and

bad, 'cos now I'd sampled both and they were the same in terms of strained tensions and awkwardness and thoughts of elsewhere.

And strangely, part of me felt sorry for Father. Always on the wrong side of the door. Never where he wanted to be and tonight, below in the graveyard.

The Twenty-Seventh Year

Hope is a curse sent to tease us
Let the rain of reality lash down
on our dreams. Don't tread softly
because they're fragile.
Toughen them up by wearing hobnail boots
to jump on their back, strengthen their spine
so they won't fold as easily next time.

(Peadar Gibbons)

Montepulciano. Monte pulciano, I loved saying that fuckin' loved it. Like yerselves, guards, I had never heard of the place until I got the letter from Mother's first cousin who was a St John of God brother based in Rome. Not a priest, but a brother, but he had the bearing of a priest and he was ultra confident. Mother knew him as Vinny but to the order he was known as Bro Fabio (which is an Italian name and no doubt earned him the trust of the natives, over there in Rome.)

Every year he came home, all tanned and neat in his black outfit. No smell of chalk of him, but the smell of a sweet eau de cologne that he used to wear. Every year he came home he brought us a toy or a book. He gave me a wonderful book which had photographs of modern Roman ruins on one side and then drawings of how the sites looked back in the day when the lions ate all the prophets in the Colosseum. He also brought us two wooden Swiss Guard dolls, colourful outfits and their sharp swords, all designed to guard the Pope, even though to be honest they must be fuck all good if they didn't stop yer man shooting him all those years ago. I still have them here in the house – a memory of a childhood belonging to somebody else.

His visit home was the highlight of every summer for us as a kid. He never stayed in the house because this was a man who was used to his comforts. He travelled the world talking to students about joining the John of Gods and so he was used to the fine things in life. Nice hotels, soft beds, fine china of the type that wasn't just wheeled out for him, like ours was. Apart from all this, he was a very down to earth man who used to tousle my hair and teach me basic Italian words like arrivederci.

He stayed in the hotel up town and sometimes the posh B&B where they'd bow their heads to him and treat him like he was a bishop and speak differently to us when we went to meet him;

not like the look down your nose sort of way they normally did. And after his breakfast he'd come down and sit beside the fire all day and chat to Mother and uncle Liam and sometimes my father, if Father wasn't off drinking. And in the days before Granny died he brought her home all sorts of relics and religious objects that she held dear 'cos they came straight from the city of God and contained shavings of timber from the very cross that Christ died on. Or so she believed.

However this one time I'm talking about, I came into the room one weekend and they fell silent as if they had been whispering about me. The three of them. And they looked up at me which made me wonder if I'd done something wrong, or if Bro Fabio and Liam and Mother had discovered the wrinkled picture of Bo Derek that I'd kept under the mattress for tossing off to. Fuck, how would I explain that? But no, twasn't that.

Seemingly a doctor who worked with Bro Fabio in the Brother of God was looking for some English-speaking young lad to spend the summer with his teenage son in Montepulciano which was some Italian place on the top of a hill. That explains the Mont bit, like mountain, d'ya understand? Anyway, the kid had no English and I had no Italian apart from the few words Fabio taught me, but he was confident that the summer there would do us both the world of good, though it would mean me giving up the Galway job.

Montepulciano...top of a hill, Fabio said. And the doctor had a house on the edge of it and I'd be living in the house with them and getting paid an allowance as well. And I'd be able to spend this money on things in the village, if there were places to spend money there, but I was sure I'd find something.

174

My fuckin' head was spinnin'.

Italy.

I'd never thought of going to Italy. If I went to Italy or some foreign country then I could start my life again and leave the old me behind. It'd be like going on one of those witness protection programmes where you begin again at whatever part of your life you want. It'd be like rewinding a cassette tape back to Track One. I could get to know the language and like the food and the people and invent myself again, because over there I'd be kinda different. The pale one who could speak English and write English. And with all the spare time I'd have, I'd be able to work all evening on my books and poems while sitting on chairs outside little restaurants, sipping a glass of that Chianti red wine stuff that they make in that region. I'd be like fuckin' Hemingway. I'd turn into a cranky cunt like him and have all the people walking by me and saying to themselves, in Italian like, "there's that cranky cunt Gibbons." and muttering " He thinks he's fuckin' Hemingway," under their breath.

And how good that would be? To have people talk about you. Even if they were calling ya a cunt, 'twould be better than not being noticed at all. I hate that, being not seen at all. Not being worth a fuckin' glance even.

As I lay back in the room that night and thought of how it would all be, I wondered if I'd miss Mother and I decided that I would, but that apart from all that, I'd adapt fine. I'd have to buy new clothes, lighter stuff 'cos it's hotter there and some nice shorts and light shoes, not runners.

I wondered if I'd get the ride there and decided that maybe I wouldn't 'cos the men were all so fuckin' handsome, with their brown square chiselled faces. I thought for a minute that I might turn queer again, but then put that notion out of my head. Maybe

175

the women there would want the opposite of that, they might be fed up of Italian gods with schlongs on them like stallions and I'd be in like Flynn. Either way, I'd play it by ear.

When the library opened the next day, I used the tickets to get six books on Italy and Italian cooking and Italian culture and read about fellas like Machiavelli who was famous for saying 'the end justifies the means' – I fuckin' liked that. I could keep that line and use it 'cos it was the kinda stuff I was doing anyway. I reckoned that if I was to meet Machiavelli or any of his descendants in Italy, that we'd get on fine, 'cos it sounded like they were heartless fuckers as well. Then there were the Borgias who were popes. There was one count there who took out the son of one of the Popes (yes the Popes had sons. Twas like fuckin' Galway) and had his soldiers ride the hole off him in the middle of the square to humiliate him. Fuckin hell. How the Popes have changed I thought..
Overall, I liked the Italians cos they seemed like mad fuckers and maybe twas with mad fuckers that I'd be best settled. Then I thought of the Mafia and was worried that I might piss them off some way, but then if I kept to myself and didn't blow too much about my writing, they mightn't notice me.
And as for the young lad I'd be minding. It'd be great. It'd be like having a little brother (just one who wouldn't have a clue what I was saying. And I could teach him stuff, and talk football with him and women. Yeah, I'd have to tell him all that shit. And generally have the craic with him. His name was Giuseppe. If he was my brother he'd be Giuseppe Gibbons. Liked that thought.
I was raring for it. I'd be giving up the job in Galway but what the fuck. Italy was much more exciting.
I was even looking for shorts and stuff and I'd applied for a

passport and I read about planes and how to not be afraid on them.
And I'd even looked up how long it would take for me to turn brown and not get burned.
And I put gel in my hair.

Then the letter came from Rome, from Fabio, with its airmail bordering and its colourful stamp and the headed notepaper with the fine gold writing inside. And when Mother read it her face seemed to drop and when her face dropped my heart dropped.
The doctor had suffered a heart attack in Rome and was critically ill, so all plans to have someone mentor his son were cancelled. I was devastated. I didn't curse my bad luck like I would have before. Now I felt like fuckin' Peig Sayers. Every attempt she made to leave her island failed with some dark twist at the last minute. I wondered if a hundred years from now people would be reading my story like hers and thinking what a miserable fucker I was. And how everything I touched seemed to go to shite.

I got over it 'cos I was only thinking about it for a month in total. But ever since then I can't stand to see or hear anything about Italy or Rome. 'Cos when I do I'd sigh and my heart would sink and I'd let this silent little howl outta me like some sort of baste. Now, if I'd made it to Italy, I wouldn't be writing this letter to ye, guards.
But then maybe I was as well off because 'tis not knowing the shite I could have got involved with if I'd gone over there.
"Maybe, 'twas for the best," said Mother.
"Maybe, twasn't meant to be."

177

The Twenty-Eighth Year

When you get a punch
to the heart,
it leaves a hole so wide
that the next punch fits
neatly through the opening.
The only feeling being
the sudden draught
of clenched fist
past open artery
that makes each next blow
all the easier to take

(Peadar Gibbons)

I never knew the difference between Green Macs and Brown Mac. But I do now. All I'd been told is that there were two McCarthy brothers from somewhere in Mayo who went to London, set up their own construction/labouring business and then somewhere along the way fell out and went their separate ways. I've no idea what they fell out over but one fuckin' hated the other and even the men they employed grew to hate the others even though it was just fate that saw them plucked for green or brown from the queues outside the Cricklewood Cafe at five in the morning.

One wing had green vans and the other had brown vans, so they were distinguished by the names Brown Mac and Green Mac. This useless fuckin' information would all have remained unknown to me were it not for the fact that Marty and Ray worked for the Green, were picked up by Green vans near the Crown pub, and brought off to work with little Green men on restorations pulling cables and gutting houses in places with fancy names like Maida Vale.

"We used to go to work through Connaught Square," Marty told me on the rare time when he phoned home. "Imagine them Londoners having a square named after our province."

They also told me that they spent one summer gutting the house which once belonged to a woman called Margot Fonteyn, but that they hadn't a fuckin' clue who she was but that she must have been loaded. And that she definitely wasn't the Margo who used to play in the Town Hall in Ballinrobe 'cos that wan was Irish. And was Daniel O'Donnell's sister.

The house had been bought by Arabs who wanted it demolished and knocked into fancy flats. I put them straight that she was a ballet dancer 'cos the Cuddys had a collection of Encyclopaedia Britannica that their father bought 'cos he had notions and which

179

all lay unread on their bookshelf, apart from days when I'd be around and I'd borrow one. My brothers would never have been into fuckin' ballet anyway so were unlikely to have known.

They told me that the first job they had was pulling cables at Liverpool Street. There were big shafts dug in the streets and that tunnels were drilled the 100 yards to the next tunnel. The cable would be pulled through, but that sometimes they'd have to go into the tunnel themselves and crawl all the way through. They told me of the feel of the cold water dripping on their bare backs, aware that at any minute the whole thing could collapse on top of them. But they said 'twas worth it for the pay they got, but it was pay that they pissed away against the walls of North London.

I've no idea where Hackney was in relation to all this, but that's where they were when the row started. And of course, 'twas outside a pub. What started off as a few fucks being thrown around between the Browns and the Greens, developed into a full blooded brawl in the street. Marty and Ray were never ones to stay out of a fight anyway so they waded in, kicking and punching as they did, each picking out members of their opposing crews, fuckers they mightn't have liked. Anyone that had a puss on them like a Brown Mac-er. But they had drink on them and were none too steady on the feet, or so we were told.

And with all the kicking and punching and screaming and staggering, they were all over the place.

And somebody was going to call the police, but then they said that 'twas just the fuckin' Irish lads flakin' each other so there'd be no point 'cos they'd all back each other up in the end and nobody would press charges. The Brown Mac-ers never used the regular law to sort out rows with Green Mac-ers.

180

None of them saw or heard the big red bus coming along as it drove under the railway bridge and onto the street outside the bar. The driver said to the police later that he just felt a bump and then heard the screaming. And the roaring and the fighting stopped and everyone rushed to the side of the bus and when he jammed on the brakes, they started roaring at him to move up a bit and then others said "don't move 'cos there's fellas's heads under the wheels." And then there were Green macs and Brown macs getting sick on the street and turning away to wipe the puke from their shirts before retching again and then letting roars out of them, the two groups of them together regretting the fuck that they'd not stopped this shitehawking a few minutes earlier before three of them had fallen under the wheels of the 253 route from Hackney central to Camden Town.

Uncle Liam got the calls... Three of them. Two from the guards, in Ballinrobe and in Claremorris, 'cos they'd got the calls from the Met. And then there was a call from some civil servant in Dublin asking if we needed help in repatriating the bodies. The bodies, yeah, the fuckin' bodies.
When we had the funerals, the coffins were closed because the undertaker felt that would be best and least upsetting for my mother who despite all their faults, had wanted to hug and kiss them for the last time. The way that she had hugged and kissed Kieran when his bloated body was lying there in the coffin and he blueish like an old man and he only fifteen. They told her that the lads had serious injuries and that it would be best for the rest of the family and friends if the coffins stayed shut, and she accepted that.

But we really knew that their heads had been popped like melons and that really it was as if they'd been decapitated 'cos there was nothing left of them there at all, much. Fuck. I wondered if they knew what was happening, even for the slightest of a split second. Did they feel anything at all? That bothered me. Just like I worried if Kieran was being held under the water by the eels at the Soldier's Hole. Were they holding him by the legs just under the water enough to fill his lungs like? Just to make it look natural. I wondered if he'd meet them now wherever they were. And what he'd make of them.

And if they'd have heads.

Mother was immune to death now. The doctor had given her sedatives to make her spaced for the funeral, but we all knew that one day, they'd wear off and that the full horror of her life would become obvious to her. In the space of thirty years, she'd buried three sons, a husband and her mother. And she not even 56. And some days it seemed to me that she did not feel the existence of myself and Seamus was any use to her at all.

Uncle Liam got drunk at the funeral, which I'd never seen before and he told me that his sister should never married my father at all, that there was 'bad cess ' with him and that if she had married anyone else, she wouldn't be sitting here a broken woman, her family devastated by drink and tragedy and she left with the two sons, one fecked off to Tipperary and me a waster, whose only saving grace was that I didn't take the family liking for drink. He told me that Mother thought I was a waster too....which hurt me bad.

And there was no call to tell me that.

I'd done nothing to deserve that.

Not on a day like that.

But he was drunk, so I let it pass.
But it hurt, it fuckin' did.

Back when I was a teenager I hoped that one day I'd move into the bedroom occupied by Marty and Ray. It was at the back of the house and had a window through which you could see across the fields and over to the Partry mountains. It was a middle-sized room and here you could play music without the rest of the house hearing it.

I went upstairs and looked into it, its dark emptiness a reminder of the days when it was a centre of noise, with cassette players belting out cassette recordings of the Top 30 on Radio 2. The walls still had football posters cut out from the pages of Shoot. Players playing for Chelsea and Arsenal and Tottenham. Players who played in London and who lived in London. Players with sideburns, wearing flares and shopping on the King's Road.

I wondered if these players had ever spotted Marty and Ray digging the streets or pulling the cables or scurrying up and down scaffolding on houses owned by dead ballerinas and rich Arabs.

I wonder if they'd seen them, these two fellas, my two brothers, sound fellas, daft fellas – dead fellas.

And if they'd seen them I wondered if they looked at them, just at them, and not through them, 'cos they deserved to be looked at, and acknowledged, if only for a second, the poor bastards, the poor bastards.

The Twenty-Ninth Year

I knead words
like a fine flour
into choux pastries
which crumble
if you look at them too closely
and try to find a meaning
I didn't put there

I need words
so I can show
the world that I'm alive
behind these
dead eyes
that `I'm more than I am
and than you think I am.

(Peadar Gibbons)

I never told the bosses at work about my brothers having been killed. I took just two days off because the funeral was at the weekend. They might have read about it in the papers, but if they did, they never said anything to me about it. They never said much to me about anything, unless they were pulling the piss out of me. They were city lads and were pricks. Not pricks like the lads from the Neale Road at home, but pricks in the sense that they thought they were fuckin' gods. They'd all band together when they'd be laughing at me, asking me if I ever got my hole or was I a virgin or a queer. They'd heard I did some writing as well so one or two of them mentioned that. And laughed and called me fuckin' Roddy Doyle. And as time passed by I noticed that whereas I was neutral when I came here, without any prejudice for or against me, now I found myself slipping back into the role that I played back home, the easy target, the receptacle for abuse and jokes and derision. And if this is the case, then 'twas me that was letting this happen, not them. I must have carried this vibe that 'twas ok to tease me, to bully me, to make fun of me. Feeling shit about myself and feeling kind of grateful to anyone who wasn't not nice to me, if you get my drift. I found myself relieved if I could have a conversation with anyone and not feel more shit about myself than I did at the start of the conversation.

I tried to ignore them as best I could, but every day when I'd arrive early to pick up my first order book of the day, I felt less inclined to work as hard as I had before. I would never have called myself lazy, but I just needed the opportunity to show people that I could do a great fuckin' job if I was let. And that's all I wanted to do. Work, keep me head down, and get on with people. And be regarded as someone that others would be proud to say they worked with. Is that strange? I mean I didn't know any of their friends or family but I kinda hoped they'd go home and say 'this Gibbons lads I work with, he's a fuckin' gas man, so he is."

But I knew they wouldn't. People don't say that about me. I suppose it's cos I'm different and not all blokey like they seem to be.

That's why I loved the Mass serving so much, 'cos the tasks were all laid out, and I did them so fuckin' well. And I thought that when I'd got this job that it would be grand and easy, that I'd be able to do it very well and that then at night I could be writing my short stories. I'd written two that year already – one about the river path in Ballinrobe and missing Cuddy real bad, called The Walk. He and I had walked there after Kieran drowned and stared into the water, the black dirty water. I found it grand and easy on the mind to be writing about something that had hurt me so badly. Therapeutic I know it to be called now. But I found that most evenings when I'd get back to the bedsit, it'd be too warm to sit inside writing or I'd be just too fucked from a day's working.

So at the weekends if I wasn't going home, I'd take the big hardback pad I'd bought myself in O'Gorman's bookshop and go to the beach at Ballyloughane and try to get words onto the page. It saddened me not to want to go home. I had always loved going into the house with a bag on my back and being thrust immediately into whatever drama was unfolding here, but it was probably selfish but I couldn't listen to another weekend of incessant sighing from Mother, and making sure she took the right tablets to help her make it through the night.

Another reason I didn't like going home was the fact I'd be reminded of thumbing again and I hadn't thumbed since that day with your man in the car. I took the bus now on the rare occasion

I'd go home, but 'twas the Galway to Ballina bus that went all over the country, stopping at every fuckin' village letting off grannies. I didn't want the guards to be checking the thumbers at the Headford Road and to be thinking of me in any suspicious way. Though ye probably weren't, but ya can't be up to ye, guards.

I'd read in the paper that ye were investigating the death of a man in a car in Carnalough Woods, but there was fuck all detail in the story. It didn't say that he'd had his head bashed or that his trousers were down and his flute was out. Ye probably kept that detail to yourselves for what ye called 'operational reasons."

No, most weekends I'd stay in the city and do a bit of writing. And I loved it, even though people who saw me couldn't tell that I was a poet or a writer.

But I could see why 'twas said that I was always handy at the auld English. "You were always thinking outside the box," said Tommy The Jink, the English teacher. He was one of the good guys, never felt me balls at all.

He said that after he gave us an essay to write on the topic of No Man Is An Island - I did mine along the lines of "Noman is an island in the South Pacific, where the Nomanese people live." He smiled when he read it and gave me a good mark. I remembered that 'cos I got fuck all good marks when I was in school. So the good ones were rare.

I wondered if I'd been from the Neale Road if I would be a famous writer now with loads of money and people pointing at me in the street and saying "there's Gibbons the writer." I always wanted people to look at me in a nice way, rather than in a pitying way. I think a pitying way was not as bad as people not looking at you at all, and looking right though ya as if you were fuckin' invisible. I don't think I ever did that to people. I think

187

everyone deserved at least a proper look or a nod.

Granny used to say to us when we were teens that "always be nice to the little people on the way up 'cos they're the ones you'll be meeting again on the way down."

I knew I'd never been on the way up to bother about coming down again, but I took her advice anyway in case I ever would.

So I was a bit downhearted when I told the bossman that I was handing in my notice. He'd been sound to me since the day he took me in and had me earning straight away. He shook his head and looked at me in disbelief.

"Jaysus, I remember you were in here on your hole begging me for a fuckin' job. And now ya want to hand it in and ya say you're not going anywhere else. Are ya sure?"

I told him I was sure and then said that my two brothers had been killed in England and that I had to mind my mother at home. "Minding the mammy at home" is the kind of excuse that would get ya off the hook on anything in Ireland. 'Tis like the old GAA one about how the star player always had a brother at home who was ten times better but wasn't playing cos he was "building a house."

He went for it, but 'twas kinda true. I was going to be minding her but the main reason I was going home was for me. I wanted to protect myself from being caught for something bad I'd done. Lately I'd been having these thoughts. And feelings. I wanted to get home, to sleep in my own bed and to start all over again. Maybe I could make myself normal if I had a normal lifestyle again away from temptation.

The city lads at work told me I was a fuckin' eejit for chucking in such a handy job. In fact they were far nicer to me in the last

188

week than they had been all along. I wondered if they'd been that nice when I was working there, would I still be there, happy out and not here in this God-forsaken town, bored, frustrated, anguished and alone?

And wanting to hurt people.

The Thirtieth Year

They say an expert is nothing
but a local lad who went away.
able to grow without fear
of the demons of his old life
grabbing him by the nuts and saying
don't get above your station, man.
Home will drive the notions out of ya
'Twill drain ya of your dreams
'til you give in to its mundane temptations
and say farewell to ambition
forsaking it for knocking balls along a green baize
and supping pints of cheap mouldy beer
and wanting rides you're better off not getting.

(Peadar Gibbons)

The year since I left the job seemed to drag on forever. I'd lie awake at night, soaked in sweat, tormented that I'd talked myself into a job and then just given it up on a whim. I'd hug the pillow and say "ya daft prick, what did ya do that for?" And I'd be giving out to myself all the night, and then I'd hear Mother coughing over in her room across the landing. When I heard that cough, it reminded me how vulnerable she was and how maybe she too would die and then I'd be left alone, just me, by myself, in a house that once held a family.

And when I'd swear at myself and talk to myself, I wondered was I going the same way as her. Would I be going mad as well? Mad Gibbons from the street, they'd say. And the kids who'd taken our place kicking football on the street would be laughing at me like the way we used to laugh at Tommy Walsh before he got hanged in his house.

I noticed too that my hair was getting grey. Not just on my head but on my chest and on me balls. Was I getting this old and me just a few years younger than Jesus was when those fuckers nailed him to the cross?

I thought of him too and he living at home with his mammy until he died, and then I didn't feel too bad, but that would be only a reprieve as every night the darkness fell, I could feel it pressing against my head.

It was as if a black curtain was pulled across and I wanted to just hug that pillow. During the day and during the night, I'd turn it over and over, trying always to get the cooler side, so that my head wouldn't ache as much. But after two turns both sides would be warm and sweaty and so I'd get up and go downstairs and drink milk and eat plain biscuits until I felt I was tired enough to give sleeping another go. And then I'd feel bloated, there in the dark.

I never had this problems at the bedsit in Galway, but then maybe I slept 'cos I was fucked tired after a day working, and fucked tired after a while wanking, and maybe 'twas because then I used to feel better about myself, and that I was somewhere where people noticed me. I wondered that if I died in the morning, would anyone give a fuck, or would anyone even find me, apart from mother? And if she died and then I died, would I be left to rot in this house with maybe the odd mouse nibbling away at my face 'til all the skin was gone. And the guards would have to kick in the door and be confronted by the horrible smell of me rotting away upstairs in the house where I was born. In the room that I was born, actually. Fuck, I'm even sweating thinking that.

I'd had this fear when I was a kid – wondering what it would be like when everyone I knew was dead. I assumed that everyone older than me would die before me and I'd be left alone in this world. But then I comforted myself with the notion that I wouldn't be alone 'cos I'd have so many friends in the street and beyond to mind me and comfort me. That hadn't happened though.

The lads I hung around with had fucked off with their own lives. Only one or two of them were still around. They were only driving vans or working in the bakery up town, but still 'twas more than I had. Cuddy wrote the odd time. Very odd time, but himself and Teresa and Lorna were living in Borehamwood now. And he was working his hole off.

I met the local lads now and again for a pint. There was a certain novelty about me for a while. I'd returned from the big city where I had a good job, so they assumed that I must have had a plan, and they envied me for being so metropolitan because they hadn't the fuckin' guts to leave the town and try to get a start at something in the city. They were saying it would be easier for

192

them to go to London than Galway 'cos in London you could fail and be out on your arse and nobody would ever know it. In Galway, the word would get back if you weren't doing well.

And then they'd envy me 'cos I used to get the ride off the bank girls, not like them who they'd barely let into the flat. I told them they were trying too hard, that they had to wash themselves and basically give a shit about what the girls were thinking, but then they'd laugh and say that I was getting the ride 'cos there was a bit of a queer in me, washing meself, and that the girls were just pitying me.

But after a few months when they'd see me doing nothing at midday or arsing around up town or doing the shopping for my mother, they began to tease me. They said I was like The Yank. The Yank was a fellow in our town who had planned to go to America back in the 1960s. So all his neighbours had a party for him before he went.

The party went on for three days and everyone had a great time. There was never a drinking session ever seen like it before in the town 'cos he was a popular guy. There were fellas falling around drunk for almost a week. No one more so than The Yank Murphy. In fact he had such a good time, he decided not to leave at all, in the mistaken belief that he could be feted like this forever if he stayed at home. However, it didn't work out that way and within a year he was tied up in a miserable marriage to some baste of a country girl. But thereafter he became known as The Yank.

I didn't like being compared to The Yank Murphy because after a while they began to slag me about coming home and living with the Mammy, 'cos they all knew that the Mammy was always a bit touched.

I had to sign on again and they gave me fuckin' grief about how

193

I'd given up the job, so the cunts wouldn't give me any money for about ten weeks, and then I got a lump sum together – two hundred and eighty quid. But in the meantime, Mother and I had to live on her widow's pension and the two thousand I'd saved from my job in Galway.

I gave them the 'minding me Mammy' line too so they eventually agreed to pay me a sort of dole, something that had to do with the number of stamps I'd paid in. It was more than I normally got when on the regular dole and was all welcome, but was still fuck all when compared to what I was earning in the job.

Because you had to state you were available for work when you signed on, after a few months, I got placed on an Anco Social Employment Scheme, where twenty of us had to help clear stones off a patch of ground near the GAA pitch at The Lough. During one of the hottest summers in history, we did back breaking and seemingly pointless work, shifting fuckin' stones from one pile to the next, eating only chocolate biscuits, sandwiches and cartons of milk which we stored in the river water to keep them cool.

I hated the job 'cos the foreman broke our balls and gave us grief. It was shite work and it made me feel like we were worse than those on the dole.

And then at night when I'd the flute torn off meself I'd get all remorseful and sad and crying and wishing to fuck I'd stayed away and vowing that I'd get away again as soon as I could.

The Thirty-First Year

Far beneath the grass it runs
alone, undisturbed, unnoticed.
Washing moss off stone,
messing with the curlew's head
as its rushing sound tells him
water is near but unseen.

(Peadar Gibbons)

I suppose 'twas only natural that I would gravitate towards the woods more and more because that was where we had our happiest moments as a family. I didn't bother cutting and chopping firewood anymore because my mother felt that having an open fire was too much bother, and that she'd be fretting herself at night wondering if she'd poured enough water on the ashes so that they wouldn't ignite and burn the whole fuckin' house down and us in it. So she got in one of those oil fired burners that had a fake fire in it and didn't require her going to the shed for timber or briquettes.

Lately she had got it into her mind that briquettes were too fuckin' dear and that you'd hardly get a night's burning out of a bale. She suggested half heartedly that I should get a load of timber from the woods like father used to do, but by the time I'd got around to investigating if it was still ok to cut timber, she'd been persuaded by Liam that she should get the oil thing in.

It cost over a thousand pounds which she paid for from her savings, already decimated over the years by funeral expenses and repairs to the house which had a big crack in one side from the rain going into the stone walls.

It was just as well she decided against getting firewood because the woods were sold by the forestry to some developer prick named Gerry O' Callaghan who was going to build a massive factory complex and homes to house the hundreds of workers who would be employed there.

'Twas one of those big fuckin' pie in the sky ideas that you'd hear from time to town in shitty little towns like this where shitty little jumped up developers too drugged up from being big fish in small ponds would get notions. They were probably snorting coke from the arsehole of some hoor when they came up with the idea of skinning down our woods and building rakes of shite there. They had to know that was never going to happen but it wouldn't stop them from clearing all our woods just to get a clear site that would never be used, because that made them look busy and flash and they wanted people to look at them I suppose, in the way that I forlornly wanted people to look at me. Maybe everyone wants everyone else to look at them in some way of their own choosing.

O'Callaghan was a smart prick, about a year or two ahead of me in school. He was driving a car at 15 and was always giving us the finger when he'd drive around town at night and we'd be just walkin' and eating chips from Tom Monroe's chipper van in the Cornmarket. He'd laugh his laugh and call us 'fuckin' knackers.' But he could never drive too far 'cos he had to go home at some stage and when the mood took us, we all took turns pissing on the door handles of his car when he'd be at home. And putting dog shite under the wiper blades.

So that's the flute who wanted to clear our woods.

Those flaky environmentalists had objected to the loss of this big natural space on the outskirts of the town. They said there were factories in the town lying fuckin' empty so there was hardly any need for more. But I didn't give a shite about all that. When I thought about the woods, 'twas the memory of us all there together, the whole family working and even mother coming down to join us for the lunch with her bag and her bottles of tea. It tore at my heart to think of that and even though I knew that everyone has longing memories of their childhood, the woods were a respite from my childhood that was sort of messed up by tragedy and drink and flutes sticking their fingers up my hole and rubbing their chins against my face and saying "this'll be our little secret now won't it Gibbons?"

197

So the diggers moved in and cleared about a mile of woods, chopping and pushing and generally made a fuckin mess of the place. While O'Callaghan and his friends might have been expecting a smooth landscape, what they got was a messy mile of tree stubs and briars.

Still, the area where we had the camp and where Dad cut the firewood was intact and deeper into the woods than I remembered, but then the woods had spread and grown a lot in the decades since. I fought my way through the brambles and branches of dead trees one day to get through to the old stone lime kiln where we'd had the picnic where Dad had told the jokes. That was some day, that was.

It was still the same way, ruined and majestic, hidden away in the heart of the woods. It was as if it had crashed here from some other place and time and had allowed itself to be caressed by the briars and the ivy that wrapped itself around it and hid the kiln from the rest of the world.

There were times when you could imagine that it disappeared altogether behind those briars and that it only appeared when you really looked for it. 'Twas like the Sacred Heart picture with the scary eyes in the house, staying the same 'til you looked at it and then 'twould freak you out.

And I felt safe here and sheltered here and when it rained I felt warm here too, as I'd sit in there under the stone arch and watch the rain hop off the leaves and the grass and see it cascading down through the high trees. I'd felt this way as a kid when I knew Father was just a few hundred yards away, as I'd hear the whee-whoosh of his bushman's saw tearing through the timber in the days before chainsaws. And now, 20 years or more on, I still felt safe, even though I knew he wasn't there or the lads weren't there. In fact it was fuckin' weird 'cos the more alone I was, the more safe I felt.

And I felt alone. Three brothers dead, my father dead, another brother away living a grand life for himself in Tipperary and Mother up in the house and she fuckin' crazy with the nerves and the anxiousness and the shaking and the talking to herself and she looking at me with great love sometimes and other times then wondering what the fuck I was doing there and the rest of them gone.

And I felt I was crying a bit 'cos me shoulders were heaving and I rocked back and forth on the stone in the kiln and the more I thought about them, the more I felt the dead ones around me, minding me, watching me, breathing their steamy breath on me. I hoped to fuck they wouldn't appear or anything 'cos that would have sent me around the bend altogether. Ya can tell the people who think they've seen ghosts because they all look a bit fuckin' touched, lookin' like they were dropped as a child.

No, I didn't want to have that scared look about me, 'cos then people would be looking at me for the wrong reasons and that's not how I wanted them to look at me.

And as I rocked and as the rain stopped I thought I heard it...the splish splash of water on stone.

A soft gentle rush.

Somewhere.

And then I remembered.

Dad was always telling us to be careful around the kiln because there was a big hole down to a water spring and some days he'd have us go down on our knees and listen through the big flag stone for the sound of running water below.

The flag stone was just a few yards away from where I was sitting and we'd been told that the river ran through the rocks below and the lime mason must have used the well for his work.

199

And when Dad told us about it first, we thought he was joking like, but he wasn't, cos we heard it.

And you had to keep very quiet, so quiet you could hear the leaves rustling and the water running softly over the stone below. We were amazed at this, it was a mile from the river that ran through the woods and the sound of the water splashing on rocks well below fascinated us.

We asked Dad to help us move the flagstone, but he never did.

"Ye might fall into it, he told us. And ye'd be drownded."

And then he'd laugh.

But back then on that day, he didn't know that he'd lose one of us to the water just a few miles from here. The same water that probably ran through this spring on its way to the Soldier's Hole, reaching up and saying to Kieran,

"I'll be back for you, someday.

Don't go far now, ya hear. Don't go far..."

The Thirty-Second Year

Bit odd.
'Twould be a sin
just to be a bit odd.
The wimmen would nod
if you were less
than full odd
You can pity in the street
those whose oddness is complete.
But bit odd is something
down to yourself.
Not like full odd which is
a legacy.
Bit odd is a career choice.
A skillset for the bewildered.

(Peadar Gibbons)

Mother didn't tell anyone that I'd stay in the woods the odd night, well as the year went on, it got less and less of an odd night and more the norm. To be brutally honest, she brought me down in the house with her everlasting morbid thoughts and her woe betide attitude that nobody in the world was as fuckin' miserable as she was.

Now I know I shouldn't be talking about my mother this way, after all, there must have been endless days and nights when she was bored senseless looking after me and my brothers when we were growing up and when there was nowhere for her to go - and nothing to look forward to 'cept for the long nights looking out the window and wondering whether, or being sure, that Father was up town riding one or both of the Kelly sisters.

And all she had to look forward to would be him arriving back down and he not in the mood for anything like that with herself 'cos he'd be spent out from it all. That's what she had to look forward to in those days, but those days must have taken their toll on her cos they left her a fuckin' shadow of herself, wrecked and haggard and her hair wasn't even done anymore. It just fell lank around her shoulders, not full of bounce and volume like it had when she was caring about herself and when she used to make an effort.

But sometimes I just wanted to tell her to shut the fuck up. She didn't seem to acknowledge at all that I also had the right to be sad and broken and to be welling up with tears all the time and to be talking to meself and to be scared in the house with all those fuckin' ghosts around to come back and haunt us because they didn't want to die when they had. Even though none of them had actually died in the house, I reckoned a small bit of bilocation wasn't beyond them now that they had passed on.

And so every night when I'd wake up and come down to the

202

kitchen for a glass of cold milk and some digestive biscuits, I'd stand there dipping them in the milk to soften them, and look out through the kitchen curtains at the endless darkness of the garden, miles without light, and tell myself 'tis no wonder me mother went fuckin' mad in this house.

But despite all of this, there were moments when she was almost normal, when she had an alertness about her that she'd had in her younger days. And on those occasions, she still worried about appearances. Even though we were the street drunk's family and people felt pity for us with all the dying and all, she still felt as if she had to keep up appearances as if it mattered a fuck now that she was past sixty five and the reputation of the family was beyond repair.

So she'd talk to the neighbours and she'd make the chit chat with them and she'd tell them that I had a good job in Galway but that I "took extended leave" to look after her. And then the other mothers in the street would nod their heads at me and look at me as if I was some sort of' latter-day saint, and me with the big fuckin' mad head on me full of thoughts about riding, and wanking, and killing half of the time...and other mixed-up shit the other half.

But I went along with it 'cos it kept Mother happy, but there was no way she was going to tell them that I'd taken to staying the odd night in the woods, because she knew that that was the kinda stuff that only weirdoes did.

"Badgers and foxes are meant to live in the woods, not young fellas who should be out building a life for themselves," she told me one night. "Let's have less of this auld gip about living like Huckleberry Finn or Tom Sawyer. You've a good education. The brother said so in his letter for ya, but you just need to apply yourself to what you're doing."

203

And there was me thinking, where the fuck did she hear this shit? Was it from the other mothers, picking up and juxtaposing the phrases together so that I'd be talked out of getting away from it all and living at one with nature.

But it wasn't that. I just wanted to be where I had been at my happiest, some place where there wouldn't be any negative thoughts, somewhere where we'd been a family at one stage. The house at home with all its empty rooms and shelves full of dog-eared comics and annuals owned by dead brothers, was a palace for the departed. Not a place to be if you wanted your heart uplifted or if you wanted not to be reminded of what had happened since I was a child.

Mother and meself, rattling around the house, passing by doors of unused bedrooms, with Seamus's kept clean in case he'd ever come and stay for a weekend, but we all knew that he wouldn't fuckin' bother to bring his wife and family into this dusty old house with its wooden plank floors and rotting wallpaper and the smell of camphor balls from within every wardrobe. Would he fuck come to stay here? So why the fuck should I?

I wasn't the first to live in the woods for a while. There were three or four others over the years who'd moved in there for some other fuckin' reason, mainly pure madness or a genuine desire to get out of the way of regular people. As people bothered less and less with stealing timber, the woods became less of a place that people bothered to visit, so you could go half a mile or more into the thickness of the forest, and nobody would ever see ya. If you had any sort of a slash hook, you could carve your way into areas of the woods where people had never gone. Deep into the undergrowth way down, miles into the woods, the only disturbance was the odd deer being bred there.

204

So that's what I did. Cutting a sort of tunnel for myself a yard wide through the thickness. The path led for about 200 yards and in there I built my camp in a little clearing. Over three weeks, I brought plastic sheeting and sticks and bits of wire and nails and a hammer and a saw and a bundle of Time magazines and Woman's Ways.

We had an old style green army tent in the shed at home. It reeked of cat's piss and mould, but I took it out, hosed it down and left it to dry for a few days and when the smell was just about bearable, I cut it up with a big leather-cutting scissors that was among the many useless fuckin' things that Father had amassed from the Council. I strung this over the plastic sheeting and trees to form a little camouflaged camp where I could sit and read and write diaries and stories and think about what a fuckin' mess of a life I had. But just tell meself about it.

Of course, I missed being able to hop up town and meet the bank girls, and I even went off the idea of wanking 'cos it just didn't seem right here in the middle of this marvellous natural place to do something so unnatural. And the fuckin Woman's Ways did nawthing for me anyway, 'cept for use as toilet paper.

I never brought the lads from the street here because they'd think it was mad and anyway when they didn't see me around they just assumed I was back up in Galway visiting friends. Me, Galway. Friends. Hah!

The wonderful thing about building a home in the woods was that I didn't have to ask anyone to let me do it. It wasn't like getting planning permission for a house, or permission to park a caravan or the go ahead to pitch a tent in a field. The woods seemed to belong to everyone, a realm in which kids and adults would run free and find fun.

But I was soon to find out very soon that this was not the case at all.

The Thirty-Third Year

If they took the trees away
I'd be lying in an open field
Unprotected, unshielded, and not a bit afraid.
Yet put in these twigs to protect me,
mind me, shield me
and I feel like they are coming to get me.
To strangle me with their thin branches which will grow
into thick beams off which I could hang myself.
Sometimes what surrounds you with love is what terrifies you
Sometimes nothing is better than everything.

(Peadar Gibbons)

You wouldn't believe the scene that greeted me the morning after me first night in the woods. 'Twas like something out of a fuckin' horror movie. Hovering around all of the trees was a low fog that seemed to have come up from the river but which made the scene look very eerie. I had just peered out of the canvas door 'cos I needed to go for a shit..and I needed to go twice as much when I saw the vista that welcomed me. So I crawled over to the nearest faraway bush and shat there as quickly as I could, squatting there in the middle of the fog and it just sitting there, looking at me as I used a few pages from the Western People to wipe me hole.

I'd worked out that I'd spent over a hundred nights in the woods after five or six months. The odd night when Mother would be bad or when it would be just too fuckin' wet, I'd pop into the house and stay in me room, but there was still nothing there to bring me back, apart from mother and the four walls and the roof.

And the cocoa and the hot water bottles.

And the porn on Channel Four.

I'd started cutting grass for a few houses around town during the summer and picked up a hundred quid or more a week doing that. And I'd the dole.

Like when I mastered the job in Galway, I got good at cutting grass and doing gardens. Mrs Doherty, the grand auld ma'am at the top of the town didn't pay me the full rate one day saying that I wasn't a qualified horticulturalist.

For fuck's sake. I was just cutting her grass.

I pissed in her hydrangeas before I left with the fucking two quid she gave me.

Miserable auld coont.

With the dole money and whatever I got from odd jobs, I built myself some shelves inside the camp where I kept the cans of food, the tea and the biscuits. Packet after packet of Pennywise custard creams and lemon creams and bags of Tayto and Club milk bars. And Shredded Wheat, I devoured that stuff with cold milk. I bought those Rinkippen bags of milk that were popular at the time and stored them in the cool waters of the stream I passed when making my way back through the woods after work. None of the people I cut grass for knew I was living in the woods cos 'twould probably scare seven shades of shite out of them if they did. I didn't want anyone to know I lived there to be honest. I didn't want fuckers from the town coming down at night to peg stones at me or even knock the camp like the Neale Road pricks had done 30 years earlier.

Nobody took any notice when I cycled down Creagh Road each evening with bags of shopping and then veered off into the woods when no cars were passing. And as soon I was on the road through the woods, I was as free as a bird, 'cos I was heading to my own place. I always ditched the bike in some bushes a mile or two into the undergrowth near the mulberry tree that acted as my landmark to stop me getting lost.
I'd never gone through the woods at night. I always made sure I was in the camp before nightfall, to get my little Calor Gas stove going and cook me tea. And turn on my radio and listen to shortwave stations from across the world like Radio Moscow and Radio Albania. Jaysus, they were boring cunts and I kept thinking how I'd hate to live in some shithole like Albania if that's all they had on the radio. They even had a king called Zog. I swear to fuck.
But I educated myself from the radio and I used to bring books

209

from the library on the Main Street. You could take out two books each week, but I had old library cards for mother and Seamus and with them all, I'd take out six books a week. Other books I'd pick up from second hand shops. I read everything. Comics, annuals, history books, poetry books. I even read books I'd read when I was a kid, like Paddington Bear and Dr Seuss books and Mark Twain and Huckleberry Finn; the Famous Five, the Secret Seven, Mallory Towers, the lot. And I got out Lorna Doone again even though I'd the copy at home that Mrs Dunbar had given me. I just didn't want it to get ruined in the woods.

I wanted to send it to Cuddy for the daughter someday. Though I'd given Teresa a copy of it years ago.

The librarian knew I didn't have any kids, so I told her that I was taking the books for Seamus' crew who were going to be visiting for the weekend.

Even though I needn't have told her anything, but I knew by the way she was looking that she wanted to know. But she quickly moved on to ask me if I'd write some poems for the poetry exhibition they were having in the library. They wanted local poems so I said 'sure, I'll do a few.'

I loved being asked. Even though I hadn't ever been published it felt fuckin' great to be asked. I wondered what she thought of me. Or did she think anything? Did she think I was mysterious, cultured, educated but in a non-conventional way. I wondered if she wondered if I'd ride her, 'cos I would. Though she was about fifty, but she wasn't your typical librarian.

But the Enid Blyton books were great, instilling a sense of adventure that I'd thought I'd lost. And I'd fall asleep at night with them hitting my nose as I conked.

On days when I wasn't working in town or doing jobs for Mother around the house or collecting her pension or getting her peppered steaks from Willie Jennings the butcher, I'd work at clearing the well at the old lime kiln. 26 years after I first tried lifting it, I'd managed to get the heavy flag-stone off using a long steel bar that propped it up high enough for me to grab it and flip it over to the side of the well. It was some weight but I used gravity to help me. I was afraid that it would slip down in to the opening, but it didn't and just plopped quietly onto the sods behind it. The water ran freely below, just as it had when Dad showed it to us back then. A lot of water had flowed through it since that day.

I don't know who built the well or who had dug the narrow yard-wide shaft down to it. Probably the poor limestone worker who needed the water for his work or to live if he lived there. I wonder had he lived there like I did, and would his ghost be in the fog in the morning, watching me have my morning shit.

I wonder if there was anyone anywhere at all in the world who gave him a thought ever...and because I was doing it now would there be some sort of telepathic connection that would make him appear to me, to sort of help me expose to the world the great work he had done in constructing the stone walls of this yard-wide well. All this work he had done and nobody ever saw it or appreciated it. I wondered if I could ever be that generous of spirit and effort. And doubted it.

But I was determined to get a bucketful of the cold water from the well to throw onto my stubbly face in the morning, to have myself woken up with a splash of the most natural liquid imaginable. Cool spring water all because of some unknown fella in the woods a century earlier.

At the very bottom about twenty feet down the opening, some

rocks had fallen down and it wasn't possible to move them so I hooked down an old jam-jar with string and dipped it into the water and after a few goes, I filled it up and brought it to the top. And I smelt it and it smelt grand so I drank a bit and it felt cool and I could feel it going down my throat and down into the pit of my stomach and it gave me a chilly feeling.

It felt great – my own water for drinking and making tay. 'Twas as if I'd grown it meself. I used water from the river for washing my clothes or for cleaning meself down below. I'd also marked out an area of the undergrowth where I'd have a piss or shit. And all the rubbish I burned, and what I couldn't burn I put into a bag and fucked it into Mary Kelly's bin when I went in to town.

And so I created my own quarter mile where I was the only thing that walked on two legs. My patch.

My own patch of green.

Fuckin' Tarzan, I was.

I remember one day that year, I lay back on the grass, drinking a bottle of Lucozade and staring up at the sun as it squinted through the trees and I thought to myself "is there anything better in the world that I'd like to be doing than sitting here without pricks bothering me and making me feel bad about myself."

And there wasn't.

There fuckin' wasn't.

Then.

The Thirty-Fourth Year

Am I just a sponge
for you to dip in dirty water
to leave me self loathing
sodden with the disregard of others?
Let me dry out in the heat
of the midday sun,
get full again
absorb my plumage
Disregard me and you will feel the
hardened edge of a dried out pan shiner

(Peadar Gibbons)

As I was saying, what I loved about the woods was the big bloody sky. When I was a kid I loved the Wombles of Wimbledon Common. I thought they were the coolest fuckers, having all those woods to themselves and only coming together to meet others out in a big wide clearing. Everything seemed to happen in the clearing. They had great names like Great Uncle Bulgaria and Tobermory and Orinoco and were a proper happy family. They had their own drama, those furry bastards, but they seemed to work everything out in the end. They spent their days gathering litter on Wimbledon Common and their motto was Make Good Use of Bad Rubbish. Anyways, I always thought there was great wisdom to the Wombles.

They didn't give a shit.

They made the woods their own.

So I found myself a clearing in the woods, and imagined I was a Womble, and in the evening time when I'd eaten fish fingers and beans and potatoes baked on the fire, I just lay there, staring up at the big fuckin' sky away above the trees. I watched the greying clouds of evening floating away to somewhere I'd never go. They looked so cosy. It was there I thought about poems, the ones that didn't rhyme, the ones I did for the library thing, and more I'd sent to Galway to some writer fella; it was there I got the notion before I wrote the story that was on Sunday Miscellany even though someone else read it out and made it sound like 'twas me but Kevin the writer guy said that's the way they did it. And sure I didn't give a shit as long as it was read out. It didn't mean I was published or anything but it was a sign that maybe 'twas just a matter of time before I made it big.

It was there in that clearing that I thought about my life and whether it'd get normal and if I'd be snapped up and become a well known writer who people would look at.

And it was there I lay the day after it happened, the thing that made me leave the woods and never go back again.

'Twas said that bad luck would come to anyone who fucked with the woods. 'Twas said that there were fairy forts dotted along the woodland, covered now by trees, but once occupying vast clearings...and maybe 'twas in one of those clearings that I got my clear way of thinking, that sort of cleared up my mind, it was as if all the channels to my brains lit up at once and consulted each other as to what would be my best plan of action.
I thought to myself one night that there are men in the world who pay an army of assistants to get told the kind of thinking that I was getting for free here in a clearing looking up at the skies on a starry night. I s'pose when ya think of it, I should have been scared shitless knowing there were vengeful little fuckers of fairies living in the same woods as meself, but in another way, I'd hoped they'd be discerning fuckers who'd know that there was no badness in me towards the woods and that in some way I was a guardian of the place.

O'Callaghan wasn't one of those coonts from the Neale Road; no, he was one of those coonts from the Kilmaine Road who just went mad with the money and the drink around the time of the Celtic Tiger and became a new money prick. He had left the wife he'd been going out with since he was 19 and shacked up with some Latvian bird. She'd driven him mad altogether and he was so fucked up on coke and drink and cars and money that he was only heading one way. But he was determined to take the guts of the woods with him for a harebrained scheme of clearing it for something that would never happen before the country went tits up.

I'd seen them down by the river through the woods a lot of nights, himself and the Lithuanian, not Latvian, I think she was. He drove a big 4X4 jeep thing and he'd have the door of the back open when he'd be ridin' the hole off her. And then he'd get out for a fag and a piss and take a swig from a bottle and after a while they'd fuck off. But I'd sit there in the bushes watching them, tugging meself the odd time at the noises she'd be making. And other nights he'd come down to the woods and just sit there and look around and be roaring into his mobile phone. And 'twas on one of those nights that he saw me ditching the bike and heading through the undergrowth, across the clearing and into my camp where I lit the gas burner, started the fire and prepared for the tea.

Before I knew it, he was behind me shouting at me to get the fuck out of his land. And I've no idea what possessed me to even think I could talk him out of clearing the woods, but I tried 'cos I wasn't too afraid of him here, but all I could imagine though was wondering if 'twas him who ripped our camp down all those years ago, and made Father drink that night and ruin the only fuckin' good day we had as kids.

And then he laid into me...

"You're only a fuckin' waster Gibbons. What have ya ever done with your life? Have ya ever rid the kind of wimmen I'm riding? Riding your hand is prob all you were good for. And here ya are now living in my fuckin' woods, the cheek of ya to ask me to come to my senses when I could have ya burned out in the morning...come to think of it, I'll have the diggers come through here first when we start here next month. Then we'll see what you'll do with your 'leave my woods alone' shite.

And he gave me a pain in me head, the mad look of him and he staring me in the eye and shouting at me like a teacher, the way

216

you couldn't stop them even if ya tried.

His incessant 'tell me Gibbons fuckin' tell me.'

Like a fuckin' lawyer he was with the questions and he knowing the answers so there was no need for the questions.

So I started to shake.

And he carried on.

And me putting my hands to my ears so I wouldn't hear what he was saying to me 'cos there wasn't one good thing in what he was saying, nor one true thing.

"Look at this fuckin' place. Is it a class of a knacker ya are with your canvas tent and all? Sure even the knackers have houses these days and you here living like John fuckin' Wayne in the woods."

I knew that John Wayne had never lived in the woods in any film I'd ever seen him in and that confirmed to me that for all his money and all, O Callaghan was as thick as shite.

He ripped down a side of the canvas.

"Oops, look, this will come down with no bother at all," he said. "Five minutes we'll have this place fuckin' levelled..." he laughed. "and you outt..."

But as he turned back to laugh even more at me and see how I was reacting to what he was doing, he yelped as I flung the saucepan of hot water into his face. '

"Fuck, what the fuck h...ya cunt."

He screamed and then I took a shovel of the ashes and flung them at his face, his shirt, the red coals bouncing off his body but surprising him all the same, as he stumbled around.

And then I just hit him with the handle of the slash hook, across the side of the head and blood started to pour out from him and he looked up and me as he fell to the ground and he held his hands in front of him, and... Jesus, it's coming back to me clear now, he said 'stop, for fuck's sake " as I brought the handle again on the back of his head and there was a 'zing' sort of noise off the blow of the timber on his head, the kinda noise you'd hear with a tuning fork, a sort of afternoise. After that he went a bit quiet 'cept for the occasional moan out of him and the blood still pouring onto the grass and me thinking that I'd planned to be sitting there that night near the fire but couldn't now.

With all the drama, I needed to piss so I went over and did that before I came back to decide what to do next. But when I went there I felt I needed to shit and it was if the whole world fell out of me onto the grass. I cleaned myself up and went over and I looked at him but he was lying face down so I couldn't be sure if he could see or not but the slash hook had done damage to him alright, fierce damage.

'Think, think, fuckin think' I said to myself as I paced up and down wondering what I'd do and how I'd get away with it.

Or if I'd get away with it.

Or if I'd be caught and go to jail for it. I swear I'd never really given a thought to being caught and going to jail for any of this. I was more worried about the repercussions that were more immediate like. Such as a flakin' from whoever I attacked. Not long term punishment.

I dragged him over the side of the kiln and wondered if I'd be able to drag him all the way to the river, but then there'd be the head wounds and the burns that you wouldn't get in a slow moving river through the woods and people would cop on.

No, that wouldn't do, so I had to make sure that he'd be put somewhere he wouldn't be found again. "Habeas fuckin corpus, I thought to myself, let them find this fucker's body, as I pulled him over to the top of the well. Twas the only place to put him, but I knew that if I did, I'd never be able to use the water there again..and I'd never think the same about it again, think about Father showing us it in the first place, and now this. Fuck it. Another thing ruined.

Christ.

I went through his pockets to see if he had any money and he did. About seven hundred in fifties, so I took them and shoved it in my bag. Then I put him headfirst in the top of the well, the shaft just about wide enough to fit him. The poor bastard had no chance of ever getting out of here 'cos he'd be facing the wrong way and wouldn't be able to pull himself up. As I pushed him in further, his jeans came loose and his arse was exposed, big fuckin' tanned arse of him from the sun beds. And I thought about..... just a thought, but I didn't. I swear to fuck I didn't.

I pulled him to the edge and let the front half of him fall into the hole, and then I grabbed his legs around the knees and pushed him down the shaft into the well below. It slid halfway down, face first, jammed by the rocks, upside down.

Just as I did, he let out a moan, a sort of grunt, which frightened me.

And then another.

So I left him there for a few minutes.

But then there was nothing.

Nothing.

After I did it, I went out and sat in the clearing, and I rocked a bit and sighed and gave voice to the low howl within me, squeezing it outta me to the trees and the leaves.

Then I lay back and looked up at the stars and I thought about yer man in the well, probably dead now. At least I hoped he was, 'cos if he wasn't, 'twas an awful fucking way to spend your last hours. Upside down in a hole and you not able to move yourself, and your brain not able to do the things it normally did, like tell ya what to do. And you may laugh at this thought, and I know ye shouldn't. But I wondered if the fuckin' Wombles had ever to do anything like that.

Had they ever to hide a body of a rabbit or something and if so, did they get some sort of absolution by lying under the stars in the clearing and thinking about it.

I wonder if they did.

Now that would be a poser for Great Uncle Bulgaria or would he have put it down to making good use out of bad rubbish?

The Thirty-Fifth Year

How low is low
when your profile is already low.
How low must you go
so that nobody will know
what you know.
If you go too low
will people know
what they shouldn't know
and must never know.

(Peadar Gibbons)

Mother was surprised to see me back in the house so much for the next while. I told her that I was getting more and more fed up of the woods and that with winter setting in, I was fucked if I was going to catch my death of cold trying to keep the rain out of the canvas. Every time I tried to explain I found myself lying to meself too. So I'd tell her again and again and because she wasn't the suspicious type, she didn't pick up any dodgy pattern to my ever growing list of reasons why I was home more of the time.

There wasn't much noise made about O'Callaghan disappearing like that. His jeep was found down near the river so everyone assumed he'd just jumped in. There'd been rumours that the fucker was up to his hole in debt so 'twas no surprise that he'd done himself. If they only knew he was up to his tanned hole in spring water and weeds and mossy rocks and with the big flagstone pulled back over the top of it all and a pile of bushes there that would mean it'd be another hundred years before anyone would move it.

They never found a body even though they searched the river; but a mile or two downstream, the river ran into Lough Mask so if he was gone there, he was fucked, and the pikes would be atin' him. And bits of him would be ending up in dinners around the town. Or in France 'cos the Frenchies loved the pike. That's what they were saying anyway above in Kelly's pub where I'd go now and again to play pool with the lads from the street.

They'd taken to me again in a big way now that I'd gotten rid of all the 'decent job in Galway' notions. Now they saw me as just one of themselves, fuckin' layabouts who'd only get out of bed before midday if they needed a piss.

So we'd play pool in the back bar at Kelly's pub and eye up the Kelly sisters who half the town knew were ridin' me father for fifteen years. And honest to fuck, I've no idea what he saw in them. Where once they might have been sexy young wans, honey trap material, now a lifetime of dirty ridin' had left them looking like shit. Overweight barmaids in a small town, fucked like the rest of us.

I'd played pool here when I was 14 and now and again I'd think I'd made fuck all progress with my life since then if I was doing the same thing more than twenty years later. One or two of them had read my story The Walk and thought 'twas brilliant. But none of them had heard it on Sunday Miscellany.

None of them were ever out of bed for Sunday Miscellany.

None of them even knew there was a programme called Sunday fuckin' Miscellany on the radio.

None of them would even know what day of the week Sunday Miscellany would be on.

There weren't many writers or poets around so I was a bit of a fuckin' novelty, as well as being a waster like themselves. They'd ask me to write poems that pulled the piss outta people and insisted that they fuckin' rhymed. Anyway, they were great for the goss and they'd nothing but hate for coonts like O'Callaghan who used to look down on them at school. Now he was dead and they weren't, so they felt they'd one up on him, even though they weren't sure that he wouldn't arrive back in the door again, throwing his refinanced and dubiously-sourced money around having staged his own kidnapping or something.

They told me that the Latvian/Lithuanian bird he was slipping a length to was fucked out of the apartment he'd owned up in Bowgate Street. But within a week, she was ridin' the auctioneer Tommy Kearney so she'd a place to rest her head again. And so every day that passed, I'd be a bitteen happier that I'd not been suspected and with every day that passed, I'd feel the worst guilt for having done it in the first place.

But then again, I reckoned that guilt was fuckin' relative. And that you'd only be beatin' yourself up over it if it was bothering ya. I felt that the greater capacity a man had to live with guilt equates to the greater capacity of that man to do evil. It was as simple as that.

If you were angst ridden over stealing a cake from Mickey Hession's shop, you'd know you wouldn't have the stomach for the bigger stuff. Me, I had that stomach. I'd had it since the day I kicked the fuckin' chair away from Tommy Walsh. I mean that was the ideal one 'cos nobody would ever think he hadn't done the whole thing himself, even though I often calm myself at night with the thought that eventually he might have slipped anyway and choked himself, but maybe then it might be a while later when he'd have changed his mind and wouldn't want to die at all.

Fuck, these thoughts came to me as I lay there in the small room at the back of the house, sleeping in a bed that had a broken base, not from any strong ridin' but from sheer fuckin' leppin on it when we were kids. Though I'd had my first dry rides on it. I'd kept that copy of Woman's Weekly with the sexy picture of Bo for many years 'til eventually it was so fuckin' wrinkled you couldn't make out her tits anymore so I threw it in the bin, wrapped up in a copy of the Western People so as not to create any suspicion.

So I'd have these thoughts in the back room - and then I'd hear Mother coughing in the front room, a long throaty cough that sounded like a death rattle and I'd wonder how long she had left and if she died now would that make things simpler for me.

Mrs Herlihy down the road had died and left the house to her son John, the guy who showed me his flute. He ran into the pub and told me "the auld queen is dead. I've fallen in for the cazzy." And inside a year he'd drank the fuckin' lot. No, I didn't want to end up like him, so for the while I just kept me head down, left the woods, got in with the lads and acted as normally as I could.

But Mother wasn't dead. It was just her spirit that had died and the rest of her, the skin and bones and coughs and smells were there with me in the house and there was fuck all you could do with those if the spirit was gone. And then I thought that maybe if she died, it'd be the worst thing that ever happened to me. Because at least she was the one constant in my life, she was the one who never gave out to me, and who was always looking out for me, even then she surely thought I was a bit of a fuckin' waster. She had to know that dreams of being a writer were bullshit too 'cos people like me don't become writers. Most writers have had some break in life that they exploit. Or a father or mother a doctor or a professor or a journalist. Me, I just had shit to deal with all the time and I had a mind that was sort of damaged through all that.

Or would her dying just make me worse?

At least when she's alive, I'd have some order on my life, even it's a boring one. As long as she's alive, I could stay in the house, 'cos I'm sure if she croaked that Seamus would be up from Tipperary saying that he wanted his share of the estate and that I'd have to sell it, and then I'd end up with just a few grand in the bank and living in a bedsit in this shithole of a town, with nothing to look forward to but just the inane company of my fellow wasters playing pool, looking at the fat barmaid and pretending I was happy.

The Thirty Sixth Year

Twould have been proper order
if the lad who invented QWERTY
just put the letters in the proper order.
How much of our lives are wasted
Looking in between the spaces
of those alluring typefaces.
How many more words would I have penned
if my fingers didn't have to depend
on the ravings of Mr Sholes.

(Peadar Gibbons)

'Twas around this time again that I started writing again. I mean proper writing, stories and stuff. Poems when the feeling hit me. I was able to knock them up at a few minute's notice. Ones that sounded like they were written by a real poet. Ones that didn't rhyme and weren't about stupid things like mountains or valleys or trees. No, I was writing poems again about my feelings. Love, anger, stuff in me head. Stuff I'd thought about in the woods before, ya know. Real love, not the wanking sort of 'horn on ya' love. Love where your stomach hurts when ya think of someone. Love where you actually meant what you were feeling and not just love for getting the ride. A sort of 'I love you' rather than 'I'd love to.' I tried explaining the difference to the lads in Kellys one night but they just fuckin' laughed at me. Thick coonts said 'sure didn't matter how ya got your hole as long as ya got your hole'. And when I told them that that sounded Machiavellian, one of them threw a head on me and wanted to fight.

And when I'd feel like writing, I'd scribble words into a notebook first and then I'd sit down at the plastic Remington typewriter that my mother had in the house from back in the days when she used to write to her pen pal in Yonkers, New York.
Mother and Oscar had been writing to each other since they were kids. They found each other's name through a pen pal ad in a newspaper and they'd become firm friends even though they'd never set eyes on each other in reality, apart from the odd photograph they exchanged over the years. We never met him, but a few times every year, he'd send over an envelope with 50 dollars in it.
His photos were always colourful and exciting. Pictures of him on vacation in Cape Cod and places like Nantucket, and Albany, and Niagara Falls and Montpelier, Vermont and Maine in the

autumn.

She had the typewriter 'cos she felt that he'd be better able to read her letters if they were typed proper like, and not in handwriting, though she had a good handwriting on her, but his letters used to come typed so she wasn't going to be outdone by some Yank.

Oscar never married. And there never seemed to be any women around in his pictures, just shots of him with his man friends from whatever he worked at. Arms around them and they all smoking and they all bronzed and tanned as well, standing by the ocean, the blueness of the water behind them.

I wondered if the sea in Cape Cod was a different type of water to that which I'd seen in Galway 'cos it was a dark rich blue, and not grey and choppy like the water in Galway Bay that I'd see when I was walking the prom in those days when I had a proper job and I could take joy in not being at work 'cos it would be the evening time.

I used that typewriter to learn to type, not the proper way where you have your hands and fingers all over the keys and where you wouldn't even had to look at them. No, I learned to type aged eight by seeing how many alphabets I could type in a minute. In the end I got ten or something which was kinda fuckin' amazing when you think about it, given that I'd not had a proper education or training.

Anyway back to the writing. I went along to a reading by a poet who was a cousin of someone up the Neale Road. 'Twas on in the old Prod church and twas full of poem-loving types who nodded and sipped red wine and ate little crackers with bits of Calvita cheese on top of them. And I'd never really drank wine before, apart from the few times with the bank girls and before that when I took a sip out of the chalice when we'd be mass serving and be cleaning up the stuff afterwards. I hated the fuckin' rich smell of it then and wondered how the hell could anyone drink this stuff and actually like it - but I got a liking for it.

Anyway a poem I'd written was one of those picked out by the poet guy to be read out, and he read it out so well in that posh educated voice of his. He asked me before if I wanted to read it myself, but I said no, 'cos I didn't want it to sound fuckin' stupid and it might not sound so fuckin' stupid if an educated fella read it out, 'cos you see they get away with shit that the rest of us non-educated types don't.

It went like this and 'twas a love poem that I wrote one day when I saw a couple in Kelly's bar looking into each other's eyes and their legs brushing against each other in a playful way. He looked like a fella who was going to get the ride 'cos he was a good looking fella and they got the ride easier than ugly fuckers. I wondered though if he'd ever write a poem for her like this, try to win her heart with words rather than just having a big dick. She seemed to be crying another day he was there with her, so maybe the big dick wasn't all it was cracked up to be.

Anyways, it went like this;

The Touch

Never has so little meant so much

As when the hearts connect

with gentle touch

and when the eyes match up

to share that trust

and ankles brush like fleeting

birds in flight.

And when tears flowed sadly on that day,

he knew his heart was

swiftly swept away.

And when the poet guy read it out, there was a round of applause in the room and then he pointed over to me and said that the man who wrote it was in the room and then everyone turned and looked at me and clapped again and I went sort of red and me heart was thumping so much in my chest I thought it would burst out through my ribcage and fall flapping on the floor like a fish dying by the side of the river when you'd take him out.
But it didn't.
And it felt great.
And people came over and shook my hand and touched me.
And when I went home that night and told Mother that I'd had me poem read out, the poem I'd written on her typewriter, she told me that I'd have been better off getting a job for myself and why did I have to get someone else to read out my poem. Was I not able to read it out meself without having to get someone else to do it?
And I didn't say anything but I went to the room and sat down and stared at the wall and wondered why people always had to take the fuckin' good out of things.

The Thirty-Seventh Year

Tormented I twist the dial past Hilversum
They're not there anymore so I spool
the old wheel down towards Tirana and listen
to mad fuckers spouting propaganda in slow English
At people who don't speak it or understand it.
I think of dogs listening to people saying you're a cat
so be proud of it, cat. Walk like a cat.

(Peadar Gibbons)

There's a quare loneliness to just two people in a house, especially if sometimes you looked at each other as if you were the strangest strangers in the world, like someone you saw in a pub, or someone you saw on a train. But it's even worse than that. 'Tis the kind of loneliness you have when ya actually know the other person but realise that they don't really care about your welfare or you about theirs. A sort of loneliness max.

And so I was stuck in this state, wondering if I'd ever be happy again.

Miserable as fuck.

Answering her call from the room or from downstairs - Making cups of tea and Bovril and Complan, sandwiches and bowls and bowls of fuckin' Ready Brek. I always thought there was something awful wrong about grown up people eating Ready Brek.

We'd had it as a kid and although I loved it when I ate it many years later, 'twas always as some sort of comfort food in some sort of fucked-up period of my life. It was as if 'twas ideal for those moments you feel shit and couldn't be arsed to make proper porridge.

But I badly needed some company. 'Twas bad for my writing as well. Writing is a confidence game. If you're happy or really sad, you're flying. If you're stuck in the fuckin' middle, then you have neither the motivation nor the inclination to write. My groupies seemed to have gone as well. The bank girls I knew had been transferred, two to Charlestown and one other to Swinford. Jesus, life can be cruel, can't it, I thought when I heard it. Ya get Ballinrobe first and then you get those other worse places.

Anyway I needed to get out more and meet people, even if people weren't willing to meet me, without getting paid for it.

There'd never been hoors in the town before. Well there were women who were hoors, but they weren't getting paid for it. Slappery auld wans who'd pull ya off down The Bowers and the likes of that, but none of those ones who you paid proper for the ride. And ya wouldn't go near some of them for fear of catching the AIDS or one of those diseases.

Living with Mother in the house meant I couldn't bring any of those quare wans back, so when the Celtic Tiger came along, 'twas great for getting the ride. Everyone seemed to be getting the ride during those years. If ya weren't getting it at home, you'd get it for €60 in one of those new apartments built just off the Main Street.

They had telephone numbers you could ring, but some of them seemed to be independent operators who saw ya in the pub and sidled up to ya if they knew you were gamey like and whisper in your ear. The first night it happened, I thought someone was putting her up to it. But they weren't. I hadn't been to one before so the first night was a fuckin' disaster. I'd never been to a place where you were buying the ride. I'd been to the massage parlours where you couldn't get the ride but ya got enough to keep ya going, like.

The first time I went to one of the massage parlours was when I took the bus to Galway. I had the number in my pocket from down off the Internet, a mobile number that I rang.

She was in a flat not far from Eyre Square, just a few hundred yards. Foreign she was, hard to tell what, but she'd an accent, so proper foreign. Like a Bond girl. Hundred euro for an hour or sixty for half an hour and a happy ending with both. I'd no fuckin' clue what a happy ending was. I assumed that any ending would be fuckin' happier than the beginning ya went in with.

"Will ya touch me down below," I asked her before I gave her the money, but she hadn't a fuckin' clue what I was on about.

"Me mickey, will ya touch that in the massage," I said to her.

"Yes, that's happy ending." she said with a smirk on her face, a smirk in half pity and half laughing her hole off at me.

'Twas grand. I took everything off and lay there on a table with a space for me face, covered me arse with the towel and she started away with the baby oil and the likes. Jaysus, 'twas fucking lovely. She'd done this before, I thought.

She covered my back with oil and stood in front of while she did it, leaning on over me with her crotch right in front of me. Through the hole in the table I could see her feet, nice and brown in her sandals. I wanted to reach out and touch them, but I didn't. I loved women's feet. There's something fierce sexy about them. Is that weird?

Then she did my legs, running her hands all the way up to me arse, her fingers lightly brushing me bollocks each time. Gorgeous 'twas. I think she was doing it deliberate like, to get me going, so that when she'd have to do the deed at the end, it wouldn't take long. Smart out these hoors were. They didn't get called hoors for nothing, so they didn't.

And when I turned over, she massaged my chest and my arms and the front of me legs. She took the towel away and did the same before grabbing me mickey and finishing me off in less than a minute. And while she was doing it, I felt like telling her I fuckin' loved her and I wanted to kiss her but she wouldn't let me.

And 'twas then I got the guilt.

Terrible fuckin guilt when the life drained out of me.

Thinking of mother at home talking to herself and with fuck all in the fridge between us, and here was I, wasting me savings on

234

a hand job that I could have done meself in half the time.

I was covered in baby oil and I refused her offer of a shower and went home with the clothes sticking to me and the smell of baby oil off me. I sat on my own near the back of the bus, with a terrible feeling of blackness in me head. I wondered if the auld free travel women on the bus smelt the oil and knew where I had been even though they really shouldn't have had a clue, but that's the way I was thinking.

I couldn't wait to get home and have a bath and scrub it all off me.

The blackness in me fuckin' head was terrible.

I had been grand right until she'd pulled me off.

Happy ending me arse.

Fuck her anyway, she had to go and ruin it.

After that, I went back a few times, using the same number but getting a different woman. And every time I felt bad once I'd come.

One week I spent all the money I had in there and had just enough for a snack box in Supermacs before making the long journey home, smelling of coconut oil, cod, guilt and chips. All that mother was told was that I'd been to see the specialist in Galway for me eyes and 'twas better that way.

She had to know that a man like me had needs. She had to know, although 'twas never something we'd talk about. She'd never mention anything like that, except the odd comment over the years that I should find meself a nice woman and settle down.

Wasn't I fuckin' settled enough? What did I need with a woman who'd be the same wan forever? Sure wouldn't you get bored with that. But I nodded all the same when she said it.

I played along in case she'd think I was queer like, which I wasn't sure I wasn't, to be honest, though I never got a horn looking at any man. So I mustn't be.

When I got the channels in for her, she had Channel Four which had a lot of filthy movies on late at night. They'd a little red triangle in the top corner and after I'd get her cocoa and biscuits for her supper and see her off to bed, I'd get the box of tissues and sit there, watching French films with women with small titties, pulling meself silly for an hour or so, before I'd get the blackness in me head again and fuck off to bed, feeling like the worst bollocks in the world and wanting to kill myself and anyone else.

Anyone.

The Thirty-Eighth Year

I'd rather die than live during the day
saturated with the misery thrown at those
who cannot die but live during the day.
Under darkness,
everyone's home.
Young, old, good, bold.
Not just the select few
who cannot die but live during the day.

(Peadar Gibbons)

There were times when I thought about killing her, just going in and smothering her with a pillow, to stop her coughing, to put her out of her misery and by fuck was she in misery? The wheezing had got fierce bad 'cos she wasn't taking the blue inhaler that the doctor had told her to. She'd leave it around the house and then when she'd need it, she'd have the wrong one, the brown one. Or was it vice versa, I don't know. One doctor told me 'twas the blue one she should have first and not the brown. And if I was confused 'twas no fuckin' wonder that she was.

And so with no inhaler to be found, she'd be wheezing away, her eyes big looking up at me, her grabbing my arm as if pleading with me to mind her, to take care of her, not to let her go 'cos she was very scared, and the terror evident in her face and she having the look of someone who was going to die and who by fuck was going to cling onto something or someone here on Earth for as long as she could.

And there were nights when she'd be staring at me in terror with the wheezing and I'd think that she was looking beyond me over my shoulder and then I'd think that she was being called up by hordes of dead people visible behind me and then when I'd look, there'd be nobody there.

And I'd feel a selfish prick for worrying about being scared at the very moment that my mother was grasping for air for her life. And then when the wheezing would subside, and when she'd get a few hours sleep into her, and the dawn would come, she'd forget that she ever needed me that much and she'd bark out something or other at me, treating me the way she did before she got the wheeze. Being all mammyish. Bossing me and with ne'er a word of thanks for me being there during the night and stopping her choking to death for the lack of air in her own bedroom.

And I'd feel bad hanging around the house every day, sitting there watching fuckin' daytime television with shows about fellas who rode their sister's husband's brother's dog and the like. Weird fuckin' stuff that the English and the Yanks got up to. And then if they weren't bad enough doing that in the privacy of their own homes, they had to go on television and tell the rest of the world about it. I wondered sometimes if I should go on a show like that 'cos my family would make great viewing, but then again half them would be dead. If you could have dead people on the show and they were all able to talk, then my family would be ideal, but then I'd be afraid that if dead people were allowed on the show, that there'd be dead people there who I didn't want to see.

Dead people who I made dead, waiting back stage until called out to give damning evidence against me. Fuck, the thought of it. Especially Terry Ward. If he came out, the knacks would have me slaughtered before I got out of the studio. Especially if they were brought on with their slash hooks and their machetes and baseball bats. And if Tommy Walsh came on, there's no fuckin' telling what he might say. He might say that he did it all himself and that he asked me to kick the chair, but then he might have changed his mind in the seconds after I kicked it, and then he'd come out and throw the whole fuckin' blame over on me. Dead fuckers, you couldn't trust them to say or do what you want them to do.

Dr Murphy came in to see Mother a few times but even he was getting pissed off with her, but then again he was a depressed fucker as well, so he probably felt sympathy for her. When we went in to see him, he was fidgeting and scratching and shaking and I wondered if we'd catch the auld anxiety off him.

Often I thought that the doctor didn't give a shit about making auld wans feeling better. It was as if he felt that they'd had their life and if they filled it with misery, then they fuckin' didn't deserve to get happy pills. One day he was seeing her and I went in with her, the fucker yawned his way right through the consultation. I felt like going up and shoving a box of his happy pills into his gob and see if they made him any merrier. But they probably wouldn't. And Mother there shaking in front of him and she looking at me to what's the word, advocate, to advocate for her, to try to explain what he was saying, but he didn't give a shit about me either and reckoned that I didn't need an explanation for the medication he was scribbling onto his little prescription pad.

He prescribed her a rake of tablets which she was supposed to take for her mood, to make her feel better.

Mother didn't help either. She told him that she'd difficulty sleeping, but he said 'why didn't ya take the sleeping pills I gave ya?"

And she replied:

"Arragh, they were in the toilet and I was too tired to get out of bed to go and get them."

Other times, she'd shame me. She told him that she probably hadn't gotten enough nutrition as a child 'cos when it came to feeding the family, the men were always first to be served the meaty bit of the stew and that all that would be left for the girls would be the watery stuff with no meat and only a small bit of veg.

"Us girls would have been better off if we'd been born with mickeys," she told him one day. And I blushed 'cos I never heard her talk about mickeys before and when I heard her say that I knew that her mind wasn't right at all. And he laughed, the miserable fucker, and I don't know if he was laughing with her or at her.

The health board sent in a woman a few times a week to mind her and wash her, using a big basin in the bathroom 'cos we didn't have a shower and getting into the bath would have been too difficult for her. And when this woman would call, I'd mope around downstairs or go off for a walk for myself and inhale the air and appreciate the nature around the town. That's the great thing about Ballinrobe, there was always a blast of nature to appreciate. The river ran through it, and I'd lately taken to walking around the river again, past where Kieran went in at the Soldiers Hole and past where Terry Ward went in. It was as if one cancelled out the other in my mind. It was all just dirty water floating along, the sudsy bits that the chemicals from the sewage plant created, looking like eyes that seemed to be winking at me and sayin' 'come on in ta fuck and less of your mopin.'
Walking around the river only took half an hour but I stretched the fuck out of it. I walked and walked and I stopped and stared and sat and thought and did everything you could do while walking around the river. I saw lots of young lads there fishing for perch and dropping jars for pinkeens and they all looked happy and they all gave me the nod, the sort of nod young lads give lads who are a dozen or more years older than them. Not a formal hello but a 'howya,' or a 'howsitgoan'.
And they all seemed nice lads and I hoped to fuck that they had more luck than I had and that by the time they were a dozen or more years older, they'd have got to fuck out of the town and got proper jobs and stayed away rather than coming home and being

caught up in a web of loyalty, and be expected to do the daycent
thing.

The Thirty-Ninth Year

Over and out
cross that threshold where
she'd peered out nervously
its wooden beams soaked through
with the steam of her front door voice.
Handprints engrained where she
stood and stopped and wondered
with the suitcase in her other hand
the brass of the handle marked
with the many times
she stepped back in and put the
case back in under the bed.

(Peadar Gibbons)

In the end I had to carry her out of the house in me arms. Out into Mrs O'Malley's car. And off to the county home. The public health nurse had been to the house and said "she can't stay here with just the two of ye and me coming and going and she mixing up all her tablets and shaking them all out of their little bottleens and me trying to get them back in the right order. Blues and pinks and blue/reds and reds and yellows."

And then making sure the right colours were in the right bottles in case I killed her by giving her too much of one and not enough of the other. There were ones for blood pressure, diabetes, shakes, fits, sleeping, depression. Mogadons, Xanax, Lamictal and other names I can't remember. And then there were ones that had to be halved and some of them you just couldn't halve 'cos the powder would spill out of the capsule and the taste of that would make her sick, and then she'd be throwing up on me and herself and the good of the tablets would have been gone 'cos she spewed them up and then you couldn't know if you were allowed to give her more again and I was shit scared of killing her.

She'd fallen a few times and was soiling herself and it felt wrong, just wrong, to be seeing my mother this way. And I knew I was useless for her. Sure what could I ever do but pick her up and clean her up and that's just not right for a lad to having to clean up his mother after she soiled herself. Although it didn't seem to bother me, I knew that if she was in her right mind, she'd be mortified to know what I had to do.

Even though she'd not been the same after Kieran's drowning, she was still a great mother. When I was a kid I used to be sweating awake in the bed at night, worrying how the fuck I'd miss them all when I got older. I knew she'd die before me and so the day would come when I'd be the only one left...and it kinda felt that way now with me carrying her out to the car.

This once fine woman who used to pick me up and swing me around was now reduced to seven or eight stone, boney, frail with her face caving in and her hands all veiny and spindly. Her brown hair now a matted grey and white and lank and down around her face and not pointing proudly at the sky in the way it used to when she went go to the auld hairdresser Maggie Tierney up the road and get it done in a curler machine that was from the 1960s and could have fuckin' blown up any minute.

It was as if all of a sudden this woman had turned old, though the truth is that she'd been getting older all those years, all those days when I was away in Galway or living in the woods. I shouldn't have been fuckin' surprised and now I felt a strange guilt for not sharing every single day with her. And I felt such an ungrateful prick.

I wanted to cry as I placed her in the car and leant over to put the seat belt around her. She seemed so frail that I was afraid the belt would pinch into her, and maybe crush her if the car had to come to a sudden stop.

And when the car pulled away, I went back into the house and all of a sudden, it felt very dark and quiet. It was if every scintilla of natural light had been drained from it with Mother's leaving for the county home. I knew then that it would be her last time ever crossing that threshold. This house that she'd lived in since she was a child was now behind her. And now it was going to be mine, but suddenly being master of the house didn't seem like I had long imagined it would be.

At that moment, I didn't feel elated but disappointed, that I'd failed in some way. That I didn't fuckin' deserve it, that my grandfather looking down from his portrait over the fire would

245

look at me and say 'you're a bad bastard, Peadar and I'm twisting in me grave thinking of you owning this house and you no better really than your mad drunken father who married my darling daughter.'

And I sat there and cried.

And just as it had after Father had died and when the funeral visitors had long gone, the ticking of the clock on the mantelpiece seemed louder, with each move of the hand a reminder of my own mortality. That in some sense it was teasing me, that the hands were pointing at me, and that the fuckin' face on that clock was sneering at me saying 'is this what you wanted, you fuckin' waster? This is all your fault. If you weren't such a pathetic person, this wouldn't have happened. Your mother would be able to see out her years in her own house. She deserved that, you gobshite...and then just as I covered my ears and refused to listen to it anymore, it fuckin' rang, eleven times for eleven o'clock and every ring a laugh in my face, saying take that, and this, and this and this.

And so I threw myself on the couch and tried to fold myself into myself but the cushions were full of the smell of old woman's perfume, the sweet sickly stuff that she'd sprayed on herself back in the day but which seemed to have infiltrated the fibres of the cushions. And that just made things worse.

Over the course of the next few months I had to convince myself that she wasn't dead, just dead in terms of the house. And I'd go days and days without ringing to see how she was or visiting and then I'd think about how I'd feel if she really were dead and I'd be guilty about not visiting her. And how I wouldn't be able to ring her at all then. And then I'd visit her and she'd sit there in the wheelchair not knowing me, but the nurses told me not to worry about it as she was getting used to her new meds and that she'd be more communicative once they kicked in.

She'd gone so long without taking the right meds that her head was a bit fucked up...and she was seeing a psychiatrist as well. A free one supplied by the HSE. Not a proper one that you pay for and lie on a couch. These fuckers had no couches, they just made you sit on a hard auld chair. I went along with her one day and the shrink, an Indian guy, asked her if she'd ever thought about harming herself, but she didn't understand the question and I answered for her, but he just looked at me and said that he needed the answer from herself, as if he was thinking there was no fuckin' way I'd know what was going on in my mother's head, and me having only watched her go mad since I was a toddler. And I kinda wished he'd asked me the same question so that he could have helped me and if he helped me then I could help mother, but no fucker was asking me any questions at all, 'cos no one gave a shit about how I was feeling.

And after that visit, she got new meds and slowly but surely, she began to come around. She knew who I was and she began to talk and she began to laugh and smile and read the paper and enjoy life in a way she hadn't had for generations. I know of course that meds were responsible and that for the first time in ages, she was being treated in the proper manner, one that dealt with all her problems. That at last she had proper people caring for her and when I realised this, I didn't feel so bad about carrying her out of the house and into the nursing home.

I thought about getting a dog to keep me company in the house at night, when it'd be dark and when I'd spend hours peering out at the dimly lit street, at the rare passing car, at the odd shout of some crowd coming down from the pub enjoying themselves.

247

And when I saw this, even though I was looking out the window of the room where I was born, in the house where I'd lived all my life, I felt like an outsider.

And then I wished that I'd let myself be more of an insider, that'd I'd followed the line of Father and gone on the piss and fucked around and been more of a prick than I'd let myself be in the early years when the map for my misfortune was being sketched.

The Fortieth Year

The midway point between
love and crazy
I stood on it,
a leg on each side
smitten but riven
by a desire to end,
to encage, wrap up,
push away, drag in
never let go for fear
the light of distraction
might shine on my scarred
face and make her cackle
at my vain attempts to deserve her.

(Peadar Gibbons)

To be honest I lost the run of meself once I had the house to meself. When Mother was there at least I had to retain a semblance of decency and normality. Now I found that I was walking around bollock naked and leaving the jacks door open when I was having a shit and not washing up until last thing at night 'cos it didn't really matter if I did or not.

I didn't worry about anyone walking in on me when I'd be having a wank to Channel Four or one of the well-worn sex tapes that Kieran Donnelly had brought back from Scotland.

And I let the grass grow like fuck out the back 'cos only the neighbours could see it and it didn't matter anymore since there were no kids wanting to play football on it.

And I just put out the bins once every few weeks 'cos if I'd be lying in bed in the morn and I'd hear the bin man outside, I'd just turn around in the bed and say "fuck it, I'll just squash in more rubbish into next week's."

I was monarch of all I could see. I did if I wanted and if I didn't it was because I didn't want to. But monarch of all you can see is grand if you can see a lot. From where I was lying, all I could see was the foot of the bed and dull-grey wallpaper.

So then I discovered that there's no fun to living like that in a house at all, and that there's no fun in pushing out the boundaries if there aren't any boundaries there anymore. So I got my act together and over four days cleaned the house from top to bottom. I went through all Mother's old clothes, the stuff that she'd worn when she was heavier and not just skin and bones. There were jackets and blazers and dresses there from way back. Numerous blouses that would wrap around her twice now if she got them, and loads and loads of shoes, all the old style from the 70s which she loved. I took brillo pads to the kitchen and got it spotless, I bought a big bucket of paint and painted all the downstairs and then did the banister on the stairs, taking time out to put a different colour on the rails. I tidied up all the odds and ends that she kept in drawers, unusual souvenirs of a life she'd lived when she was young and had real hopes of a life a million miles from the one she was going to live.

I ripped up the old carpet from the stairs and the rooms and got the fella in the carpet shop to give me a good deal on some left over bits from a big hotel job he was after doing, so I ended up with five-star carpet for fuck all. And it felt great and smelt great. And on the last few days that I'd be walking around bollock naked, I'd sit on it and roll around on it, just to feel the sheer luxury of it all.

And I took down the curtains and washed them and ironed them and although they still looked a bit creased, they had a cleanness about them that I hadn't seen for a long time.

And then I went out and got meself a girlfriend. A proper one. Not one that you'd ride for the one night and only see now and again for another ride for the one night. I mean one that you'd love and have your heart beating before you met her, that type.

So I went to the Valkenburg on a Sunday night 'cos there was fuck all point going on a Saturday night 'cos there'd be too much competition and shape throwing and pushing and vomiting, and I knew I'd only get distracted and not be able to cope at all. And only feel worse about meself I was getting rejected all the time, so I made up me mind that I wasn't going to put myself in situations where I'd know I'd lose. 'Cos when ya lose all the time, it just feckin' gets to ya. And your head hurts and you don't think straight. And you feel angry. And I didn't want to feel angry, I wanted to feel loved and loving. I wanted some woman to look

251

at me and say 'jaysis I'd love that fella to mind me, just to mind me and care for me."

So I went on a Sunday night. And that's where I saw her. Claire McMahon. With a brunette head on her and slightly protruding teeth and nice cheekbones that made her look like Pat Benatar. I fuckin' loved Pat Benatar and lately had graduated from wanking off to the Suzanne Vega cover to the Love Is A Battlefield video. And jaysus if you try wanking to that you've a job on your hands to keep up, literally.

Claire worked in the County Council office in the town. Some sort of temporary clerk of some sort. God knows what the fuck she did in the County Council in Ballinrobe. She'd probably have been the ones writing Father's paycheque back in the day, but he was long gone before she arrived.

She was sweet and pretty and played badminton and liked walking and reading books and going to the library. I'd know all this 'cos I used to follow her from her flat on the Main Street when she'd go for walks or to the shop. She headed out at seven o clock every night, for a walk around the Bowers. She had a friend Katherine who went everywhere with her. Katherine had a great body but a shit face and she was mad into getting her hole — but Claire was different. She went to the daily Mass at 7.30 on Monday, Wednesday, and Friday nights, which was kinda weird but comforting in itself. 'Cos I knew the plainer she was in terms of outlook, the more chance I had.

I'd had my heart broken before. So I knew I had to be careful. I didn't know if I'd be able for that again.

On a Sunday night, she went to the Valk with Katherine, so I went along one night and bought them both a drink. Katherine stayed around as we chatted and that made it easier. And Katherine got pissed and talked a lot about looking for a farmer from out Ratheredmond way or someplace outside the town. "Someone with a big arse and a bit of a belly," she said. You haven't got a big arse so you'd be no good to me," she said. "I need the big arse 'cos as they say, to drive a big nail, ya have to use a big fuckin' hammer." And she laughed and Claire laughed but reddened.

And so I told Katherine that she was looking for the wrong things if she was just focusing on the big hammer. I said to her that what she needed was someone to fuck with her soul, the prospect of some fella making her soul come, was far better than someone just rutting away at some other part of her for a few minutes.

And Claire and herself looked at each other and thought this was the weirdest thing they'd ever heard from a fella in the Valk; that it was fierce poetic and then when I told her that I was a bit of a poet and that I'd had a story read out by someone on Sunday Miscellany, they were fierce impressed.

And Katherine began to cry and said that I was a lovely fella and that Claire could have me 'cos although 'twas probably true what I was saying, she'd wanted nothing more that night than a good auld dirty ride from a fucker from Ratheredmond with clay and her skin under his nails.

So Claire and I met in the Valk on many Sunday nights and we went for river walks on the Bowers and I showed her where Kieran had drowned and when I'd mention that she'd squeeze my arm real tight. And we used to come back to the house and watch films, not dirty ones, bur French ones like Jean du Florette. Films that you'd talk about afterwards, and I'd learned how to cook

253

dishes for her, spaghetti bolognaise, and risotto, and a broccoli one served with pasta covered with cheese, and lightly toasted under the grill.

She lived in a flat at the back of the hotel up town and said her father would kill her if he knew she was spending nights in my house doing the bould thing, as she called it. And she was good at the bould thing. Slow and controlled. Not taking the lad off ya with any lepping around, like.

And I fell in love with her.

Big time.

The Forty-First Year

I just don't see it
Or so she said and so
I don't question it,
but just myself
because if I can't see it
then I am so much less
than she who can see it;
and if she can see it and I can't
then she can see what I am
and what I amn't.
And God knows what else
she can see
but hasn't the heart to tell me.

(Peadar Gibbons)

I loved being in love, seriously. I never knew that such a feeling would fuck ya up so much, in a nice way and in a shit way. There were nights I squeeze my naked self against hers, spooned under those blankets, with the dead man's clock tick-tocking away on the mantelpiece downstairs and the house having an air about it that it didn't have for a long time. I'd be there clutching her, smelling the back of her neck as she slept, and I inhaling everything about her, my tongue tipping at the chain that went around to the little cross in front. And I wondered why the fuck I had taken so long to find love, to strip it away from sex and sweat and energy. And to replace it with charging myself into her power source and letting her dictate how my stomach felt. Just by being herself. And there were times when she looked just ordinary, as I know I did, but in those times she was the most beautiful woman in the world 'cos at those times without her makeup and her county council uniform she was mine. I don't mean that in any weird stalking possessive way, but I felt that those times when she was like that, she was like that for me and for herself and for us.

And I was just myself.

And I didn't feel that I had to pretend to be anyone else when I was with her, you know in the way you are with other people like, letting on you're someone you're not.

I never knew that you could feel like this, that you would be so fuckin' all consumed by someone. And falling in love proper like for the first time at this stage in my life gave me an insight into songs and films and things and I started seeing her face in everything and every place. But love is an awful dangerous emotion to be fuckin' around with 'cos when you fall in love you are cutting out your soul and handing it to someone else, saying 'here hold this for me and whatever you do, don't drop it."

And you knowing fuckin' well that it can never be held aloft forever because people's arms get tired.

And they start to thinking what am I doing with this eejit when I could be doing so much better for meself. And the world would be a better place if people didn't keep thinking they could do so much better for themselves, better than they were now anyway.

There were times when I even considered telling her about stuff. And how I was, but then I thought that if we ever had a fight, she might tell someone. 'Cos she told me stuff that she'd told nobody else, stuff she felt bad about; stuff that was eating her up inside, but nothing like my issues. Hers were more normal, day to day things. Stuff she'd done on her friends. She told me she'd slept with one accountant while going out with another. And then when she started going out with the other fella, she'd rode the other lad as well. Proper order, I told her. Serves feckin' accountants right for having sex anyway.

She even mentioned that we might have a kid. Really. And we joked about it and how she picked the name Thomas after her granddad and I picked the name Lorna like Lorna that was Cuddy's baby.

And she thought Lorna was a really literary name and it is, like in Lorna Doone which is where I read it and told Teresa Sheridan about it before she gave it to her baby daughter.

But we could have a Lorna too, although Cuddy might think it was fucked up or something, but he's in London now, so I'm sure he'd understand.

And I thought Thomas was a shite name, but she was from East Mayo after all so I said nothing and hoped to fuck it'd be a girl child we'd have.

And the idea of having a kid didn't freak me out. I thought it would, ya know, having all that responsibility to keep it alive and clothed and fed and all that, but now, the more we discussed it, the more a good idea it seemed to be. And the idea of having my own Lorna and having to go out and work and having to get food for her and come home with stuff made me feel really proud about the whole thing. And I didn't care if we didn't get married before we had the kids and all that.

I didn't bother much with the lads when I was going out with Claire. To be honest I was embarrassed by them and their wastery ways and to be really honest I didn't need them. and when you're fuckin' selfish and in a relationship like this, you just don't need other people. In fact, other people just get in the way.
And because of the niceness of what I had with Claire, I knew there was never any way I was going to find this with any other person, So if I was with any others and if she wasn't around, I felt that my heart wasn't at the centre of things and that the further away from her I was, the less happy I was. And the more distracted I was and the less attention I'd be paying to them and all the shite they'd be talking.
And then there were days when I thought about how so fucking happy I was, that I'd go off into a corner and cry to myself at the thought that someday I would not have this. It was like a grown up version of that dream you have as a kid when everyone is dead.

Then I went and met Claire's parents. At a wedding. And I went and forgot my jacket so I had to ring Snugg Murphy to drive down the county with it to me, and I don't think her mother was that gone on me. She had a very teachery way about her. A sharp face that didn't break into a smile when she met me and then I got the thinking that the reason they didn't like me was that I didn't have a proper job and would be of little use to her daughter in the marrying stakes. And when they heard I did a bit of poetry, they lifted their fuckin' eyes to heaven and overall it was very awkward. And at a fuckin' wedding it's kinda hard to get away from the thoughts of marriage and prospects and futures and so on. And there were times when I didn't want to talk about futures. I just wanted the present to go on forever, to be the present forever, the sex and the slagging and the red wine and the cooking and the house being clean 'cos I wanted it that way for Claire all the time.

And I didn't really mind if Lorna and Thomas never came along 'cos what we had was magic, but Claire was getting her head turned I think.

Or maybe she was just turning her own head.

At the wedding I got to meet many of Claire's friends too and while they were great craic and all, I got the feeling that they thought I might be sort of just passin' through because Claire hadn't told them a lot about me. And then I met two former boyfriends she had and they were all working away with decent jobs in Castlebar and Galway and not scratching around writing poems like me.

And they were the two accountants.

Fuckin' accountants.

Who both trusted her but who I knew they shouldn't.

And when it ended, it ended fast.

With Claire it all came to an end above in fuckin' Croke Park at an All-Ireland final between Mayo and Kerry.

259

Kerry got two early goals, so the game was over after about five minutes.

Five minutes after that, so was Claire and Peadar.

She said she hated that we'd drifted. And I didn't really think we had, but 'twas just her way of getting out. To say something like 'you just don't see it.' Or you just don't understand. And there was no answer to any of those questions really 'cos if you said you did and then couldn't explain it, you sounded like an even bigger dick than you would have if you admitted responsibility from the word go.

And when I pressed her on it and told her I'd make a better effort to be something else, to be whatever she wanted me to be, she told me that I just didn't see it, that I just didn't get it.

And whatever you can train a blind man to do, you can't train him to see, so I resigned myself to my blindness, and bowed to her superior knowledge about the things I just didn't see.

And I bowed to the knowledge that whatever the rights and wrongs of the situation, she'd always think there was something in me that made me unable to read certain situations or do the right thing, and because of that I fuckin' hated myself and almost wished us to end, even though it made me miserable and vowing never to fall in fuckin' love again.

And on the day she left the house for the last time, I felt that I'd died. That a piece of my heart had just been ripped out and thrown on the floor.

That someone had jumped on it.

And squashed it flat.

And made it worthless.

And spat on it.

And I knew then that nobody was ever going to love me ever again.

The Forty-Second Year

When did one start
giving a fuck
when giving a fuck?
God be with the days
when all ya worried
about was yourself
and ya hammered
away without one eye
on the clock.

(Peadar Gibbons)

I know you won't understand this, ye being guards and all, but then maybe ye will 'cos ye spend yer whole lives dealing with mad fuckers and all; and maybe this is the kind of thing I shouldn't be saying. Or anybody should be saying in normal circumstances, but these aren't normal circumstances. Yet I have to say I'd missed how good it was to feel that I'd had the courage to see someone's life end. Doctors and midwives always speak about the unbridled joy they feel when they are present at the birth of another human being. They talk about the uplifting experience there is in the practical application of their skills. The fact that they've helped in some way in the transformation into life. And that's noble, it is. Really.

But nobody ever gives much thought to the sense of exhilaration and emboldening that one gets when you are present at the death of a person. Maybe it's more morbid, less joyous. And this is especially the case if you are a willing partner in the commission of the deed that brings this person's life to an end. And I don't mean this in the sense that you wanted to see a person hurt before they died. I never had that motivation. I was always reactionary and not premeditated, so there has to be sense that what I've done is more considered and less bad.

But there is a real heart-racing blood flowing excitement to seeing someone die, not in the sense that it'd give ya a horn or anything. Not perverse like that at all. I have to admit I've never had the horn as someone died near me, but that would be proper sick, so it would. That'd be like those fuckers that I used to read about in the News of The World.

That paper was full of serious weirdoes who planned what they were doing, who weren't just encountering it as part of their lives like I had. Marty and Ray had told me one of the times they were home that they'd been living in a place called Muswell Hill in

263

Cricklewood and there was a fella named Dennis Nielsen who was a fierce sicko altogether. And he did that sort of stuff. No, I'm just saying or trying to explain to ye what it felt like and how it was a nice sort of feeling, although a sort of feeling that you could never share properly with someone. A sort of nostalgic one. The kinda feeling you'd get when you'd meet an old friend of your father from way back and who you never expected to meet again. The momentary warmth of a familiar encounter. Feeling it fast and then mourned as soon as it had ended. But when the feeling came back or when the want of that feeling came back, it was hard to keep it all to myself.

She was Lithuanian. Or Latvian. She had the most unmerciful name on her. Not like the Poles or the Russians. I didn't even try to pronounce it. She wasn't O'Callaghan's Lithuanian. She didn't tell me it, but I'd seen her name on a wheelie bin outside the house where she lived with three other women down the street. I didn't know that she was a hoor even though in the back of yer mind I thought that all those Eastern Europeans were good at the auld sex. It was as if they'd discovered it a hundred years before us or something.
I was playing pool in Kelly's with the lads when she was there and when she was outside having a fag afterwards out the back she just came up to me and said "pull your prick for thirty euros." Which I rejected 'cos the full ride was just sixty.
And a wank is never a half ride.
Never in a million fuckin' years.

I'd rode a few wans here in the house before, apart from Claire. Five or six times, up on the side of me own bed, once on the couch downstairs, another time on the stairs, but never in the big

264

room where mother and father used to sleep. 'Twas the biggest bed in the house and I'd never even slept in the fuckin' thing. I'd aired the bed clothes every six months or so cos the smell of the mothballs was sometimes overpowering. And it looked fierce inviting. A proper bed.

But overall the room looked like it hadn't changed since I slept in that cot in the corner. The cot was long gone, but the chairs with the clothes on them to block off my view of the bed was still there, with an old tweed skirt of mothers hanging off the back of it.

I was amazed with the body she had when she threw off her clothes, fuckin' like a supermodel she was, like Helena Christensen or whatever her name was. I couldn't believe that she looked like she did.

And she moved and swayed above me with me in her, and she looking like she didn't give a shit and looking she wished she was anywhere but here. And she even picked up her phone at one stage and looked at it.

And then said something to me that I knew was shit. Something that ended with 'baby.' Yes baby" or some shit like that.

And me doing nothing to encourage it, really.

And then she kinda laughed at me and chewed her gum and laughed more.

And then writhed more and more.

And oohhhed and aaahhed and said more 'baby' shite.

And I knew that she wasn't like Claire or the bank girls. And I felt I was a fuckin' eejit for even thinking that she'd give a shit about anything I did or said to her. And the more I thought about all of this, the less hard I became and the less hard I became, the more uncaring she seemed to become.

265

'Do ya wanna fock or not?" she said to me but I wasn't hearing her. At all. 'Cos I'd lost interest and felt shite for thinking that this was any kind of love at all. Sure love isn't love if you can't show it to other people or tell people about it. I could hardly tell anyone about this wan.

And then I saw myself — over at the cot, the little face looking out through the bars, through the gaps in the chair where my father's trousers used to hang, where mother's tweed skirt would act as a makeshift curtain and where now this wan's leopard skin miniskirt was draped over that very skirt.
I could see my little face looking at me straight in the eye, staring at me and letting a little laugh out of him, out of, whatever the fuck. And then he threw his head back, this cheeky little three-year-old and he pointed at me and laughed even more and more. I wanted to go over and punch him in the face to make him stop laughing at me and I swung out and hit and hit and kicked and punched again at the dark shadows of the night with the head boiling on me and me closing me eyes and lashing out and crying and kinda roaring...
And when I'd stopped and when I reached up to switch on the light over the bed I saw her lying there, her face bleeding and she not talking or moving or groaning and she broken like a doll with her arm twisted skewways and her naked body not at all sexy now that 'twas covered in blood and her face not pretty anymore 'cos her teeth were smashed and one of her eyes was open and the other was closed and dark.
And when I looked at the chair, the little fucker was gone — he'd been laughing at me and now he'd fucked off and left me here on me own with a badly beaten Lithuanian or Latvian and not a stir out of her. And me not knowing what the fuck to do with her.

I took Liam's car out of the yard where he left it on nights when he'd be going for a few and wouldn't want to drive. It was a dark night, not much of a moon. And I was sweating and I could still smell her. Could smell the sweat of myself and the perfume of her.

I'd no idea if she was still alive but she was well limp when I put her into the boot in the dark of the yard. 'Twas easy to drag the clothes onto her 'cos there was fuck all and no buttons.

I was nervous driving down that road. 'Twould be just the night you'd meet the guards or someone would crash into ya or something. But nothing happened.

There was a bend in the road after the Liskillen wood. Only a handful of houses down there, mainly auld bachelors who'd lived with their mothers. A road with maybe a handful of cars every night.

I took her out of the boot and put her at the dark side of the bend, left her there, lying on the road. I was shitting meself in case some car came around the corner and thought I'd hit her, but there was nothing coming.

You'd see the lights for half a mile away anyway if there was. Nothing would be coming down here until after the pubs were closed. And that was at least an hour away. So I left her on the road in the dark of the corner at the worst part of the bend.

And as I drove away I put the sight of her out of my mind. Her lying there, unable to move, if she was even alive.

And then I went home and cried because I hoped that I'd dressed her right. And I cried because after all the thoughts I'd had about being a father with Claire, I remembered that once this woman was a child that a father and a mother had put to bed and worried

267

about.

That there were loads of Saturday nights that they'd checked to see if she was sleeping and warm and comfortable.

And here was me, arragh fuck it, it doesn't help thinking. It hurts. It fuckin' hurts.

And the howl within me started up again like some sort of a keelin' banshee.

And then I tried to sleep, back in my own bed.

But it didn't come easy to me, not easy at all.

And then my accomplice, the clock downstairs, tick-tocked its mocking noise past closing time.

The Forty-Third Year

When pouring hot tay
keep the spout low
to the cup tho
it may look ok
to be showing off
and pouring from
a great height.
It might feel good to
hold the pot way above
to be guiding the trail
of golden liquid down
a straight line to the delph.
But the higher ya hold it
the greater the splash
and parched bystanders
get spots of hot tay
into their eyes
scalding their
innocence.

(Peadar Gibbons)

Now, guards, I've no idea if you'll believe me or not, but I don't know who I felt more sorry for — meself, the Lithuanian bird, or Paddy Grimes.

Paddy had told ye that he'd nothing to do with it. And that should have been that. But then you'd expect him to say that, wouldn't ye? But in his own mind he didn't have a fuckin' clue whether he did or not and he eventually told ye that and ye went and prosecuted him for dangerous driving causing death and he lost the licence and the only way he had of getting to town for the only human contact he had.

And he was never more than a five-pint a night man anyway.

And he'd been making the same journey home every night for forty years and he'd never been in trouble before. But still ye were very fast to nail him. But then hey, listen to me here who's talking and me who set it all up. But I was hoping it'd be one of the Maguire brothers who'd have been normally lashed fuckin' drunk flying along that road that would have done it, some cunt like that who deserved a doing anyway for all the dangerous driving he'd done over the years. Not Paddy fuckin' Grimes, the most harmless man in Liskillen.

And because ye did him and because ye took away his licence and left him without a way to get to town, he went worse on the drink after that - drinking bottles of whiskey at the kitchen table and generally going fuckin' mad in the head.

And he hated the way people tut-tutted at him for running over that nice Latvian or Lithuanian girl who worked in the supermarket.

And the way he had denied it and then the way he continued to deny it after they found the blood on his car and the way the lads in Kellys' pub said that he hadn't drunk that much. Just a few pints, five or six, enough to put him over the limit, but he'd drunk more before and never had an accident.

And anyway what the fuck was she doing there on that road anyway and then they were saying that she might have been down there servicing one of the auld farmers, or maybe Paddy Grimes picked her up and brought her home and something went wrong and he ended up running over her. And he such a nice man and he living there in that cottage on his own, just a lovely auld bachelor who probably never got his hole anyway.

And sure maybe that was it, when you come onto something late in life it can ruin your judgement 'cos ya haven't had the steady slow run into it. So maybe he was discovering ridin' and he went mad.

His sister the nun in the States came home to see him and told all and sundry that 'twas the drink that got him into this trouble in the first place and he driving over that poor foreign girl and squashing her to bits with his heavy estate car and then leaving her there on the road until the guards came the next morning and saw her blood and brains on the underside of his bumper and Paddy inside in the bed with the smell of the few pints off him.

Whatever the story, the reality was that Paddy Grimes was fucked after it. He stopped going to Mass 'cos he felt people looking at him. At first he sat further back the church from the pew where his family had sat for generations. Where he'd sit in and leave his tweed cap on the seat beside him. A holier man you would think you would not see. Sure it's always the quiet ones who are the worst, the people said.

Even Mother heard it in the county home. Her wits were coming back to her now 'cos they'd 'regulated her meds' as the nurse said. So she no longer looked at me as if I was some class of an amadán. She was now telling me she loved me and that she didn't miss the house and that she was comfortable here but that sometimes she got terribly frustrated when she realised that she might never be leaving this place alive...and I'd tell her to shush and not to be thinking such stuff.

And then she'd say something like "Yes, it could be worse. See that poor Paddy Grimes the way he has gone and everyone thinking he was an innocent auld soul."

And I'd have to nod.

And sometimes when I'd listen to the chat about Paddy, I'd have to stop myself from interrupting and telling them wasn't what happened at all, but I figured it was better for me to keep my fuckin' mouth shut.

And then I'd feel guilty and then other times I'd tell meself not to be daft and that sure how the fuck was I to know that he'd be the one to come around the corner that night.

And that 'twasn't me that made him drink the five or six pints and that he should have known that was enough to put him over the limit anyway and that if he was a better driver he might have avoided her, even though 'twas a bit difficult to do given that I'd placed her so near to the road.

Oh, me fuckin' head was sore with the thinking about him. I thought then about going out into the fuckin' street and roaring out that 'twas me who did it, that Paddy was just caught up in it, what do they call it, collateral damage. Yeah, Paddy was collaterally damaged by it alright. Because I didn't come out and confess, he was sat there at home with the terrible thoughts in his mind and he shamed like he'd never been shamed before in his life.

And a redness in his cheeks and a thumping in his heart every time he set out. And still there when he'd be sat at home alone.

And that howl in him would be rarin' to get out.

This was the year he took out his shotgun and shot himself in the head, but the poor bastard squinted and grimaced at the thought of it, and moved at the last minute and the gunshot took off his ear and a fair portion of skin from one side of his face. And it left him roaring then on the floor for a good few hours until the neighbours came in to check on him.

And found him with half his face missing.

And when people heard that he'd done that, they reckoned that made him all the fuckin' more guilty 'cos they reckoned if he was really innocent, he wouldn't have tried to do himself. So the sister nun came home again and she got him sorted in the psychiatric home in Castlebar, 'cos he was demented with the pain and the horror of what he had done to himself and the horror of what he thought he had done to the Lithuanian bird.

And the house he lived in just got damp and cold and empty and soulless.

He with his wheelchair and his bad walk now and his disfigured face would never be back in it again. 'Cos the dressings had to be changed every day to take away the purple shiny wet leathery look off the badly damaged skin. And he'd frighten people with the look of him.

He got the odd visitor in the home in Castlebar and I was tempted to go along myself. But 'twould be hard to explain to him why I'd want to do that since I'd never had many doings with him at all.

And then I was thinking if I saw the state all of this had left him in, I wouldn't be feeling the happiest after it, so maybe 'twas better I didn't. 'Cos when you see some things, you just can't fuckin' unsee things.

So I just left him there to shuffle up and down those corridors with the screams of the truly mad ringing in his ears and the fine lines between horror and reality blurred into a foggy streak in the roadway to his mind.

The poor poor bastard.

I'm truly sorry.

The Forty-Fourth Year

I don't sound at all
like the person I want to be.
I don't come from where the person I want to be
comes from.
My words spill forward from this mouth but
a line up wouldn't link them to me
They are not mine.
Are they strangers in my body
or am I a stranger in theirs?

(Peadar Gibbons)

I want to be normal. How do you become normal? I mean ya hear this shite about how people change their lives and take it easy and become new people, but I've never really known how they do it.

Like when you hear that people in hospital beat illness by fighting against it, I just wondered how the fuck you did that? Do you push and shove and battle against the illness? Do you strain yourself like a constipated auld dog? Or do you lie there and stare it in the eye like you're trying to freak it out or something. The same with trying to be extra normal. If you seemed too normal, you come across as a fuckin' weirdo. What exactly is normal? I mean you could describe half the people in the town as normal, but how do you take on any of their individual 'normal' characteristics without making yourself so different from yourself that you have people thinking you're mad. Do ya understand what I'm trying to say here?

Fuck, my head hurts so badly and I've this pain and strain in my chest that's not a heart attack but just something that I know isn't doing me any good. Stress or something. The head feels like I've been slapped around the place, though I know I haven't.

So I needed to relax big time, but the more I tried the harder it got and the less relaxed I was. If you know you're stressed, you get even more stressed trying to be less stressed.

I went to the doctor and said that I was trying to be more relaxed but then he was asking why I needed to relax given that I was a chilled out sort of poet so I shouldn't need any more relaxing. And when he suggested sedatives, I pictured meself stumbling around falling asleep in the middle of the day...and anyway it wasn't sleep I wanted. Or the type of sleep I was getting anyway with deep deep sleep and then terrible fuckin' awakenings when I'd sit bolt upright and the sweat would be pouring off me.

And when he suggested anti-depressants, I read that you were always kinda duped into getting those and that when you tried to get off them, you'd fill up with loads of thoughts about killing yourself. And that'd be a worse state of affairs to be in. I mean you'd be shitting yourself more about that side effect than you would about the real need to be on the fucking things in the first place. No, I had no intention of killing myself. I just wanted to feel better, to feel normal, to look normal, to live normal.

And when the doctor spoke to me about things, I realised that maybe I was normal already, just that I didn't feel it. He could have been saying things to humour me as he was prone to doing and as I'd seen him do with Mother, but the impression I got from him and from a lot of people was that I was someone who didn't stick out from the crowd, that I was just one of the boys from High Street and that I couldn't be more normal if I tried. I was like extra-normal, with no decent job to me name, getting the dole, writing poetry, and keeping the head down.

Shopping for the normal stuff, never in trouble with the guards, never any worse than the next eejit who lived in the street. And he said that everyone thought I was very relaxed 'cos I was a poet. I wonder if he thought I was making a living out of it, and if he did, maybe others did and then I'd be kind of a normal normal.

But even with this realisation, the feeling didn't get any better. I hadn't been out much for a while. I wondered if I got me hole would it make me feel any better, so I did but 'twas shite, with some young wan who "wanted me to be happy too" 'cos I made her damp awful fast and who insisted on pulling the flute off me with no effect for twenty minutes before I cajoled her into stopping by saying I was more of a giver than a taker which she loved but which I knew was pure shite - but which she thought

277

was lovely.

And then I'd listen to Sunday Miscellany and I'd feel annoyed 'cos I remembered the time I was on it and I thought then that I'd get book writing big time after it, but then it didn't happen and now the fucking music and the way they spoke on Sunday Miscellany made me want to reach over and switch it off and then put the pillow over my head, a head full of fucking regrets at things like that. And the people who spoke on that programme had a certain way about them. I'd say they came from homes where everyone read books and not just the odd fuckin' child who was shite at sport.

They all sounded happy and joyous and they had a spring in the way they read their stories, because they were all probably writing books and stuff and knew that they'd have their stuff read out on the radio eventually. And another way they were different from us was that they all had voices just made for reading out their stuff on the radio in public. S'pose that was the true test of them as writers. Whereas I wrote well and sounded shite, they wrote average and sounded average so they had an advantage all round. And so I'd listen to `Sunday fuckin' Miscellany and hear these people with great voices reading out shite pieces of prose about the day something terribly fuckin' ordinary happened to them.

But in their oddness and middle-classness they weren't fuckin' normal either. So there had to be a middle type of normal – normal as in just plain ordinary. Above the kind of normal as in crazy strange normal like me and below the kind upper crust niceness that was a normal as well.

And so I tried to do things that other normal people did. I started going to evening Mass. I shopped in the small shops around the town. I cut the grass at the back of the house in the garden that nobody could or would ever see apart from the overlooking neighbours and often I'd wonder why the fuck I was doing it. And I'd sit in the grass and fall asleep in the sun and dream the nicest of dreams and then the weirdest of dreams. And this year I was having the dream that I'd had as a kid, when you knew that in the natural order of things, everyone else in your family would be dead before ya, but the natural order of things wasn't living with our family at all.

No, the natural order had been taken up by the hole, and spun around and then dropped into our house with all sorts of people dying when they shouldn't and others living when they should be dying. And when you'd have that dream as a kid, you could shake yourself awake and try not to imagine it, and convince yourself that that was all donkey's years away and that by then you'd have loads of friends to ensure you weren't lonely anyway. But it hadn't turned out that way for me. Mine had turned out the exact fuckin' way I thought it would, with me alone, friendless 'cept for those fools I played pool with, and those who I paid to have sex with; nothing but darkness for real meaningful company and me mother below in the county home and she half dead anyway in me mind.

Sure how the fuck could I be anyways normal with all that normality going on?

The Forty-Fifth Year

I'm getting to me
pissing me off
irr-it-ating myself
Can't stand to be
in the same room
stealing my breath
looking at me and wonder
why don't I just scram
and leave myself to myself.

(Peadar Gibbons)

At first I thought nobody would notice me 'til the day in the shop when I saw a little kid looking at me before saying 'why are you nodding all the time? Is something wrong with your head?" And I looked away and then saw that his parents were looking at me and I nodded again. I think now that if I'd said something funny then, like laugh it off or make a joke of it, that I might have coped with it better. But no, I didn't. I had to make a scene, and told him to fuck off and then his father said "don't you fuckin' use language like that in front of my son" and when I told him that he'd said fuckin' as well, he spat in my face, so I ran out of the shop and stopped a few yards outside and then walked the rest of the way, more and more conscious that I was nodding.

Where the fuck did this nodding come out of? Was it something I'd been doing for years? I hadn't noticed it before but it was with me now. With me all the time, well not all the time as like I wasn't continuously nodding like one of the handicapped kids you'd see in Romanian orphanages.

No, it was like I'd nod when I felt under pressure. If I looked in the mirror I wasn't nodding, but when someone would speak to me, it'd come to me.

In the end I decided to go to the doctor, this time a woman doctor, to see if she could recommend something to make me stop nodding, like a relaxant for my neck or something, but then I thought if I did that, I mightn't be able to fuckin' nod when I needed to, like when people would ask me shit. It'd be like Botox for my neck. "Oh fuck, what am I going to do," I roared at myself one night upstairs in the room.

And then I nodded again.

And again.

Even when I pressed my head hard into the pillow, I found myself nodding. And the more I resisted, the more damage I thought I was doing.

But the doctor said that there wasn't anything actually wrong with my neck. It was just that I'd developed a habit and that just as quickly as it had arrived, it would go again. But there was something about the way she said that made me not believe a fuckin' word she was saying. Then she slyly added in that it might help if I considered taking some Xanax. I knew Xanax was one of those fuckin' pills Mother was taking and see the way she ended up. I didn't want to carried out of my own home in a couple of years after being found in a puddle of my own piss and shit.

So I told her no fuckin' way was I taking Xanax. But then she said if that was the case, there was nothing she could do for me. All I could do was go home and rest and try not to be getting meself into stressful situations that might bring on the nodding. No, I nodded, and thanked her and left and then I realised that I'd no hope of ever shifting it because my whole fuckin' life was a stressful situation.

And my family's life and all this personal cloud I seemed to be permanently walking under.

I wished that life hadn't been so fuckin' unfair. I knew there had to be other cunts going around who were worse than me, but who weren't in the slightest affected by it. I wonder if I told the doctor of the stuff that I could feel in my head, would she take more notice of me then? I suppose to her I was just another middle-aged fuckin' loser in a dead town with no job who was surprised that he was feckin' depressed.

After a few months, I did crack the nodding.

But I replaced it with swallowing.

I found myself fearing that I'd swallow me tongue. Even in bed, I'd sit up bolt upright swallowing nothin' but air and then touching my tongue with my teeth just to make sure it was still there. I'd the tip of the tongue cut off meself. I'd seen on the paper that if you swallowed your tongue you could fuckin' choke to death and that nobody would have a fuckin' clue what was wrong with ya until it was too late.

Especially me there in the house alone, sure who'd find me and then I'd get all sweaty and upset and cry and then I'd nod again and swallow and cry again and fuckin' roar at the wall. But there was nobody the far side of it to hear me 'cos the neighbours had all died away as well and their kids in Dublin were waiting to sell the fuckin' place to whatever poor unfortunate would buy it, with its mice all coming over to the heat of my house. I'd put down the kind of poison for the mice that would make them want to get out quickly to drink water but all that succeeded in doing was driving the little cunts crazy and making them make it halfway through my attic and under me floorboards where they'd die screaming and then rot and then the smell of them would be all over the house until I'd lift the floorboards and drag out what was left of them and fuck them in the bin outside.

Then I feared I was going to choke on some food, so I'd be eating small forkfuls, even when I got a dinner in the cafe up town on dole day, I'd be swallowing and gulping down water to make sure it all went down and then when I'd see others looking at me and then looking away if I looked at them, I'd start nodding again.

Even if I turned away from them and faced the wall or the window, I'd have the feeling they were looking at me and I'd scratch my head to stop myself nodding, but I fuckin' would. So many days, I just got up, dinner half eaten, half fuckin' starved and I go home, nodding all the way and scratching and swallowing until I'd turn the key and go back inside the darkened house and cry meself to sleep.

I wondered if the badness that was inside me was poisoning me in some way and making my body go all fuckin' weird. What next, I wondered? What ailment would next be visited on me until I gave up all of me badness and resigned myself to a life of oddness.

I always felt that the capacity of a person to do bad things was in equal measure with his capacity to live with the thoughts of those bad things. And while I was always confident that I could pack away of lot of the bad shit into me head, maybe now I was failing. Maybe I wasn't naturally a bad fucker at all. That was alien to me and that I was reacting against it in this way.

And maybe that's why I have come to the station to admit things the way I have. I'm crying for help.

The Forty-Sixth Year

Dawn is a bastard to your thoughts

When it should be soothing,

trailing its fingers along your scalp

blinding your lobes to what went in the hours before

confirming the rightness of all that was said and done

but no, it laughs and pokes its spindly digits in your eye

pours cold water on your comfort

laughs and makes your nice words seem jumbled and rude

throws light on the areas that like the shade.

Makes what seemed right, seem so wrong.

(Peadar Gibbons)

I'd no idea why I did it. Honest. It might rank as one of the most irrational fuckin' things I've done in my entire life, and I've had a few. But he deserved it and that's what makes me accept this more than many other things. I won't be haunted by this but it was still a fuckin' stupid thing to do because it endangered me on so many levels.

I was in the Lakeland Hotel at the final night of the open reading session of the writers club. This was a gig where the public were invited in, but apart from the 30 or so regulars who attended, only a few stragglers made their way in from the bar to the little function room on the right hand side.

The evening was going well. I was on the list to read my story *Knowing Mary*. It was about an old woman who lived up the street from us. We used to do odd jobs for her and she'd give us money.

Her husband had been the ticket collector in the cinema, the guy who'd fuck ya out if he caught ya messin' or wanking, or both, in the middle seats upstairs. So because we were good to his wife, Mattie'd let us into the cinema downstairs through the emergency door that led out into the ditch beside the river. He'd have been fuckin' fired if the owners of the cinema knew that, but they never found out and so Mattie was a sort of hero to a whole generation of us young lads from the street where he was born and bred. As for the cunts up town, he made sure they were charged full whack.

But Mattie was a ferocious smoker, practically atin' Woodbines and then Sweet Afton and then easing down to Carrolls in the years before the cancer took him, leaving him a shell of a man, like a ghost. I remember the last time I saw him, the eyes had shrunk back into his head. I was only about fifteen and he scared the shite out of me, with a face like a raccoon on him, the shape of his skull coming through his bones, and that yellow look in his skin.

He was in the ground a few weeks later and poor Mary was left by herself, sitting there by the window staring out at the people making their way to and from the cinema where her beloved had worked for so long. She told us once that she'd never smoked 'til she met Mattie and he'd pass on his fags to her when he'd chewed his way halfway down one of them....and now after his death she was carrying on his legacy, devouring the fags one after another, often going without atin' so she could smoke instead.

Even though we knew 'twas fuck all good to us to be doing odd jobs after Mattie had died 'cos he couldn't get us into the cinema no more, we did them anyway. And then she'd offer us tea and biscuits but we'd turn them down 'cos we were afeared of getting the cancer off her. But sitting there in the darkness with her, she'd tell us stories about how she met Mattie and how they ran away together and how he told her he'd own his own cinema some day. He never did, but got to work in one for thirty years. She died about a year or two after him. And the basis of my short story *Knowing Mary* was built on how that year was spent and what she told us.

So you see how I was fuckin' proud of it all. How it meant something to me to write about someone I knew. Not a fictional person like others wrote about. Not a made-up flute. But a real living person, well one who was dead, really, but you know what I mean. So 'twas like writing about me own mother 'cos Mary was like family, being a kindly neighbour.

When she died, we were the only young fellas at the funeral; all the other fuckers who'd gotten free tickets from Mattie never bothered their holes showing up.

287

So the story meant a lot to me. 'Cos I felt I was giving her the obituary she'd never got. I was too young to do a piece from the pulpit when she died, so this was my way.

And then that fucker ruined it. Sitting there with his pint and his fat belly. Scratching his balls with his thumb. Only came in 'cos the bar was warmer in there.

Only came in to laugh at us.

Ignorant prick.

He started early on in the story. I was up at the microphone holding my pages, and the leaves shaking, and me hoping I wouldn't nod or swallow. He started laughing at the bit where I'd read how Mary had died from cancer of the throat.

"Too many blow jobs, did she?" he roared up.

I stopped and went red.

And tried to start again.

Do I go back to the beginning or do I let the interruption bother me into distraction? I stopped and went back. He laughed and others with him laughed. There was no bouncer there 'cos twasn't the kind of fuckin' gig you'd think you needed bouncers for.

Then he started again.

"Were ya riding her, ya gay fucker? Did ya hear the bones crackin, did ya?"

He looked around to laugh but nobody laughed with him this time.

But he laughed anyway, before taking a big gulp out of his pint.

And then I did it.

I picked up the Ballygowan water bottle that was unopened beside my microphone.

And I caught it by the neck and fucked it down at him, hitting him on the side of the head, knocking the pint glass all over him.

A solid thud, the thick end of the bottle catching him on the temple. Fuck. I didn't mean to hit him that hard. He went down, so he did, didn't have a clue what happened him.

But others did. His friends had seen the bottle coming, and they came up onto the stage to get me. The auld dears in the club started shrieking and shouting, so I ran out the side door and into the lobby and into the street. They were shouting 'come back ya quare cunt," but I ran. Realising that I looked daft, a man of my age running. A man of my age doing something like that. 'Twas ok for young lads to run but not fellas my age. After a few hundred yards, I knew that they weren't coming after me, and then I was afraid they'd get into a car and come around the town and find me, so I ran down the Bowers by the river over the bridge, across the Green and climbed in the back wall of the house, avoiding the streets.

The next day I was going to go in to ye in the garda station to tell ye what happened. I knew ye'd heard that a fight had broken out but there didn't seem to be any report on it or anything. I rang Michael Clarke the organiser and he was less friendly which was surprising 'cos I was only defending the integrity of the event. But then again, I s'pose fuckin' a bottle at someone wasn't preserving any integrity either.

I thought he'd be more sympathetic. He said something about freedom of expression and having to deal with criticism and all that and that I should have been more prepared for negative reactions, but I thought that was absolute bollocks, but didn't tell him that then.

He said that the incident had ruined the night but he accepted that I'd been provoked, badly provoked.

He added that the writing club were disappointed that I had

reacted the way I did. He said they were shocked to see me do something that seemed so alien to me. They felt that I was a nice man with a great talent for the writing but that maybe it'd be better if I let things cool down for a while and didn't attend again until the autumn.

Take the summer off, he said, but I knew in his voice that he really hoped that by the autumn I'd have gone off this writing lark and that the petite and precious ladies and gents of the Robe Writing Club would be just as happy if they never fuckin' saw me again.

And they never fuckin' did.

The Forty-Seventh Year

I've fed you all these years
with stuff I've not shared
wrapped in code and half truth
written in sun and half light
trusted you to remind me
but then you got greedy and wanted
heartier meals, more of my soul.
Slapping me with sepia negatives
of moments that never happened
in a life less ordinary.

(Peadar Gibbons)

Every night when I climbed into the bed, it was staring at me, the fuckin' thing, with its embossed red cover and its fancy gold writing with its name and the year stamped on it. Sitting there lording it over all the other books, the books that'd be read in two weeks, the one-night fucks unlike itself which had a whole year in its pride of place, and then eternity in the drawer where I kept the forty or so other diaries.

I'd leave it there on the locker or on the floor after I'd finished writing it the night before. But then there'd be days on end when I hadn't the heart to open the fuckin' thing and try to recall the few memorable events of the previous two or three days. Once or twice, I'd gone weeks without filling it and so I'd stay up drinking coffee downstairs to see if I could think of something, anything, that would let me put any sort of scrawl on the page for that date. I'd be scratching my head and almost roaring at myself for failing to remember anything of note that warranted being put in the pages. Some days I'd just write in shit like "got up and had breakfast, went to town," and so on.

If I couldn't remember anything I'd leave the pages blank but those blank pages tormented me, big gaping holes in the book that was supposed to act as my recorded memory. And the big gaping holes were like mouthfuls with teeth missing. I'd started when I was about 12 and the first one was just a few lines about what I watched on television mainly. The telly was new to the house so anything I watched was fuckin' memorable. *The Man from Atlantis* with Patrick Duffy, later Bobby Ewing; the *Gemini Man; Alias Smith and Jones* and then big rip roaring English dramas like *Poldark, Clayhanger,* and *The Onedin Line.* They all got their lines in the diary, those TV dramas from the late seventies. And from then on it soared. Every Christmas I was gifted a new diary and so it became tradition, like socks and slippers.

Every year I wondered how the fuck would I stop writing a diary. And would that be the year I'd die? I had thought about not buying one but lately every year Seamus's kids in Tipperary sent it to me as a gift for their sad solitary uncle in Mayo. They knew I read books and was handy with English so they in their teenage innocence were not to know that they were giving me a gift that would turn into the most ungrateful and demanding thing in the world. If they gave me a naggin' wife it would have been a better gift, but sure I hadn't the heart to tell them not to give me that fuckin' thing.

In the end it made me feel small because I wouldn't have bothered to fill it in. And it made me feel shit about myself when I ignored it. There were nights when I wouldn't be able to sleep cos I hadn't the heart to fill it in. There were nights when it put me off wanking 'cos of the way it made me feel rushed and under pressure for not giving it the attention it desired. I felt kinda unfaithful if I'd started tossing off before I'd done the diary and then when I'd not manage to do either properly, I'd be fuckin' maudlin and cranky and twisting on the pillow, flipping it over and over trying to find a cool side but failing miserably.

Over the years I had special diary codes for when I did things. I used to write 'eventful nacht' on the top of a page if it was worthy of mention. Something like a ride or a good night of drinkin' or a good night of poetry reading or if I had craic with the lads or something, anything that was out of the ordinary, anything that differentiated those nights from the thousands of other boring nights.

Some of them I'd look at over and over again to see if the 'eventful nachts' even constituted a proper month if lumped in all together. A fuckin month of 'eventful nachts' is not enough for a man of 47 years to have. What would be the point of any book if only 30 of the 15,000 pages were any good, even if the rest were for context. Sure a book like that you'd fuck in the bin. I wondered what was the point of reminding me of days that were so forgettable to start with that I struggled to remember them a few days later.

What was the point then in keeping those forgettable notes for consumption years later? Yes, they have been handy for trying to put some shape on the fuckin' state of my mind for the purpose of this admission. They provide a context for you to understand, and a context for me to understand.

As I read back through the small scrawl over many years. I can see the scattered bones of a family crushed by tragedy and drink. I can see why I was a nervous prick when I could have been much better. And that that nervous prick then became an older nervous prick and carried with me the scars of that time. I know I put a lot of the scars there myself, but I'm trying not to justify it, but to show how good people can become bad people if bad things happen to them.

So why am I telling ye about this, guards? It's because this was the first time that I realised that I'd written oodles of shite about a life that meant nothing. To me I mean. I know and ye know that my life impacted on other people's lives, but none of that would have happened if they hadn't collided with me in the first place. If they'd not bumped into my life, they'd have been grand, and I might have been grand, and ye'd never be reading any of this now.

294

And my diaries are a reflection of that life – years and years of seeming nothingness, nights spent in solitude and isolation when they should have been spent socialising, meeting friends, making me some sort of normal so that I could free my head of the shit it holds.

Who would ever read these notes and pages? What were they all for? So that I'd know where I was at a certain day in time? Who the fuck cared? Did I really care? No. If anything the diaries made me depressed even more when I'd read back the stuff that I deemed memorable. Diaries should have been fun, something to reflect on happy days, but mine were just one piece of sadness after another. There was rarely a day gone past that I'd like to relive again. I just prefer to take my chances with what the next day brings rather than harking back to others. But then maybe my view of it all is coloured by the fact that I know what happened in the days and months and years after.

And so that was why I stopped writing them this year. I finished the last one and said 'no more." I have them all in a big box in the attic, all organised in chronological order, some of them yellowing, others bulging from having old photos and receipts and job application letters and postcards from places.

That's where they are and that's where ye'll find them. And if ye do take the bother to go through them, then maybe I will have been justified for writing them because after all these years, they'll make some difference, they will matter.

'Cos they will tell the tale I've been telling.

And as a writer, at last some of my stuff will be read and pondered over and made sense of.

And there's not much more that someone like me can ask.

The Forty-Eighth Year

Somebody out there.
Don't ya just love it
when somebody asks you
a question you can answer?
When you don't have to say
'sorry I'm not from around here'
Or 'I've no idea what you're asking.'
'Cos you're able to think on your feet.
There isn't much knowledge that you
have that's yours only
Even Mastermind experts share a knowledge
of their chosen subject.
Only a few have knowledge that nobody else has
Because you're somebody out there who knows.

(Peadar Gibbons)

The temptation to pick up the phone and ring was something terrible. I was watching Crimecall and there was his face. And Grainne Seoige reading out his details and the big picture of him in the background. And some guard going on about him. Well-known Sligo businessman. Fifteen years ago this week. Brutally killed in his car in Galway. Blah blah, fuckin' blah. Upstanding member of the community. Upstanding member alright, twas upstanding member in my hand, I said to myself. But I didn't laugh.

I just said it out loud, spitting crumbs.

To myself, 'cos I was the only one there watching it. Sitting there and me lashing into a toasted cheese sandwich, crusts and all, and a big mug of cocoa with the powder not properly stirred floating around on the top.

No known enemies or reasons for his death. Family and friends shocked and distraught. Wife was on pleading that someone out there knew something about it and that they should come forward blah blah fuckin' blah. No enemies in the world, family man....

Yeah yeah, if he was such a family man he wouldn't be offering young lads money to pull him off, the dirty bastard.

And ya know, then for a while I began to lose any sympathy I had for him at all. It wouldn't have been so bad if he'd just been some auld queer fucker who ya wouldn't expect any more from than to be pulled off by young lads, but here he was living a life of lies to his family and wife. I can be damn sure I wasn't the first one he paid money to 'cos he was so fuckin' casual about it. He knew what he was doing for sure, he did.

And as I watched the programme more and more, the less concerned I became for him and the family and more for the gorgeous woman garda who was talking on it. She so pretty with her hair pinned up at the back and ya knowing only too well how much better she'd look if that hair was let fall down around her shoulders. I loved touching women's hair though a lot of them weren't too fucking keen on it. Even the whores I brought to the house. You could touch every fuckin' part of them with every part of you, but if ya stroked their hair, or ran your hands though it, they went apeshit. I always wondered why. I never argued the toss with them about that. I just went along with their wishes like, out of some sort of weird fuckin' respect.

I remember I was drinking the cocoa when I watched that programme. Mother had a carton of it in the press from way before and although I wasn't sure if 'twas gone off or not, I made myself a cup 'cos I'd heard that there was going to be a programme about cold cases and that this was one of them. And I wanted to relax and sit down and watch programmes like ordinary people did. Sit and enjoy them like.

This was the first time I'd heard guards talking about one of the things I did. S'pose all the others looked like they just happened and that there was a rational explanation for all of them. But this was the only real loose end, even though it wasn't any more premeditated than the others.

This was one where I didn't have time to clean up the scene, to remove all trace of myself, to have an exit strategy in my head that I could follow. No, this was one where I just fuckin' ran and ran and ran. And maybe I'm still running from that one. But as I watched and watched and listened and heard what they were saying, I was thinking that this was one that still made my heart race. And I wondered why I had done it and was it purely for the money I'd lost that week or did I do it 'cos I enjoyed it? And would I have done more if I'd gone to a hotel with him or something, and if I had, my whole life might have changed. 'Cos I might have been happier that way. If I'd gone that way, if ya know what I mean.

His name was Kevin. I had heard the name at the time but had never really thought that much about it, because I'd never bothered to read up too much about it.

His wife looked pretty, but drawn. She was probably a looker in her day but time wasn't kind to her. She had that look of a Prod about her, ya know the kind of good looks worn down by time and work ethic. She was the kind of woman you could imagine organising a church fete or something. Making fresh scones and two kids hanging off her at the gate of a house with a long drive, that sort of look. The kind of woman who looked as good with her hair all scrunched up back off her face.

And as she told her story, she started to cry and I wondered if in the fifteen years since, she had moved on at all. Had she married another man or had she been taken in by Kevin so much that she vowed never to love another? Or maybe she knew that he kicked both ways and was ok with that, but then if she did, she mightn't have bothered to keep looking for answers. And if she hadn't moved on, she was a serious waste of a woman, even though it could be argued that she was a waste of a good woman anyway given what I knew about Kevin.

She seemed very genuine about her appeal. She seemed like she was someone who had been hurt very badly and that she was hoping that there would be some way of getting rid of that hurt if she knew what happened to her Kevin. But I fuckin' doubt if meeting me and asking me about what happened would ever reduce her pain. If anything, 'twould make it worse. 'Cos she would find out how senseless and pointless the whole thing had

299

been.
Which it was.

So the line 'someone out there must know something...someone out there, something...help...mystery" kinda resonated with me. I had often heard families saying it on the news for different things but until now it never made sense. I'd be thinking that those lines were always aimed at mothers who might have noticed their sons coming in covered in blood or wives suspicious about where their husbands were on a particular night, husbands coming in smelling of sex and crime and guilt.

I never really thought that the 'someone out there who knows someone' could actually be the person who did it.

And that kinda freaked me out and then as I looked at the screen and the presenter looked into the camera and the pretty garda looked into the camera, I could see that they were talking to me. To me.

This was a programme about reaching out to one person and that person was me.

That in the whole country who were watching this tonight, I was the one to whom it related, the only one would could answer their questions, the one who had not been found and might never be.

And for a while I felt special and I got the horn on meself thinking that I was important after all, but sad that nobody out there knew about it.

And never might.

And for me that was the saddest thought of all, that my torment might never be explained, that my loneliness might never be recognised.

That my difference would never be appreciated.

And as the credits rolled on the programme, and the numbers came up, I was tempted to make the difference, to do something daft, to take the big step.

But I went over to the phone and took the cable out of the wall for fear I'd take a fit and ring the guards, in my sleep.

And then as I stood there, panicking, crumbs on my chin, I looked down at the cable wrapped around my hand and thought the darkest of thoughts about how I came to be in this place with nobody in the world to love me, not even myself.

The Forty-Ninth Year

This is not an everyday.
So grab it, inhale me
standing before you.
When they slide off your lap
and say more please more
you will tell them how I stood
and asked for understanding
and gentleness and respect
and how your pupils pierced mine
and afforded me
a shoulder for this burden.

(Peadar Gibbons)

I never thought that my fiftieth birthday would be just a lot of nothing. I had assumed that there would be some sort of minor celebration. Some family, some phone calls, the odd card from mother or Liam or from Brother Fabio in Rome.
Something.
Anything.
But not this, sat there in the back room in Kelly's with Snugg and Bertie and the lads and we playing pool and they laughing at Moira Kelly bringing in a swiss roll cut in the shape of a coffin and a 50 scrawled out in the top with a knife and one solitary candle and they all singing Happy Birthday. 'Twas like something out of a fuckin' bad dream.
And with Moira's saggy tits hanging down into it and the rolls of fat around her middle and the stains under her arms, 'twas as if I wasn't even there but I laughed along with them anyway.
"Your life is over," they joked, "so that's why we did the coffin thing. Fifty means it's all downhill from here now," they said, and I knew they were right. And after I'd eaten a slice of it and then decided to go for a piss, I fecked off home instead without even telling them I was off.

I wondered if I would now be spared the torture of ever having to go in through that dreary fuckin' pub again.
And as I made my way down Bridge Street, over the Robe at the Bowers and up home. I passed the barracks and saw that there was at least one guard there 'cos the squad car was outside.
I took a deep breath and I decided 'fuck it,' here goes.
So I went into the house, threw off my jacket, put on the kettle and started gathering stuff. And then I wondered if I should at all. If it was just a gung ho idea that would seem shite when I woke up the following morning in a cell.

I wondered if I'd had a wank, a good wank, would I get over it? Would it make me change me mind, but 'twas the opposite. I felt drained and useless and pointless. What was the point of me? I'd always told myself never to wank when I felt down 'cos all that does is make ya feel further down. However empowered you feel with a loaded gun, ya feel fuck all when you've emptied the barrel.

So why the fuck was I doing it? S'pose you could say it's a sort of cleansing. Couldn't I just leave things alone and go on the way I was. I'd never been in any sort of real trouble before. Mother was always afraid of that. "We don't want the guards coming to the door," she said, even though they came once for Kieran 'cos his ball went through Delia Fahy's window and sent glass scattering in on top of her as she ate her tea. When she died a year later, he woke up one night crying saying that maybe the glass went into her sugar bowl and that it killed her slowly. But he was talking shite, 'cos she died of the cancer that had seen the bottom bit of her tongue black and crusty. And not through any terrible glass poisoning.

I didn't even know who I'd be talking to. When the older guards were here, you knew them by name. Some of them were my friends' fathers. They were the old style guards who'd kick seven shades of shite outta ya if ya did anything wrong. We'd see them hauling in the knackers for robbing and they screaming inside as they were slapped by two or three guards. And then we'd laugh at them when they were let go but the fuckers would get us again another time when we'd be on our own and not so brave.
The new guards now barely fuckin' said hello to ya. Not pug faced like the old guards, these were straight looking feckers

with degrees and an education that only served them to deliver new ways of insulting ya.

And these are the fuckers that I'd have to convince.

On my fiftieth birthday.

Imagine, it would be fifty years since Dr McMorrow delivered me in this house. I sat on the bed in this room that had seen so many births and deaths and now it would be the last place I'd sleep before I had a big occasion of my own. I'd lived a life free of big occasions. No wedding or children being born. Just deaths and bad stuff. In here, they waked grandfather before we were born, in here they waked Kieran when they got him out of the river; in here they waked Father after he got the heart attack and now here tonight I'd put my head down for what could possibly be the last time in this house. But fuck it, they're only walls around spaces. They could be knocked in the morning and gone. 'Twas what's in your head that matters. Those walls are impregnable.

But I couldn't nap. I wondered what I'd need. I got a carrier bag and went around the house gathering some socks and some jocks, soap, my razor, my glasses case, my tablets, and then I looked at the bag. Was this all I was going out with? All the dreams I had in this house, the hopes dashed time and time again, Italy and working in Galway, Claire, Sunday fuckin' Miscellany, the writing club. A life that had a river of sorrow run through it, bursting its banks every time I had a chance to do something better.

So I sat there on the bed and wished myself a happy birthday and wondered if I'd get any mention of it above in the garda station when I'd be filling in any forms. Would they be filling in the sheets and say happy birthday to me? Nobody had said a proper happy birthday to me for a few decades now. A greeting where people meant it.

Mother was too old in the last few years. Even at her best before she took to the bed with the depression, she struggled to believe that her youngest son could be in his forties.

And that three other sons didn't even get that far.

I remembered back to the time when she remembered all our birthdays and she'd get a proper cake from Mrs May the baker for the tea and she'd take out the candles which were used for all our birthdays, rickety half-burnt ones that were blown out seconds after they were lit for fear there'd be any prolonged unnecessary joy in the house.

And so I went. With the carrier bag with the stuff in it. Pulled out the door behind me, shaking the brass handle to make sure it was closed, 'cos sometimes with the air vacuum in the small hall inside if the inside door was closed, it took a bigger pull to close it.

And I walked the two hundred yards to the barracks.

And walked up to the solitary guard at the desk.

And when I said to him that I'd done bad things and I wanted to explain, just to explain, he just sat back and looked at me and I knew he said 'fuck' under his breath but then started to smile at me. He had an empty mug in his hand and I got the feeling that me coming in here was getting between him and that mug being filled with tea.

— What sort of things?
— Bad things.
— Serious things?

306

— Yeah, serious things
— Like robbings?
— No, killing.
— Killing?
— Yeah killing.
— How many 'dya kill?
— Five.
— Five?
— Yeah five.
— Jesus five's a lot. Are ya sure?
— I'm sure.
— And you want to confess to them all?
— I do.
— Why?
— Cos it's my birthday
— Your birthday?
— Yeah.
— Today?
— Yeah, today
—What age are ya?
— Fifty
— Fifty?
— Yeah, fifty.
— Jaysis, that's a quare auld landmark. And were ya celebrating the birthday?
— I was, in Kellys
— Kellys?
— Yeah.
— Was Moira there?
— She was.
— Did she give ya a birthday kiss?

— No.

— Fuck, that's a first.

— So?

— Well, Peadar, this is a lot to be landing on me on a Sunday night. Are ya sure about this?

—I am.

—Were ya drinking much for the birthday?

— No, just a Becks.

— A Becks? Sure that's not drinking.

— 'Twas all I felt like.

—You're the poet aren't ya.

—I do a bit, yeah. Was on Sunday Miscellany.

—Were ya?

—I was

— Sure why don't ya go home and write it all down for us. All of it. — Don't leave anything out. Drop it in to us when you've it done. No hurry.

And with that, he just leant over and patted me on the shoulder and said.

— And a happy birthday to ya. Fifty, ha. That's a good one.

So I left. Prick.

An hour later, I'm back, sitting here again. Confused, angry, even more frustrated. Wanked again 'cos it couldn't make me feel any worse. Took me longer 'cos I'd done it so recent like. Thought about Moira Kelly and the swiss roll to get me going. I fuckin' love swiss roll.

And then I start to feel like shit.

Nobody takes me seriously.

"Write it down" he said, the fuckin' prick with the smug face on him. Good fuckin' lashin' he needed. Fuckin' Tory Island station posting or a violent Love Ulster march, That's what he needed. And then I wondered if I said nothing, would he even remember I was in. I could go in and apologise tomorrow like. And say 'twas the drink.

That was almost two months ago. Fifty days to be exact. So I've torn into it since then. Writing these pages. Writing it down. As he said. I'll give him fuckin' 'write it down.' And I've printed it all out, on the library printer. Cost me €17.

This evening, I go back. I'm not dealing with a regular nawthing guard this time. I rang up and found out that Sergeant Conneely is on duty. I know him from the time the lads were killed in England and he came to the house to let us know. I told him that I want to talk to him about something and could he meet me and he said he would. I think he thinks it's about some shite to do with the youth club and the creative writing programme but I know it's not and you know it's not.

Wish me luck.........

EPILOGUE – The Fiftieth Year

I met Peadar Gibbons as an adult for the first time six months after he became a patient at the Psychiatric Unit in Castlebar. My father Peter Cuddy had lived just down the street from him in that Irish town on the western side of Ireland, the town where I was born and lived in until I was five years of age. Even though Dad was nearly two years older than Peadar, they had sat together at school and raided orchards and played pool in an Irish pub. They had loved Irish girls and drank copious amounts of Guinness and cocoa. They all had dreams that in the main lay unfulfilled. They had lived together in an age when opportunity failed to knock loudly on the door of their existence. Together, they endured life and remained friends even through the alleged horror of the revelations of the last year.

It was late last year when Dad called me in New York to say that Peadar had got himself into trouble and had a large document of notes which he felt should be made public. My memory of 'Peadar The Poet' was of Dad's gentle friend who always seemed a little sad and a little mad, but I was not prepared for what Dad was about to tell me. I also never knew just how much my arrival impacted on both of them.

To be honest when Dad told me Peadar had a story that needed to be told, I had not expected much, because Dad was always suggesting great stories to me that in essence were anything but. In recent years, cognisant of the effort he went through to get me into university, the long shifts worked in London, his pleas with me to become educated so I wouldn't have to work nights, I was acceding more and more to these requests. To be fair, some of them were of niche interest to the type of readers in the American magazines for which I wrote articles. Eric Feltz my agency editor who first got me published in Vanity Fair and the New Yorker was amused at the types of suggestions that Dad had made. There were five legged donkeys and then there was the mother and daughter from the town whose lives had spanned four centuries. But none was to have such an impact on Dad or on myself as the tale he told me seven months ago.

This time it was personal.

This time he was in it.

And so was I.

Dad had always felt sorry for Peadar because of all the tragedy that befell his family - their friendship was cemented in later life when Dad's years of emigration in London featured in Peadar's short story The Walk. The story was selected to be read out on the literary Sunday Miscellany programme on the national Irish radio service RTE, although it went unnoticed in the town they grew up. Dad always said that Peadar had a great way with words, but had a "horrible tongue on him when it suited." His copybook was full of poems that Peadar had scribbled there, mainly satirical pieces aimed at teachers and classmates and girls and bullies.

Last night, I looked back at all the books that I'd kept since I was a child. Books that came to London with me when we left Ireland when I was just five. Books I now know were bought and chosen by Peadar The Poet. These were books that gave me a 'gra' (Irish for love) for words and writing. From there I graduated to more advanced ones. From there, I advanced to reading Lorna Doone, without knowing the significance of that book and the choice of my own name.

His solicitor who secured Peadar's notes for me on the basis that they may have been merely been the product of an unsettled mind, said that one of the gardai said it was "the most elaborate and entertaining confession" they had ever received, and because of that, its credibility could swing wildly in either direction.

Even after reading the notes, Dad feels that Peadar was a victim of circumstance rather than a criminal. My opinions on the matter differ substantially but as an objective journalist I have tried to be as true as possible to the style in which Peadar wrote his notes. There are some beautiful sections of prose and lucid thoughts, and there are many coarse sections and words and for that I apologise for anyone who has felt offended. To this end, I have held back my end of the story until now because I have wanted the story to be Peadar's, laid bare for all to see and judge. I got involved because I now know more about my early life and the life my father led in that small Irish town. I also know more about the gentle nature of my mother Teresa, who died from cancer more than two decades ago and who was to never see me reach the heights I have reached in my career. For that I am sad, and I thank Peadar Gibbons for letting me know this beautiful, frightened, young woman.

If I am being honest about this task that I originally undertook at the behest or badgering of my father, it resonates of the relationship that Dad and Peadar had with their own fathers. I wonder if I had lived beyond four years of age in that street, would I too have grown with the same paternal tensions that both men suffered and brought with them throughout their lives?

The text has been left almost unamended so as to give you a true sense of the frustration he suffered and to contextualise how he felt throughout those fifty years. The book does not seek to condone his actions, nor does it seek sympathy for him and his situation. Many others have had similar setbacks in life and have not gone on to do what Peadar claims he did.

In order to comply with his request that I look at his story, a copy of Peadar's notes were retrieved from the gardai (Irish police) by a solicitor hired by his brother Seamus. When I met him in the psychiatric unit, Peadar was sedated and medicated with a drug which aims to relax the body without disabling the mind. He had already been questioned more than a dozen times by criminal psychologists while the Cold Cases Unit of An Garda Siochana was actively investigating the historical cases, but the details are so dated, it was almost impossible to prove any culpable guilt. His attorney Joan McEvilly has claimed that the notes were in the main "the ramblings of an unsettled mind," and so for the duration of this investigation, he voluntarily agreed to hospitalisation to undergo treatment in the psychiatric unit in Castlebar, County Mayo, Ireland to unravel the entanglements of his brain.

I spent two weeks reading and re-reading the notes in my home in Queens before I flew to Ireland to meet Peadar. He looked pale and drawn in his hospital bed, his eyes widened by medication and shock, his movement stymied by the drugs, his time spent reading plays by Brian Friel and Tom Murphy. He cried when he met me. He said that he regretted that he had given the notes to the gardai because he said they did not appreciate them. He said that he had written a 50th Year of the notes and asked me to join these in with the previous 49. I told him I would, but that the context of what had happened since his birthday would have to be included prior to this.

This is what he wrote from his hospital bed.

"There are times when I think I'm dying in this place. One time when I didn't know what time of the day it was, I felt myself floating in the bed, as if the bed was tilted backwards and I was being lifted and I wondered if this is the moment when I die. And I waited for some signal that I had died. Would the view suddenly change or would I just be left there floating? And then I wondered if I had actually died and that everything in front of me hadn't changed. So I moved my arms to see if I was still alive and they moved.
And the nurse came and handed me a notepad for me to write down any requests I had for my funeral, what music I'd like, what'd I'd like said from the pulpit; where I wanted to be buried and all that shite. And I started to write even though 'twas writing that got me into this place. And then I realised that maybe that didn't happen at all and that this pad was the one the guards had given me to write down any more information I had about what happened in the past.
At night it's worse. With my glasses off, the room to the left where the nurses are looks like a blob of light and with myself tubed up and trying to sleep on the propped up pillow, I dreamed about being in a big roll of cello tape unravelling and floating

down from the sky, the hiss of the descent in my ear, the soft mist of the moisture of space bouncing off that cello tape and hitting my face, and then landing on earth with a bang that jolted me awake. But I had been awake all along, dreaming with my eyes wide open. And when I thought I'd died I was convinced I ended up in Hell. And I wasn't fuckin' surprised, but the place was empty and boring.

And that instead of being fiery and hot, it was chilly. Mind numbing things just happened over and over again, like the same dreams about floating in cello tape, all with the same ending.

And then the nurse would come in and ask was I alright and why was I shouting and sweating, and I'd say I was alright, even though I wasn't.

Sometimes with the bed facing away from the light I can never know exactly what time of the day it is. Bright fucking room where I wake early each morning, thinking the light coming through means its midday and then they bring in food and I don't know whether it's breakfast or dinner or tea.

The brother doesn't come to visit me anymore. He did the first few weeks but then as he heard more and more about what I'd done, he got angrier with me and called me a 'stupid evil cunt' and that he was glad that Mother was across in the county home and wouldn't get to hear about this.

I thought back to those days when I'd sit on the vinyl tiled floor, rubbing the dent on it where my nose had hit when I fell. I was happy then, sitting there with the fire behind and Granny and Mother chatting away....but Kieran's drowning changed all that. The sun was shining in the back window in that vision, but when I think of later when Mother would be at the kitchen sink, scrubbing potatoes and talking to herself in a louder whisper, the place was darker.

315

I thought about killing myself in here, or that I might kill myself when my mind was soft. I saw a pen and wondered if I plunged that into me heart, would that do it, but fuck, it probably wouldn't. Then one of the cleaners left a container of cleaning fluid on the table near the bed and I thought about drinking that, but then that might just burn up me guts.

And then I thought I'd seen a ghost, I woke up and there was a man with his face half eaten away looking at me from the door and glowering at me and saying something to me, but when I looked again he was gone.
And then I thought I saw him again a few other times, but I don't bother telling the nurse this shite anymore 'cos they don't believe me. But his face looked horribly shrivelled as if he was rotting away, and I was wondered if that was Death calling me.

Now I just want to sleep. It seems like my life has gone on forever. I want to hug that fuckin' pillow like it was my best friend in the world. And I want to be back on the floor in Ballinrobe, playing with my wooden toys and Mother not talking to herself like in the days before I got to know death. And the fuckin' thing stuck its claws into me.

***

On July 4, exactly 50 weeks after Peadar Gibbons was admitted voluntarily to the Psychiatric Unit, he was eating breakfast in the dining room of the unit when he was attacked by a fellow patient. In a shocking incident that lasted less than two minutes, patient Patrick Grimes used a kitchen knife to stab Peadar seven times in the chest and once in the face. The two men grappled as Peadar tried to grab the weapon from his assailant and managed to tear at Mr Grimes' already badly-scarred face.

But his wounds were too serious and he collapsed into a pool of blood in the centre of the canteen. Unit staff who rushed in took the knife from Grimes who was crying and screaming at them to stay away. Patrick Grimes is the man referred to as Paddy Grimes in the notes written by Peadar., the man who was blamed for killing the Eastern European woman.

Peadar Gibbons was treated at the scene by a doctor and was rushed by ambulance to nearby Mayo General Hospital where he was declared dead 30 minutes later.

Four days afterwards, he was buried beside his father, his grandmother, and his three brothers in the plot just around the corner from where he grew up. Only about 80 people attended the funeral. My Dad and I were among them. The priest did not say much about Peadar. And the hearse stopped for a minute at the corner of High Street where he had grown up, and when it did, my Dad started to sob uncontrollably, and so I held him.

If by any chance you are reading this in some form, book, electronic, magazine, whatever, then perhaps at last Peadar Gibbons will have succeeded in having his work published.

317

How that would have made him feel?
If that had happened thirty years before it did, perhaps the published story would not have been as interesting as the one that tragically evolved.

God rest him.
And his victims.
Goodbye, Peadar.

— Lorna T Scully, New York.

****